THE ANONYMOUS BLACK FILES

Urban Sex Therapy

KM CUDJOE

Contents

Prologue	1
Initial Interview	3
Case File #14 – Salim & Naomi	14
Second Interview	31
Case File #23 – Malik & Tanisha	39
Third Interview	66
Case File #31 – Victor & Zakia	77
Fourth Interview	95
Case File #17 – Salim & Naomi	108
Fifth Interview	135
Case File #25 – Malik & Tanisha	146
Sixth Interview	165
Case File #35 – Victor & Zakia	176
Seventh Interview	198
Epilogue	212
Book Club Question	225
Relational Survey	227
The Anonymous Black Files 1.2: The Interviews	228

To all the couples who 'keep it real' with their significant other.
Even when keeping it real is much harder than keeping it fake.

Caveat:
The stories of the Case Files are fictional, a product of the author's imagination.
The relational advice in the doctor's Interviews, although highly informative, are derived from the author's experiences.
This work of fiction was designed to stimulate thought on the evolution of relationships in this new millennium, and to entertain.
Respect yourself, your body, and who you share your temple with.

<u>Always use Protection</u>

YOU'VE BEEN WARNED.

Prologue

You are now being granted exclusive access to the *Classified, Confidential Case Files* of one of the most highly successful, underground sex therapist in America.

A body of work being revealed to the public for the very first time, from an individual so sought out and revered for the effective, yet controversial teachings that he has given to his clients, that he has been nicknamed by the psychological community – the *'Picasso of the Phallus infused Yoni'*.

His reputation, and his name, preceded him over the course of his illustrious career, but due to issues of safety and security, today he is only known as *Dr. Anonymous Black*.

Dr. Black has agreed, under the strictest of conditions, to give his first, and only, exclusive public interview to an unnamed magazine publication, and only on the condition that his identity remain anonymous, and the names of his client's changed in order to protect the innocent.

Take heed to these teachings.

They're insightful, yet gritty. Sexually explicit, yet informative. Uncultured, yet thought provoking.

Welcome to the future of sex therapy.

Initial Interview

"Kiara, come on, we gotta get it moving," Dr. Black prattled, punching in an eight-digit code on a steel grey wall safe hidden behind a framed retro 1930's jazz festival poster; a final thumbprint disengaged the door. "Transfer and store everything on externals. Don't forget the *Confidential* and *Classified Case Files* in the file cabinet. Level-1 Clearance only. The numbered and initialed files, ignore. Ten minutes, everything you can get your hands on, and we were never here."

Kiara nodded, and rushed over to a ninety-degree workstation in the corner of the office.

Twenty-inch *Apple* monitors, four screens, two keyboards. An ergonomic, state-of-the-art workspace. Black screens raining flashes of green numbers like a scene from the Matrix were jolted awake from a state of sleep. Two thumb drives were inserted. Kiara leaned over the workstation, back arched, her navy blue and white *Phillip Lim* trench skirt slicing down the side to display a little too much thigh as she typed with the proficiency of a hacker on a high-stakes heist to transfer gigabytes of vital files on those portable drives.

Digital family photo frames, and a platinum plated desk pendulum were swept with a wave of her hand off the edge of the desk into a white cardboard bankers box. Several framed degrees were stripped, one by one, from an office wall and stuffed on top.

In three steps, her three-inch navy blue *Christian Louboutin* heels took her to a massive, marble top wooden desk, the centerpiece of the office. More personal items – four digital photos, a stainless steel water bottle, two African artifacts – were transferred into another cardboard box before Kiara reached under the desk and clicked a hidden button under the center drawer.

The left wooden panel underneath parted like tiny elevator doors with a whisper quiet buzz, followed by the right. Six stacks of bills wrapped in five-K denominations, leather-bound ledgers, external drives, and levels of white labeled CD's with *Case File* numbers and initials. A cache of secrets hidden on four shelves were wiped clean in under a minute, and stuffed to the brim in Kiara's large, cream and white, alligator-skinned *Coach* handbag.

"Black, the *Deceptive*, and *Deceptive Interview* hard copy files..." Kiara ejected a CD from a modem under the desk, unsleeved, and stuffed that in her *Coach* bag so rough she almost snapped it in two, "...they're just as important. Remember, some of our original client files weren't stored on CD, and if anyone finds this place after we leave..." Kiara peered over her shoulder behind the doctor, "...who in the hell are you?"

She popped up, and sprinted to her purse hanging by its strap on a coat rack by the window.

Dr. Black spun around.

There was an individual standing in the office entrance, frozen. Well-dressed, black, late-twenties, shoulder-length dreads tied down in three large cornrows. A razor sharp goatee. A weathered, black leather satchel hung from his shoulder. That mirror image of a younger *Lorenz Tate* stared with the same suspense as someone would stumbling upon a crime scene, probably due to him walking in on the chaos of what was once an immaculately decorated office being stripped of all personal belongings.

When Dr. Black noticed Kiara still rummaging through her handbag, fully aware of what she was going for, the wrath her paranoia could unleash, he blurted, "Kiara, hold up, wait! He's good."

Dr. Black threw his hands up to calm her. It took a moment, but she took heed to his advice. She rolled her eyes, brushed off his interruption, and resumed her quick pack up of their belongings.

Dr. Black returned to their unannounced guest.

"Hey, how's it going?" Two men shook hands. "I forgot we had our meeting scheduled for today. Is it the fifth already? Damn, time really does fly. Well, don't just stand there by the door with it open like. Come in, step in, close it behind you. While you're at it, uh, make sure you lock it too.

"I gotta admit, you kinda caught me a little off guard here, so we're gonna have to conduct this exclusive interview with me and my general manager, Kiara, doing a little...(clears throat)...*spring cleaning.* You're from the magazine, right? Cool, cool. What was the name of the publication again? Forget it, doesn't really matter. What does matter is the reputation I've managed to generate from the counseling I've given to help keep couples together. As you could imagine, longevity in a relationship is very difficult now a days, especially in this digital *'Find em, Fuck em, and Flee'* era."

Dr. Black noticed the individual before him flapping open the cover on his satchel.

"What are you doing? What is that, a recorder?" Dr. Black calms at the sight of it. "Do I mind if you tape this? Not at all. Photos for the spread? Ah, I would prefer for my physical appearance to remain...somewhat of a mystery. I was never big on being in the media spotlight. I would prefer to let my reputation and teachings speak for itself, instead of allowing distractions of my image to go public which may...*interfere* with that. Focus on the *message*, not the *messenger*.

"What exactly is my program that you've heard so many rumors about? Relax. We'll have more than enough time to get into all of that. Well, not *that* much time, but enough time to give you a little history lesson. Pardon self, where's my manners? Please, have a seat. Just move those three white boxes on that leather chaise, and place them right there on the floor. Excuse the mess.

"Care for something to drink? No. Suit yourself. Where do I begin? Well, as you can see by the brass name plaque my second half just tossed in that white cardboard box, I go by the name...well, you can just call me, Dr. Anonymous Black. Dr. Black, or just Black, is cool. I've been practicing sex therapy for almost a decade now.

"Where did I get my degree? Up front kinda guy, I see. Let's skip the formalities, and go straight into the heart of things, because we're short on time. Let me help you. First, put down those notes. Second, forget about whatever you were prepared to ask me, because trust me, this isn't gonna be your typical interview. My life story, and the journey into the field of sex therapy, is a long and complex road to travel down, and being that we're a little pressed for time, I'll give you the short and sweet."

$$ $$ $$

"Back when I was incarcerated in...yeah, you heard me right. Prison. Behind that 'G' wall. Don't judge. *He who is without sin amongst you, let him cast the first stone.* Happens to the best, and worst of us. Joseph. Samson. John. Peter. Now although no light shone down on me, nor chains miraculously fall from my hands and feet, I can say a revelation unfolded, an enlightenment in my brief break from society.

"I guess you could say I was a college prodigy who fell victim to the allure of the street game, and you know, the 'law of averages' thing. No need to burden you with the messy details, but twenty-six kilos changed my life, and pushed the pause button on it for a little over three. First and last time, I promise you that. Prior to my fall from grace, you could say I was dedicated to my field, focused, and doing the right thing. Attended UCONN. President of the debate club, graduated at the top of my class with a Bachelor's in psychology, studying for my doctorial. A year later, I worked for one of the state's most popular counseling firms, before I branched out just a couple after that to launch my own.

"Low and behold, while working as a psychologist, a notorious client I counseled posed a very compelling offer to me: handle some business on the side, make a quick five grand. That was the first time. Tens of thousands of dollars later, a solidified position in a drug cartel that I'll leave unnamed, and I was commissioned to move one of the biggest packages they paid me to handle. Hence, twenty-six kilos. I thought I was under the radar, a ghost, too smart to get caught. Wrong.

"Funny thing, when one is confronted with something like that – trapped in an eight by twelve foot concrete box for twenty-two hours a day – one can spend that time in one of two ways. *One*, squander that *opportunity* away, because it is an opportunity, by immersing themselves in frivolous things, thinking of someone, or some entity, to blame their current circumstances on, or any of the other trivial nonsense the unthinking mind can waste their energy on.

"Or *two*, take responsibility, take control, and use that time productively. My journey began by doing a lot of soul searching. Forget the career, the money, my connections, my clients, how I was going about advising those who sought out counsel. None of that. Only myself. Working, improving, and reflecting on myself. Asking myself on a deeper level: **who was I** as a twenty-seven year old black man at the time? What was the essence of my entire being? Doing so, I began to pinpoint and review the flaws in my character, mainly the relationships with *my* significant others.

"You see, I was always smooth with mine, looks and style to back. What my younger peer's today call 'swag'. I *was* lit, *still* lit, *always will be* lit. Hell, I had so much 'lit shit' in my repertoire I was crushing more cuties than a college brother selected as a first round draft pick for the NBA. The only problem: just like most of the other brothers who dealt with the criminal element in that fast lifestyle, I think we all carried within ourselves a disproportionate amount of trust issues. Trust with who we did business with. Trust with who we could get close to, what to expose. Trust with even our own women.

"I've dealt with issues of trust prior to associating with that street element, but my dive head first into the underworld only made things ten times worse. And if you incorporate this kind of thinking into your personal life, a question begins to linger: how can you have a meaningful, successful relationship with your own woman if you don't trust her?

"The answer – you can't. That's an oxymoron, a contradiction in terms. Yet, the more women I dealt with, the more ingrained I became in that lifestyle, the more I allowed that mentality to infect my bloodstream, the more I...yeah, Kiara, all of them. Delete everything we're not taking. This place has to be a shell when we're done, like we were never here," Dr. Black mentioned to Kiara; he returned to their guest.

"Where was I? Oh yeah, the trust issues. Based on the exposure of women I dealt with, I began to reflect on if I could ever be in a healthy, productive relationship. I began relationships with women with the expectation of these women holding out the potential to separate themselves from all those who failed miserably before them, only for them to fall into the same category, and before I knew it, I classified them in a clump with the rest of them.

"I was wrong in doing that. Wrong to think another woman could correct the mistakes someone else made before her. Wrong to think another woman could fill the void of love the previous ones failed to fill. Wrong to believe something, or someone, *outside* of myself could correct something that was from *within*.

"It was then I began to ask myself a series of questions: what is this mysterious thing called love, *for me?* Is it for me? Is it different from lust? Infatuation? Was I confusing the sensation I felt experiencing an explosive, all night 'fuck session' with a beautiful, physically appealing *friend with benefits*, and the time spent alone with a woman I respect and value? Or were those feelings one in the same if I experienced 'love' in doing both?

"Then came the most essential question: would I ever find that *one* woman who I would truly want to spend the rest of my life with, my *entire* life? Or was that some fairy tale I should have discarded and dismissed like the cartel I was cliqued up with which led to all those years suspended in time, and that half state of death? Decisions needed to be made.

"**First**: I needed to be honest with *myself*. I was *built* a certain way, *thought* a certain way, *viewed life* through the lens of my experiences, trials and tribulations, and I needed a woman to accept that in it of itself. **Second**: I needed to appreciate that *I am the sum total of my experiences*. Every experience I lived through made me into the man I am today; I could not *un-learn* what life and fate unfolded for me. **Third**: that I couldn't pattern any of my *future* relationships from the mold of any *past* relationships, successful ones included.

"I could take tried and true base principles – honesty, loyalty, openness, respect – and incorporate them into my relationship, but it would still be unique from any other relationship before it. What I needed was a woman who could appreciate the eccentricities in my character, while at the same time, on my end, being accepting of the fact that she had past experiences herself."

$$ $$ $$

"My journey began by refreshing myself to one of the most important things I embarked on while I was on the inside – *the importance of acquiring knowledge*. I was already equipped with schooling and past experience in the psychological field, but it wasn't fluid, I didn't breathe life into it. I was riding the coattails of the fathers of psychology before me; Maslow, Freud, Jung. When I delved into literature again, I approached things from a different angle, read materials that could have been considered a little unorthodox compared to traditional psychology.

"In those three and a half calendars, I consumed hundreds of books, ate the meat, disregarded the fat, and incorporated those principles into my character. Yet and still, I wasn't satisfied. Why? Because on that journey, I learned that I was still perceiving things all wrong. Psychology, as a field of study, in my opinion, cannot per se, be classified under the traditional guise of science. *Science* is the rational and systematic study of the *facts of reality*. *Psychology* is confined to the study of *conscious living organisms* who possess the *faculty of awareness*.

"In a *scientific experiment,* let's say at when a pot of distilled water begins to boil, the process can be repeated countless times, always leading to the same result. In a *psychological experiment,* let's say how someone would respond to a violent encounter, with every individual being just that, an individual with their own unique perspective of the world, their likes and dislikes, their vices and pet peeves, coming from their own cultural, age and gender differences, you would never be able to replicate or predict down to the minute detail the results. Every experiment would be different. Meaning, all the women I encounter will be different, and will not respond to me, for the most part, identically to the previous ones before her.

"Remember: I had to work on myself, my relationship with the world, before I could truly help someone else, especially another couple. Based on this revelation, I took a more hands-on approach in trying to get a deeper understanding of the psyche of myself, and others who were similar to myself. Conclusion: after I read countless books, and formulated a new theory on how to view relationships, I interviewed as many couples as I could who had the patience to let me interview them about all of their past relationships.

"After gathering all of this evidence, I began to see one obvious recurring theme – we all just wanted to be happy in our relationships. Sort of a common sense conclusion to come to after hundreds of hours of studying, right? Yet, how is it if we all just wanted the same thing out of life, why was it so hard for us to find it? I found out why.

"I took it back to the beginning: the simple basic concept of...yeah, those books too, Kiara. Those are the most important ones. Not those, but all of those," Dr. Black pointed to a shelf stacked with books, "Put them in the Benz out back. Remember we parked in the alley, off the street, because...well, you know. Just take everything out there while I finish this up."

Dr. Black returned to the journalist.

"Where was I? That's right, the beginning. An understanding of the simple basic concept of: *aloneness.* I learned the full extent of this aloneness concept when I was locked up in that prison cell. One man amongst thousands, yet stood alone. In there, I had no choice but to reflect on who I was as a man. And as a mature man who was looking to dedicate himself into a long-term relationship with another woman of like mind, I had to understand that we would both be entering into each other's lives from that basic concept of aloneness.

"I'm not talking about being single, or holding on to any ties from past relationships for a sense of security, but the fact that we entered into this world a single entity, and will leave the same way. I needed to *under*stand this concept completely in order for me to fully *over*-stand how that would affect me sharing my life with someone else. Sort of like how I would have never been able to fully define the darkness without grasping its opposite, light. Big without being exposed to something small. Black without ever viewing the color white. The pleasure of enjoying a big meal without ever experiencing the pangs of hunger.

"I had to learn that being alone comes with the condition of self-responsibility. That no one could think for me, feel for me, live my life for me, or give meaning to my existence except myself. To be frank, when I fully grasped this concept, it was a little overwhelming to me. I also came to see that this fact was one of the most fiercely resisted and denied facts of a great many people out there.

"Little did they know, myself included at the time, that such resistance only resulted in countless problems. As an individual man, I know I am linked to all other members of the human community. An inhabitant of the universe linked to everything else that exists. Yet, at the same time, appreciate I'm a single point of consciousness, a unique event in a private and unrepeatable world. Until I *over*-stood this, I knew I would never be able to *over*-stand, or share those moments of serenity and bliss I experienced when I felt myself to be alone, yet one with all that exists. A being who..."

Kiara rushed through the office door, panted, "This meeting is over. We have to go – now."

"Are you sure?" Dr. Black instinctively stood from the sofa.

"Yes. I just got the call. They're on their way. We have to go, *now*," Kiara repeated, stressing every word. Just as fast, she rushed out the office, her silky, shoulder-length locks bouncing chaotically behind her as she disappeared around the corner.

"Ah, change of plans. We're gonna have to finish this interview at a later date. What's the problem you ask? Again, nothing you should concern yourself about. Just a tiny, little, minor discrepancy I'm having. I do have to say: sometimes what you see, may not be what you get. When can we continue this? Here, how about this."

Dr. Black double-stepped over to Kiara's *Coach* bag, flipped through a couple of files on thumb drives, retrieved one.

"Per my policy, once I reopened my new firm, I began to encourage my clients to document some of their most personal encounters for my psychological studies. I had plans to go over this with you before concluding our first meeting, but being that time is of the essence, take it with you. Watch it, study it, tell me what you think of the findings.

"In a couple of days, I'll contact you to reschedule this interview. Although this file is only one of the many couples I'm counseling, I think you'll come to agree that their approach on life, and how they maintain the spark in their relationship, is quite beautifully unique. By the way, I would really appreciate it if this little mishap could somehow *not* find its way into your final edit. No need to tarnish an otherwise productive, fruitful meeting, huh? Remember, a couple of days. Peace."

Case File #14 - Salim & Naomi

Salim entered his townhouse suite, closed the door behind him, and tossed his mahogany leather, attaché case and dark blue pinstripe blazer indifferently on a black leather ottoman in the foyer.

"Naomi, please tell me you chef'ed up one of your specialties tonight, cause the god is starving."

A set of keys attached to a white gold keychain, and matching money clip, slid across a thick, dark green marble coffee table in the living room.

"Maybe that breaded chicken dish, with your famous style of Mac & Cheese. And if you really want to make it a good night, tell me you made some dessert too," Salim added.

A stack of envelopes were scattered across the coffee table aside a couple of works from *Diderot* and recent issues of *Robb Reports;* credit cards, gym membership, light bill, cable. Junk mail. One by one, Salim glossed over them, and tossed them with a flick of his wrist right back on the coffee table. He just assumed Naomi felt the same way from the manner in which they were scattered about.

Salim loosened his tie with each step, and headed straight towards a sliding walk-in closet designed in polished wood resembling a wall. He knelt on one knee, moved shoeboxes aside, revealed a digitized safe hidden underneath a floor panel. A Glock 9MM was removed from his waist, he placed it atop close to a hundred grand in cash wrapped in bank tape; there were several passports, leather-bound ledgers, and documents neatly aligned within.

That had become only one of Salim's rituals after a long day of work – stash his weapon away, document his day's progress, soak in a visual of his secret finances.

Salim had been running his promotions company for close to five years. It took less than one year to get it up and running, and only another six months to partner up with the right sponsor to catapult their business well into six figures; not an easy feat considering the competitive field. He was just that good, Marketing and Advertising his element.

Another ritual: scan over one of his most prized accomplishments which skyrocketed his company to success – a glass encased poster in which he booked the *Young Money/Cash Money* triple team threat of Lil Wayne, Drake and Nicki Minaj, one of the hottest label's at the time, to a sold out venue, *The Stadium,* one of the hottest clubs.

There were times where he lost countless moments just staring at it, dissecting every minute detail. Well, Nicki specifically, and that black cat suit she crushed with that seductive look over her shoulder, back shot. Not that evening. What held his focus is what sat in the center of a brass and glass table in the den: a crystal chessboard, by its side, a copy of *Ars Amatoria* by Ovid.

The crystal pieces weren't set up to begin a new game. To the contrary, there were less than ten pieces spotted over the face. End game. White, distinguished by the ivory accents inside, checkmated black, onyx accents, with a clever stratagem of a rook, two pawns, and a bishop.

Salim knew he couldn't touch it. To reconfigure the pieces for a new game would have opened the door for ridicule. Naomi won the last game; the last three to be exact. Just to think, in the beginning she hadn't the slightest interest in the game. It was Salim's keen interest in the centuries old game, which sparked a similar interest in his soul mate.

While it may have taken others years to get a deeper concept of the game – formulate strategies, project three and four moves ahead, study their adversary to play not only the game, but their opponent as well – for Naomi it took mere months. She made it a point to tout this gift to Salim. Rub it in by reminding him of the price of such losses: the winner could have any fantasy fulfilled for one evening. As it stood, she was up three. For the past couple of years they engaged in other such games, with chess currently trumping Scrabble, all of which in the recent past Naomi claimed victory to.

"You know we're gonna have to run that last game back, right?" Salim made his way to the kitchen, cracked a stainless steel fridge door. "No more being nice to you and playing you with my 'B game' either, cause you might actually think you're doing something."

Salim twisted the top off an ice-cold *Corona*. After taking a hearty gulp, an eerie feeling came over him when he realized he might have been having a conversation with himself for the last five minutes. He stood motionless; sensing, listening, processing.

"Naomi?"

No answer.

$$ $$ $$

That was weird.

Salim knew he remembered seeing Naomi's Lexus in her parking space. Her *Chanel* pumps were at the foot of the recliner in the living room; on the seat, her compact black *CK* clutch.

Her leather trench was even slung over the side. Salim took calculated steps through a darkened hallway, passed their daughter's bedroom to see that it was empty, and headed to the master bedroom.

DJ Khalid's *'Major Keys'* rumbled quietly in surround sound with animalistic growls behind their cracked bedroom door. Pops of light flickered from a seventy-two inch smart screen inside, cast a dim glow, affecting an almost angelic silhouette around the entrance. Salim prod the door open with the tips of two fingers as if he should have announced his presence in his own home.

The room took on a soothing aura.

Naomi had a habit, her pastime, collecting exotic oils. Turkey. France. Persia. India. Fragrances from foreign lands. Salim could detect mere moments prior to his arrival that she laced the entire place with a sweet aroma; a heavy scent of jade. A massaging leather recliner vibrated whisper quiet in the corner, next to it, a small end table. Aside from a night lamp, there was a bottle of Grey Goose with two half-filled glasses on ice; a quarter of the bottle was consumed.

"Hey baby," came Naomi's voice in a light, sultry tone.

Her greeting alone informed Salim that she was buzzing like crazy. He turned to the TV. On the screen, erotic images flashed, scenes from a porno, *Black Angel,* what Salim knew to be one of her favorites.

"Do you like what you see?" Naomi asked, her voice dripping in invitation.

A hazel-skinned porn star, Olivia Winters, looking as sexy as she wanted to be in two dimensions of *Smart technology*, so clear her image could have easily been mistaken to be right there in the room with them, was laid out, spread eagle, on the center of a plush white leather sofa, ass hanging off the edge, legs held high in the air, taking a thorough dicking from someone irrelevant to Salim.

She took close to a foot of that thick, vein-embossed, black phallus dipping in and out of her like a champ, her face twisted in the erotic throes of ecstasy every time that Mandingo long-dicked her deep with calculated strokes, but Salim was sure that's not what Naomi was referring to.

Salim knocked back a few more gulps of his beer, downed it to less than a third. A part of Salim found himself drawn to the vibrating recliner in the corner and the relaxation emanating from it. That is until the lure of their custom king-sized draped in a delicate white silk canopy parted down the middle and fully raked back to give him the perfect view inside became too strong of a temptation to resist.

"You know I do," Salim uttered smoothly making his way bedside.

He soaked in that feminine specimen positioned invitingly on the center of his bed, donned in nothing but a pair of cherry red, paisley boy shorts, and a matching paisley bra, like he'd never seen a spectacle so magnetizing in his entire life. Once Salim came within range to stand only a few feet away, she began to squirm across the surface of white silk sheets as if his presence ignited raging hormones she could no longer contain.

Salim finished off the rest of his beer, downed it to suds. He debated on if he should knock down a few shots of that Grey Goose. He could see from Naomi's planning that he had a long night ahead of him, and strong liquor always did the trick of bringing out the true freak in him; what he could see it had already done to her.

Just as quick, he decided against that.

He didn't want to blur his faculties too much.

Naomi invested energy into planning and execution, so he wanted to cherish that moment, savor it with a relatively sober mind, experience and remember everything it had to offer. Salim placed the empty beer bottle on the nightstand by the bed. He only managed to unbutton the top three buttons of his sky blue *Kenneth Cole* dress shirt before that anxious presence melted into his personal space. She reached out to rest her hands over his with a set of perfectly manicured, Gucci-tipped fingernails to stop him.

"No. Let me," she said softly.

She took her time, preceded sensually down each button, stripped him of his shirt, slacks, peeled his tank top from over his head. Salim stood before her, bare, in only a pair of black silk boxers. His eyes were sliced heavily in lust. He could see hers were too – she licked her lips deliciously, then lowered them to his waist.

The weight of his erection began to stiffen, gradually harden, but he was far from being as proud as he knew he could be; although the devilish glare in her eyes was sure to accomplish just that if Salim continued to stare into them long enough.

The eyes were the windows to her soul.

Everything that could be revealed was speaking to him through them; hunger, lust, desire, passion. She crawled from the bed to lower herself to her knees on their plush white carpet before him, peered up at him through those same desirous eyes, bowed before him, became his sacrifice, her offering to his flesh tabernacle. Her petite hand slipped into the slit of his boxers, nimble fingers circled around him.

"How long have you been planning this?" Salim asked, fragments of passion filled his voice. Her delicate hand managed to fish out and free his erection through the slit. It only took seconds under her firm caress to get his thick, close to ten inches stiff, pulsating within her hand.

"About a week. I did win that last game of chess, you know," Naomi said, pronouncing her win as if she was victorious in all aspects. That gentle hand managed to coax out a few small droplets of his essence, two fingers smeared it all over his bulbous head. Her other hand cupped his heavy bloated sac to massage him lightly.

"Yes, you did," Salim breathed heavily, "and *this* is your fantasy?" Salim remained glued to her tongue brushing deliciously across those plump red kissers, the way she licked her lips, before she proceeded to swipe up his essence with the tip. She began to lick all over him like a flesh lollipop.

"One of them," Naomi mentioned.

Salim released a throaty moan when those soft wet lips wrapped around his knob. Her tongue licked fiercely at the tip inside, she sucked expertly on the head, her saliva-coated hand slid in a circular motion from his base to meet her lips, she squeezed him up in her mouth trying to siphon as much of his natural nectar as he would supply her with.

"But not quite the whole fantasy."

Salim fought to keep his eyes locked on those lips sucking all over his erection, how those eyes attached to those lips made it a point to stare up at him the whole time to soak in his reaction, gauge the pleasure her lips provided, but couldn't help but to be drawn to the movement coming from the corner. A hand weighed down in platinum and diamonds – three-karat tennis bracelet, charmed bangle, two diamond rings – circled around the neck of the Grey Goose bottle on the nightstand and drug it across the surface.

The massaging recliner shut off.

Naomi moved across the room toting that bottle of liquor, her gallant stride strong, her strut confident, smooth, like she was floating on water to take Salim's side after knocking back a few more shots. She peered down at the female on her knees before her husband, the woman bobbing her head up and down, sucking all over his dick, then sliced her eyes up to him.

A mischievous grin rippled across her lips.

"In order for this to be my fantasy," Naomi said, lightly running her nails down the female's back as she would a kitten to make her purr, "I would have to get in on this too."

$$ $$ $$

Naomi took it upon herself to alternate the images of erotica on the screen for another before she officially introduced Salim to that feminine specimen who already introduced herself to him by acquainting him with her lips and tongue.

Her name was Madie.

She was full-blooded Puerto Rican, fresh off the island, Boricua to the bone. Five-foot-five, one hundred and forty something pounds of physical power. She came equipped with milky, butter pecan skin, ferocious vixen curves, and thick, jet-black, spaghetti string curls that flowed over her crown down to the center of her back.

She spoke broken English, held an uncanny resemblance to *Selena* due to their similar characteristics, mainly around the eyes and the way she coated her thick lips in a bright shade of beet red lipstick, but it was her slim waist, wide coke-bottle hips, firm round ass, and powerfully thick thighs, making her debut in that expensive, designer cherry red paisley set, that really paired her with the Latina legend.

Salim lay completely stripped, down to his bare essentials in the center of their huge king-sized, with Madie equally stripped in her butter pecan birthday suit, snuggled up close by his side. From the moment she first laid eyes on his powerful Asiatic physique – his six foot, two hundred and ten pound frame of chiseled flesh, his almond brown skin, and throbbing ten inches covered in veins – she hadn't been able to take her eyes, or her hands, off of him.

The second scene Naomi decided they were to indulge in was one of Salim's favorites – strictly ménage-a-trios. One well-endowed brother servicing two, extremely curvaceous women in their sexual prime; exactly what he had before him. Naomi started those sultry scene of events from the beginning, episodes they both knew to be over four hours long, and sliced her way through the folds of the canopy at the foot of the bed like a human feline.

She crawled over to her husband on her hands and knees, her short, spiky, a la circa Hallie Berry haircut styled to perfection. She held Salim locked in her line of vision, stalked him. Salim remained silent, perfectly still.

He just watched her.

Her heavily mascaraed thin eyes and high cheekbones. Her undiluted blue/black skin glowing in the dark. Her 36C-24-43 inch powerhouse measurements as she rose upright on her knees and reached around to unclip her bra, the last article remaining to take her down to her born day; she tossed it indifferently over her shoulder for it to land next to Madie's crumpled designer jeans and half-shirt that read, *'Got Milk?'* across the chest at the foot of the bed.

Two layers of chocolate with a creamy caramel center on the surface of white silk.

"Look at you, laid up like you the king," Naomi said in a fluffy voice.

Salim sat propped up on huge down pillows against the headboard with his arms stretched out; one of them was coiled around Madie's shoulder palming her breast, his legs spread wide as if it was some unspoken invitation to Naomi.

"Get it right. I'm the god," Salim corrected, quite sure of himself.

"That you are. And who am I?" Naomi ran her French-tipped fingernails from the heel of Salim's foot up his right calf, and traveled deliberately into the center of his thighs; he shivered from the sensation.

"My beautiful Asiatic goddess."

The title he bestowed upon her got a wicked smile out of Naomi. She used that as her sign of permission to pay homage – she smoothly circled her fingers around his shaft, then eagerly secured her lips over the head.

Salim melted, groaned, an ecstatic, "Ohhh...that's what I'm talking about, my queen," poured from his lungs.

Naomi ventured there enough times before to know exactly how to push all of her husband's buttons; push all of his buttons, maneuver the levers, and even twist a few cranks. That was the difference between Naomi and nearly every other female Salim ever encountered. Naomi *genuinely* loved to perform oral, a woman with an insatiable oral fetish. *She* got something out of it, and not just the gratification of being aware of how much pleasure she delivered to her significant other.

Salim paid little attention to the images on the screen. Madie on his side watching with intent eyes as Naomi worked his dick over something serious with her hands and mouth provided more entertainment than any visual of some faraway strangers.

Naomi perfected the art of sucking dick, and within just a few minutes of showcasing her talents – she took close to a ruler's length of his thick, black shaft down her throat to his neatly trimmed pubic hairs, a couple of times, as if to show off her talent to that little Puerto Rican voyeur, performed tricks even *Superhead* would salute – could sense how her skills, and the excitement of the event she planned for the evening, was pushing him dangerously close to the edge. That prompted her to cut him short; she smoothly sucked up the entire length of his shaft, kissed the head of his dick coated in saliva with puckered lips, and released him.

"Naw, chill, don't stop." Salim instinctively reached out to guide Naomi's head back over him. He gently caressed the side of her face inches over his throbbing erection. "Wisdom, what are you...what are you doing? Don't stop. You got that shit feeling so fucking..."

"Easy, Sa," Naomi purred with a smile, "remember, this is *my* fantasy. Not yours. Mine." Naomi winked at him.

She turned and set her sights on Madie.

Naomi went on the attack, and crawled to hover over her

like big game claiming the prize of prey after the hunt. Their lips met, Naomi tongued Madie down with passion, dominated her. A murmur of muffled whimpers vibrated from deep in Madie's chest. Salim thought it was only a product of Naomi applying her talented tongue on her, rolling it in waves in her mouth, sucking on her bottom lip. That is until he caught glimpses of Naomi's hand deep between Madie's thighs, exploring, stimulating, tickling her fleshy petals with the tips of two fingers.

Salim sat back to luxuriate. Lust-filled squinted eyes scrutinized every second of Naomi, his wife, reducing that little badass Boricua to putty under her touch. She fingered Madie knowingly, curled her index and middle finger under her hood, stimulated her G-spot, rolled her thumb simultaneously in circles over her wet clit, and tongued Madie down like they were lifelong lovers making up for lost time.

Madie panted stifled breaths of, "...Aie, mama...aie...aie dios..." into Naomi's mouth.

She squirmed, spread her legs wider, anxious, thirsty, her pussy greedy, she raised her hips up off the bed to roll them in perfect synch with Naomi's hand. When Naomi thoroughly wet her fingers between Madie's thighs, sensing she had her right on the edge of an orgasm, she withdrew those soaked digits and raised them to their lips.

Both women licked all over Naomi's saturated fingers, both determined to savor most of Madie's natural flavor to themselves. Naomi finally fed her those two fingers, which Madie sucked like a small dick, until she pulled them from her lips to kiss her again. Not for long, just enough to feed on Madie's sex from her own tongue. Naomi kissed the side of Madie's neck, sucked on her earlobe, and whispered into Madie's ear. There was no hesitation on Madie's part. She anxiously folded over in the next breath to take Salim back in her mouth.

"Do you like her?" Naomi asked, taking her place back by her husband's side.

"I do," Salim confessed.

He cleared away loose strands of Madie's long hair that partially veiled her face, and made sure he got a real good look at her plump, red lips stretched around his erection sucking him so beautifully.

"I knew you would. I know you got a little thing for the Spanish mommi's."

Naomi spoke to Salim, but kept her eyes on Madie. A woman studying the skills of another woman unleashing her skills, sucking all over her man's dick. On the scale of technique, skill, overall talent, Naomi rated her at about a six. That was being generous. It wasn't too hard for Naomi to tell that Madie probably hadn't had the fortune of enjoying such a glorious piece of black flesh in her twenty-four years of existence.

Not the way she struggled to fill her red-coated lips around his huge bulbous head. Not the way she could only take him down to about half no matter how badly she tried to squeeze him in her mouth. Not the way she groped at him with both hands, with her caramel fingers appearing unusually petite circled around his thick black shaft.

Naomi received an internal sense of pleasure out of that.

Yeah, six was generous. Time to up the ante.

"Do you want to fuck her?" Naomi posed flatly.

$$ $$ $$

Madie's slurping became more vocal, sloppy, animated, she moaned pleasurably, and tried to stuff even more of Salim in her mouth. Naomi wasn't sure if it was a product of her voicing the possibility of allowing her to experience all of that meat digging up in her thighs, or if Madie sucked him so passionately to make sure he answered in the affirmative.

"Do you want to...*watch* me fuck her?" Salim returned quite coolly considering the request, and under impressive composure considering the intense pressure that bombshell applied, bobbing her head up and down in his lap. "Is *that* your fantasy?"

He didn't leave Naomi much room to respond before he leaned over to kiss her; he snaked his tongue deep in her mouth, as if he could no longer resist. She appeared mouthwatering to him at the moment. Her lips, her chest, her ass. He reached over to fill one hand full of it.

Oh, how he loved her ass.

Salim was convinced that his woman, his wife, his one and only, had the roundest, most perfectly shaped natural ass. Better than any other woman he ever dated. Another hand slipped between her thighs, searched for heaven. Despite the foreign mouth sucking between his thighs, he wanted to soak in her flesh, that tight, wet silk he knew to be dampening his wife's fleshy pussy lips from their carnal foreplay. Naomi refused. She only allowed Salim a taste, a slight touch of two fingers sampling her wet lips open before she stopped him cold.

"It is," Naomi confessed.

She lifted Madie's head from her intense ministrations, and helped to position her over Salim. She held her husband's rock hard erection at the base, his saliva-coated black shaft pointed like a dagger to the ceiling, and even used a couple of fingers to slice Madie's fleshy petals open for his entry.

"I want to see you fuck the shit out of her. *Punish* her! Blow this little pecan bunny back the fuck out!"

Madie instinctively arched her back, and with her eyes closed, took him in slowly with her mouth agape, mewling out an almost pathetic, "Aie…papi…grande penga. Aie dios…es grande. Por favor…es pacito…es pacito, papi," the more Salim filled her tight, wet crevice with his thick slab of black flesh.

Salim took his time with her.

He knew how to *make love*, and he knew how to *fuck*, and the way that little *Selena* look-alike responded to him, he knew exactly how to fuck the shit out of her to give her exactly what she came for. He palmed her meaty ass cheeks in both hands, an ass that wasn't nearly as fat or firm as his own woman's, opened her up from behind, and slowly worked her hefty but petite frame up and down…up and down, side to side, with each thrust feeding her more and more of his rock hard flesh.

It took some time, effort, and concentration – that little bad ass Boricua was surprisingly, and deliciously tight – yet slowly but surely, Salim exhaled a throaty, "That's it, mommi, take it for the team. Cause I'm getting *all* of this shit up in there," and managed to squeeze himself all the way up in her to the hilt, grinding it up in her from underneath for good measure, nestling her snugly on his lap.

"Aie…papi. Dame…dame mas. Feel sooo good. Es good. Por favor, dame…dame," Madie moaned when she felt every inch of him deep in her belly.

Salim gripped her ass tighter, and pulled her down on him even closer; he purposely ground it up in her with the most wicked of intentions to open her, deepen her, make her little petite ass feel every inch. She folded over, stuffed her tongue in his mouth, tongue kissed Salim with an unbridled lust, moaned, panted, and cut off her own cries of ecstasy that filled every crevice of their lavish master suite.

Salim felt a warm hand cup his balls. Naomi massaged him delicately between her fingers. Her other hand found the small of Madie's back. Every time Salim danced Madie up to the tip of his dick like a slow rising '64 Chevy Impala on switches, Naomi fiendishly pressed her hand on the crown of Madie's ass to ease her down to impale her with all of her man's pipe.

"There you go. Don't run from it. Get used to it. Take it all in like a champ, *J-Lo*. You're doing good, you got it. Don't let him win. Be a big girl, back *him* down. Don't keep running from it, bang back on that dick," Naomi urged, like a corrupt coach on the sidelines.

Salim began to fuck that Spanish girl so smoothly, so strong, with such rhythm and finesse, that it took him less than five minutes of straight long stroking that pussy from side to side, up and down, with a corkscrew snap of his hips on the down stroke, for Madie to cry out, "Aie dio...aie dios! Oh, FUCK... papi...papi...I'm...I'm cumming. I'm cumming!" and squirt her orgasm all over him.

She threw her head back to the ceiling, eyes rolling in her head, fingers clutching at his tattoo, muscled chest. She cried out to the savior in Spanish, and shook violently on top of him like she was having a climatic seizure, all of which only enticed Salim to not let up for a minute. In fact, her moans of ecstasy only urged him to switch positions, flip her over on her back, spread her sweat-glistened, caramel thighs wide, and long dick her little ass even harder like she disrespected him by giving him the pussy.

The bed rocked underneath them to a smooth rhythm. Madie was snatched from one dimension of pleasure to another. Her head bobbed like she was nodding to the beat; pants of excited breaths popped from her lungs. Salim threw her thick caramel thighs up over his shoulders, reached underneath, palmed both of her ass cheeks, spread her open wide like a massive, three thousand page legal textbook, right down the middle, and began to lay down the law, pronouncing judgment on her.

He manhandled her, bullied the pussy, busted her open, a melody similar to mixing macaroni & cheese in her honey pot. He contorted her petite body into the most compromising position, left her helpless, utterly vulnerable, tossed her sturdy frame under his weight, dug that pussy out, deepened her, left her with some elasticity forever lost, left her pussy gushy, sloshy, spitting up cum, the whole time growling animalistic pants of, "Yeah...yeah! Fuck...you think...this is? Take this...take all...this motherfucking...dick!" banging on her pleasure box from all angles for a good twenty minutes, straight, with Naomi lying next to them.

Naomi observed her husband behind the mask of a perverse smirk. She analyzed in his performance, his technique, studied the way he slowly chipped away at her arrogance, conquered her conceit, broke that little badass mommi down to the last compound who fought through it all, took it all, until she could take no more, and finally shrieked out for a final time when she came for the fifth time, "Papi...papi...pa...pi...aie dios mio! No mas! No mas! No mas!" tapping him excitedly on his thigh, her unspoken signal of waving that proverbial white flag.

Salim slowed his pace, took his time, and hit her off with just a couple more long, deep, all the way in, all the way out thrusts, just to make sure he worked the last of Madie's explosive orgasm out of her. Just to make sure she remembered his manhood, and that moment. He gradually eased his thick, black, cum-glazed, veiny chunk of flesh from her insides, unsheathed his Excalibur from her womb, his weapon that bodied her, rendered her to a panting pile of flesh, and soaked in the results of his handiwork.

Madie's entire body was damp with sweat; she shone in the afterglow of several orgasms. Salim beat that pussy up like Tyson in his prime. He left her open, custom-fitted for *his* comfort, deepened, and soaked, enough to puddle and fuck up the white silk sheets underneath her ass cheeks; she left a *huge* wet spot, tears of joy about the size of a volleyball. Salim fell out on his back between Naomi and Madie, slightly winded, his thick dick still stiff and strong, shining like a glazed doughnut from being drenched in Madie's multi-orgasms.

"Damn, Sa. You really tore her little ass up. Why'd you do her all like that?" Naomi asked mockingly, peering up at Salim with a sly smile. A few beads of perspiration bubbled up on his forehead. He was panting throughout his horizontal workout, but just as quick, came into full control of his breathing. "I told her she couldn't handle you. Handle all that dick, or that stamina, but she said she could." Naomi chuckled. "I knew she couldn't."

Madie lay spread out on her back, on the edge of the bed, she struggled to catch her breath. Winded, beat down, exhausted, she became the mirror of a woman who reflected the image of someone who just got thoroughly, and savagely, and severely fucked.

Hair disheveled, lips flush, eyes sliced low, handprints and red marks on her ass, thighs, ankles, she breathed in labored pants like the end of a five-mile run, nonstop. Naomi glanced over to her. When their eyes met, Madie cowered, shied away, embarrassment humbling her. Her look spoke volumes, her demeanor that of a woman who couldn't face the fact that she took on a challenge she clearly couldn't live up to.

"So, did you like my fantasy?" Naomi questioned.

Salim ran his hands up and down Naomi's hips. Her waist so slim, stomach so flat, thighs so thick, so smooth, so chocolaty black, her hips ballooned out something incredible. The weight of her succulent C-cup hung too close to his face to avoid the temptation – he wrapped his lips around her right nipple, nibbled at it tenderly, rolled his tongue over it. Naomi's ecstatic giggle sounded like music in his ears. Salim worked his hands down and around to palm her ass. He massaged her round bubble in complete admiration.

"I did like that," Salim sighed, positioning his wife perfectly over his waist, "I liked that you enjoyed seeing me enjoy myself. But all this beauty right here," Salim parted Naomi's ass cheeks, spread her open from behind, and guided her over his erection to slide that pussy he custom-fitted himself in for the last seven years down so smoothly in one stroke till he sat her in his lap.

"I *love* this even more. Love this more than anything on this planet. More than any fantasy you could ever bring home to me. Because you, my queen..." he began to stroke her, with passion, like he'd been given a second wind, staring deep into her eyes the whole time, "...ain't nobody fucking with this shit. You are my one and only, true fantasy in the flesh."

Second Interview

"Naw, right over there. You don't think it would look better on that wall, next to the picture?"

Kiara stood by Dr. Black's side, studied his point of view, said, "It's ok, I guess," clearly not so enthused. "Not like it would be in the armoire. On the wall, it looks forced, like you're trying too hard. In the armoire it shows more tact."

Kiara placed the framed degree on one of the armoire's several lighted glass shelves. She positioned it, took a step back, moved it again, then moved it for a final time before she gave her slight nod of approval.

"There. Now doesn't it look better like that?"

There was no denying her eye for detail; Dr. Black could only nod in concession.

"You're right. It does." Dr. Black agreed, standing by Kiara's side, appreciating her detail for decor.

The end result – she designed a five-shelf, oak and glass, seven-foot high armoire with various degrees and honorary plaques highlighting both of their accomplishments over the years. A really nice collage of their credentials, individually, and as a team. Kiara moved on to her next course of business. She lifted out a twelve-inch wide, digital photo frame from a white cardboard bankers box; several of them were piled up in different areas of the office.

"After your last choice, you know you just committed yourself, right?"

Kiara curled her lip, kissed her teeth, squinted, and playfully nudged Dr. Black on his shoulder. She wheeled a *Replogle* floor globe next to the armoire, then reached in to rummage through another bankers box. She didn't have enough time to remove a *Movado* crystal mantle clock and place it on the desk before a sudden distraction diverted her attention; she lifted her eyes to the main door at the head of the office.

"Looks like we got company again."

Dr. Black peered over his shoulder from unpacking one of many boxes to notice the journalist standing by the door.

"What up, my dude? How are you doing? It seems like we keep meeting under these conditions – you walking in on us and witnessing crazy chaos. For the record, this time it's a little different. For one, I'm not scrambling to pack my shit up to bounce… I mean, relocate. I'm actually unpacking, to stay. For two, I'm here at my new location. A real step up, huh? So, what do you think? Nice, right? Twenty-fifth floor. Beautiful view of downtown. Garaged parking. Do I validate? That's funny. Seriously. Yeah, I'm sure my client's will really appreciate and welcome the new adjustments. Enough of that. Here, let me make some room for you."

Dr. Black removed boxes from the seat of a brown leather sofa, cleared a space on a glass coffee table before it.

"Care for something to drink today? Yeah? Changed your mind, huh? That's what I'm talking about. Relax. This interview doesn't have to be all stuffy and 'quote/unquote' by the book. That's why my client's come to me for therapy. I don't confine, or limit the philosophy I advocate, to textbook theories or psychological hypotheses. I think outside of the box. Tailor my therapy to accommodate each couple, maximize the pleasure for both of them, and their relationship.

"What's your poison? Tequila, Brandy, Henny, Vod... Henny? Henny it is. Kiara, would you please be so hospitable as to find the Henny and a couple of tumblers for our guest. I'm almost positive they're in that box right there. Good looking out."

Dr. Black's eyes drifted off on her for a moment, lost in admiration.

"I swear, I don't know what I'd do without her. One thing's for sure, I'd be lost. No question. Ok, where were we when we left off last? Oh yeah..." the journalist handed over the thumb drive, "...that's right. I left you with one of my *Case Files* to review. So, did you reap the...*scientific benefits* of it?"

Dr. Black laughed.

"Of course it was gonna be different, explicit, maybe even a little unorthodox for some people's tastes. As a sex therapist, I've been exposed to an almost endless bouquet of the pleasures of the flesh. Trust, this interview isn't for the meek, or timid at heart. Naw, this is real life shit right here. When my client's come to me, the one thing I insist they agree on is full disclosure. All of their innermost thoughts and desires have to be on full display. Personally, I believe that's the problem with so many couples out there now – they don't know how to keep it one hundred with each other.

"For so many, it's all about manufacturing an image, portraying a role, acting. I won't tolerate that subliminal, pseudo-image bullshit. We leave that childish, front-a-role shit at the door. Remember what I said in my first interview – it's about keeping it one hundred and being honest with your significant other. If you wanna lie and scheme on the government to get around some taxes, lie to the police and courts to dodge some charges, and possible jail time, those are *external* issues, that believe me, come with their own set of consequences.

"But to lie to your partner, your long-term significant other, your wife? That's *internal,* personal. I would never advocate that you indulge in either, only point out that your sole obligation should be structured around the preservation of your family – wife, significant other, kids, kin – and swell to expand outside of that. Your obligation begins with your immediate circle.

"Honesty. Openness. Respect. That's non-negotiable with your wife, with your committed significant other. They go hand in hand if you expect to make a long-term relationship last. So yeah, when my client's go in, they go in hard, and it might be somewhat...explicit. I make no apologies for that. Not if you have the patience to see through to the end how powerful my methods are, and the benefits my client's receive from the jewels I bless them with.

"As for Salim and Naomi, is their relationship a little unorthodox? Some may view it as that. I'm sure there are many people out there who will find *something* negative to say about them. We live in a 'culture of cancelling' anything unlike we see the image of ourselves in. Yet, there's one thing no one can ever accuse them of, and that's being dishonest with each other.

"I enlightened them to how honest communication consists of them having the willingness, and courage, to be who they really are, to show themselves for who they are, to own those feelings, those thoughts, those desires. To give up their self-concealment that they used for so many years as a survival tactic, to tear down those barriers, those emotional walls they built up, and to stand mentally naked before each other.

"They've done that. As a result, they reported that they've never been happier. Will their methods work for everybody? Of course not. Will it for some? Only they would know. That's the beauty, and mystery, of two beings, two complex minds, attempting to coexist as one. Diversity. Variety. It may boggle the mind of one how the other doesn't have a taste for cherry-covered cheesecake, considering the other couldn't fathom the notion of passing up on a chance to taste it on their lips. The key is for them..."

Kiara approached toting a sterling silver tray, atop it sat a matching bucket of ice, along with a bottle of Hennessy and two tumblers.

"Thank you. I'll take it from here."

$$ $$ $$

"Back to what I was saying. The key is for them to be themselves. Not who they think their significant other *wants* them to be, or who they want to *pretend* to be, but their true selves. That way everything they do, it will be genuine. I teach them the doctrine of egotism, a philosophical doctrine that holds self-realization and personal happiness to be the moral goals of life."

Dr. Black used silver tongs to pluck cubed ice from the bucket, four to five clinked in each glass.

"Romantic love is what follows, which is motivated by the desire for personal happiness." The tumblers were splashed half full. "Here you go. As I was saying, these are the tools in my philosophy, the keys that I advocate to promote a sustainable relationship. Salim and Naomi, they have what some may...(a light sip)...describe as a...whoa! That's good."

Another sip, a little more, Dr. Black reclined comfortably in his leather office chair.

"Somewhat of an understanding in their relationship. Again, it may not be for everyone, their sex life, and it surely won't solve all of their problems. But one thing's for sure: they are by far one of the happiest couples I've had the honor of building with concerning the growth of their sexual development. I'm sure you witnessed portions of that on tape. They weren't always like that. Naomi, for instance, came from a deeply religious background. For years, practically her whole life, Naomi was taught to have an intense hostility to sexual pleasure, to basically scorn this earthly life.

"That to enjoy life on this earth to the fullest ultimately meant spiritual evil. Granted, it was somewhat extreme, but nonetheless, this belief was deeply rooted in her, and caused her many years of anguish. Don't get me wrong, she still believes in an Almighty God, a loving and merciful God, yet no longer penalizes herself for the feelings she has for the same sex.

"Salim, he was a different story. Although he didn't come to me with the same set of issues as Naomi, he did come to me with one severe dichotomy in his way of thinking: his view of his ideal woman. He had an ideal of one kind of woman he desired *sexually*, and one woman he admired *psychologically*. One that was the ideal for every one of his secret sexual fantasies, and one that he wanted to put a ring on, marry, bring her home to moms, and spend the rest of his life with.

"His problem: he found it impossible in his way of thinking to see them as one in the same. A woman who could put a veteran porn star to shame from her 'head skills', who would swallow him down just as thirsty as she would ice water on a hot summer day, who would bend over and happily offer him options, who not only had no problem pulling another woman into their bed for *him* to enjoy, but enjoyed her *herself*, couldn't possibly be 'wifey' material.

"Yet, strangely enough, that's exactly what he wanted – a wife. Someone who he could build a life with, rely on, trust, experience memories with, be his best friend. Only, he viewed that ideal of a wifey to be some virtuous nun who couldn't possibly *reduce* herself to do any of those things. Do you see the dichotomy, the conflict?"

Another few sips.

"When I started building with Salim, I'm talking on some real deep shit, he related to me how he reduced virtually all of his past relationships to something he could just have fun with. *'Bitches'* he could run game on, seduce, and ultimately snatch back up to his lair so he could, as he so colorfully described it, *'Buss their guts wide the fuck open, big dick style, and blow their backs out'*.

"In his mind, he couldn't possibly take any of those women serious. They were buss downs, jump-offs, wet work, brain surgeons, late-night creep shots, T.H.O.T's, slore's, or any other dismissive label he could think of to give them. Because the one thing he couldn't give them was a chance at anything serious.

"As you could imagine, both of his ideals couldn't possibly continue to coexist at the same time, because if the object of his fascination couldn't be taken seriously, if he viewed his ideal sexual fantasy in the flesh as a negative, then it would have been impossible for him to form something meaningful with someone whom he really didn't respect.

"I have a little analogy that I like to share with each of my couples. I call it: *The bank of love.* Just walk with me on this one for a second. Imagine a bank being your significant other, having the capacity to save your memories like money. The only catch – there's never any withdrawals, only good and bad investments. Looking at it from this point of view, your first encounter, good investment, is a receipt for a deposit. Your first date, first kiss, the first time you made love, all of your beautiful memories, good investments. Even your first fight, arguments, all deposits in the bank of your relationship.

"Now just like with any bank deposits, over time they will begin to accumulate. Individuals who jump in and out of relationships, they have no emotional credit, no currency. Couples who have been together for ten, fifteen, twenty years will no doubt consider themselves millionaires. But let's not forget what the late, great Notorious B.I.G. said: *'Mo money, mo problems.'* You like that? Yeah, you do. I see you smiling. Or is it because you knocked back your whole tumbler to the head? Thirsty are we? Here, have some more."

Dr. Black poured more into the journalist's empty tumbler despite slight resistance.

"No, no, I insist. Don't get timid on me now. You just started to loosen up. Remember, this isn't your 'quote/unquote' textbook interview. By the way, do you have a significant other? I know this isn't about you. No need to get all defensive. Just a question. Do you? You do. Something serious? It is. Six years you say. Wow. Yeah, I would consider that serious. Ever think about putting a ring on her finger, skipping down the aisle on some Cinderella shit, giving her your last name? You find that funny?

"Maybe I am getting a little personal. Just curious. The reason I asked is because I hold strongly to the belief that two individual souls who have a fundamental spiritual likeness, a mutual psychology, and an equally compatible sexual appetite, that finding their soulmate should be regarded as the highest priority to them. Do you think you found your soulmate? Don't answer that. Speaking of finding a soul mate, here, your second session."

Dr. Black hands over another thumb drive.

"It's another couple. They're a little different from the first. Been together a little longer, a little older. More…well, I don't want to spoil it for you. I'll let you see it for yourself. Then you can give me your opinion on if you think they're soulmates. What's today, Tuesday? The following Thursday, six o'clock, we can go over your findings. I have three appointments earlier in the day, so after six is the best I can do.

"Try to *over*-stand their psychology, their motivation, their stimulation. Because just like any other couple I travel with, although there may be some underlying similarities, fetishes, they are all uniquely different in their own way. Also keep in mind, like I said before – everything you see, isn't always what you get. Perception. Until then take care. Peace."

Case File #23 - Malik & Tanisha

Malik had been planning and looking forward to the weekend all week.

He finally made it to the end. Friday night. He planned to make it a big night out. He rarely took the time out to enjoy himself anymore. With three kids between himself and his wife, and being so engulfed in both of his sons' football leagues, which included volunteering to carpool and referee two days out of the week, the extra duties really started to take a toll on him.

Then there was his baby girl, Shadrika. Sure, her love for science and biology would be sure to pay off in the long run, because there was no question she had a bright future ahead of her in bioengineering, but those payments to the after school programs he enrolled her in really started to put a dent in his pockets.

Malik didn't want to think about any of that at the time.

He checked out of his position as foreman at the construction company he worked for, and set his mind to check out on any responsibility he had in his life for the night as he skated over to the local barber shop to get his fresh fade touched up for the weekend. His barber was an artist with them trimmers. The tapered cut and razor sharp edge-up really brought out the waves Malik had been nurturing for the past six months. His wife fell in love with them after his seven-year stint with braids.

Step two: bring the kids over to his nephew's house to watch them for the night. Last but not least, check out the new outfit he copped just for the occasion – a crisp white *Polo* dress shirt, a pair of stone-washed *True Religion* jeans, a pair of grey and white high-top *Polo's*. Malik laid each article out across the bed. He was never really one to go all out with that fancy shit. He preferred the simple and clean look. And that night, he pulled it off to perfection.

He went for his jewelry box. A thirty-seven inch, white gold, diamond-cut, Figueroa link with the white gold Jesus piece medallion flooded with ice. Well, the 'diamonds' in the face were cubic zirconia's, but no one would ever know it. He was going out to stunt. Besides, the chain was real gold, even the medallion, and the matching bracelet. Yet, on his budget, with three kids and a wife, who could afford to splurge on thousands of dollars worth of jewelry that he hardly ever wore anyways?

After a long hot shower, and a thorough brushing of his teeth, Malik strolled back into his bedroom consistently brushing his waves, wrapped only in a towel. There was a full-length mirror attached to the back of his bedroom door. Malik paused for a quick inspection.

"*Whoa.*"

That image staring back at him told him he'd better start hitting the gym again. Two hundred and forty-eight pounds, five foot eight. He'd always been a stocky type dude, carrying somewhat of the same running back frame he trained for since his high school football days, but the light four-pack he flaunted before graduating gradually dwindled into a keg.

One of his rough bear paws slapped the side of it a few times; it jiggled heartily. The gym definitely had to be penciled in and squeezed into his schedule within the month. Malik looked around instinctively, knowing nobody else was there, and stripped the towel from his waist. He twisted his body from side to side a few times, gained momentum, his flabby dick swung wildly to slap against both of his thighs. That seemed to wake it up a bit, crease a smirk across his lips. Malik straightened up stiff as if he was the lead man on a college fraternity 'step' team.

"Atten-chun!" Malik saluted himself in the mirror, slammed his heels together, body stiff, a military stance, "What are we gonna do tonight? *I said*, what are we gonna do tonight, you maggot? We gonna go out...and...straight wild out!" Malik chanted, he crouched down low, clapped his hands and stomped each foot to the rhythm. "Go out and wild out...get drunk and have fun...see ass and get right...break night till the sun."

Malik 'stepped' around his room butt ass naked, twirling an imaginary baton, just to pretend to smack it against the carpet quite impressively, entertaining himself as he made his way over to the dresser. He got dressed, dabbed on a few drops of cologne, and for the first time all night thought about his wife, Tanisha. She had to pull some late night hours at the law firm she worked in as a paralegal due to some big case her boss took on. She'd been complaining about it for the past two weeks.

Well, maybe not that much.

Neither of them could deny how the extra money would more than make up for the long days and short nights. She knew Malik planned to take a night out on the town, and decided she needed a break herself; she planned to leave work that night, and head over to her sister's. That space apart would be good for them, a little time to enjoy themselves, to themselves, some breathing room.

Breathing room Malik planned to take full advantage of.

$$ $$ $$

All it took was a couple of minutes after Malik pulled up into the packed parking lot of a bubbling nightclub for him to know he was out of the loop. It had been years since he did the nightclub thing. Even back in his college days he really wasn't that into it. He knew it had something to do with one of his main experiences in them.

That's where he met the mother of his first child, Ebony.

He was only seventeen at the time, but hanging with the older heads, he easily camouflaged himself amongst them to sneak in the club. Ebony was twenty-five. Malik didn't even notice her until they were leaving; he spotted her out in the parking lot with her entourage a few cars away from his boy's ride. His boys ran down on her girls, so he pushed up on her. It seemed like the logical thing to do at the time: him and three of his boys, her and three of her girls.

They all hit up the after-hours spot, then followed it up by pairing together to get separate rooms at a pay-by-the-hour hotel. Malik fucked her all night. Two condoms first, the rest, four more nuts, unprotected, in every position until the sun came up the next morning, all with the assumption that he would never see her again.

Nine months later, Ebony popped out a little girl she named Erica.

There were questions.

She even admitted he was one of *four* other potential fathers; two being guys she met at different clubs earlier in the week, one being her long-time boyfriend, slash suck/fuck buddy, of three years. She was a club girl, lived a party lifestyle, what his team referred to as a 'ratchet', (a dirty gun, used for a one-shot kill, then discarded) and didn't have the slightest of intentions of curbing her three-night-a-week club, fuck-for-fun lifestyle.

Oh, how he was riddled with guilt in the beginning for praying the child wasn't his, especially after he took his time to get to know her for the person of who she really was – he genuinely didn't like her. Nothing about her, *except* for how good, and how tight her pussy and deep throat felt on that one night she let him play in her waterfalls.

She was a THOT, but an exceptionally *good*, exceptionally *talented*, exceptionally *gifted* THOT.

Destiny wouldn't spare him such a fate. A blood test confirmed it – Erica was his, and he was, in essence, stuck with the likes of Ebony for the next eighteen years.

She put him through hell for most of them too – drug him back and forth to court for child support, denied him access to see her, used their child as a pawn to hurt him, he even went to blows till they spilled blood with one of the many guys she spread her legs to who tried to tell him he couldn't see his own child whenever he came around – until just a few years prior when his baby finally turned eighteen and went off to college.

Such an experience tarnished any good memories of hitting up the clubs for Malik, but he wanted to do something different that night. And for that particular nightclub, which proudly toted the reputation of catering to only the 'grown and sexy' crowd, he decided that *something different* would be to check that off his 'to do' list for the evening.

Within forty-five minutes of what time rendered a foreign atmosphere – the animated, rowdy crowd, new music, tight surroundings, and new faces – things started to become a little overwhelming for Malik. With four beers circulating through his system, he couldn't deny he was feeling good, floating on a nice buzz, but things were definitely different. He only danced two songs with two different females, one song each, before he put a stop to things and took his place by the bar.

Part of it was because he knew he was having *too much* fun with that last girl. All the way Asian, half-naked. Made up to look like an actual Barbie doll, with pigtails to match. Could have been *Asa Akira's* twin sister. Absolutely drop dead gorgeous. A little too thin and not curvy enough for his tastes, but could move that thin, petite body of hers to R&B on the dance floor like nobody's business.

She gave him her back throughout the whole song, arched herself so lewdly before him, and grinded her little ass squeezed in a tight jean mini-skirt all over him, appearing to derive pleasure from the stiffness she felt growing in his jeans every time she nudged herself into him.

Yeah, definitely *Asa Akira's* sister.

That was bad.

Not nearly as bad as the next sista he had to curb; a doppelgänger of *Taraji P. Henson*.

Finally, the worse: what he was confronted with at the bar when he turned to his side after he felt a pair of eyes burning a hole into him. A chocolate cutie, about five-foot-two or three, four inches higher in heels, but still built low to the ground, resembling an older, thicker version of the gymnast phenom, Simone Biles. A girl that was sexier than a motherfucka. A little on the thick side, which made it even worse.

That was *just* Malik's type.

He loved them with a little weight. Those types, in his experience, not only came equipped with a nice set of firm, fluffy tits, some huge thighs, and a fat ole ass, but packed underneath all of that some juicy ass, tight ass, sweet ass, slippery ass, slick ass, wet ass, good-good-*good* ass pussy.

Yeah, in his experience, women with a little extra weight on them, always came equipped with what he called *'that grease'*. And he was sure that little brown-skinned cutie, rocking them tight *Shirley Temple* curls with light brown accents covering most of her face, toting a bright, mesmerizing smile, who he could see was staring at him from the moment he stepped to the bar, would be sure to put a few black hair companies out of business – permanently! – from the lifetime supply of *grease* she had stocked up between her thick thighs.

No matter how much he tried, Malik couldn't resist turning his attention back in her direction.

A skintight black dress made her D-cup cleavage spill out the top, and was so short at the bottom, one false move and she was in jeopardy of displaying an illegal amount of her thick, almond brown thighs; a large belt with a huge button emblem flattened her stomach as much as it would permit. She wore light jewels, heavy make-up, and four-inch strap stilettos. She was at the other end of the bar, by herself, just like he was, nursing on a neon green drink.

Approximately five hundred bodies within their vicinity, but the way their eye contact connected them, it told them they were both alone in their thoughts and desires.

Malik inspected his surroundings, and tried to make out the features on the many faces that soon came to be all just a huge blur in his eyes. He knew his wife's friends, nor any of his, were really the club type. That didn't stop him from knowing there was a possibility, a small chance, and just sheer bad luck, that he would approach that little powerhouse and be spotted out by someone they knew.

Another two songs played out.

Malik finished off his beer, ordered another. He could see the female who held his attention, waiting for him to make some move he pretended he really didn't want to make, obviously grew impatient; after turning down the forth guy who asked her to dance, she finally said yes, and gave her hand to the fifth.

Malik had to reposition himself closer to the dance floor; he made sure he kept his eyes on her. He wanted to watch her get her groove on, so he did just that. That's the only reason why he came out anyway: to enjoy the *sights* of pretty faces, nice tits, and fat asses.

And enjoy he did, because...*damn!* That girl could really move.

Malik sipped his drink, and admired her from afar. The guy who she was with, she really didn't want him. Naw. He was only a side dish, an alternative. Sloppy seconds. He only got that pleasure of grinding all over her because Malik didn't push up on her. That could have been him all day if he wanted it. He just didn't get at her because he was a married man.

A night out to relax, have a couple of drinks. *Look,* only look at the plethora of different pussy and ass. That's what his plans were. After that, take it on home. Take out his sexual frustration on his baby, his boo, his wife. Pick her up from her sister's on his way home, and punish her severely from what that little brown-skinned cutie started.

Then again, he did come out to have *some* fun. So...what could one little dance hurt?

Malik thought about his days before married life. He was smooth with his. Game came natural. Talk game vicious. Smashing pussy was the least of his concerns. All he had to do was channel those days of yesteryear to the present. A few more gulps on his beer, press down his waves with some smooth strokes of his palms, slick back his eyebrows, and he was good to go.

Wait.

Hand cupped over his mouth, breathe. Malik popped in a breath mint just in case.

Malik stepped to her like it was nothing. The thought of her rejecting him never entered his mind; one of the many beauties of being confident. The theory proved correct. All it took was for him to enter into her personal space, give her his bedroom eyes, and hit her with a few dance moves, for her to instantly sway away from the brother behind her, and close the distance to him.

Malik wasn't quite sure how it happened, but within minutes, their legs were criss crossed together, she was grinding her crotch on his thigh, and he had two hands full, palming her puffy round ass, with his lips secured like a suction on the side of her neck in the middle of the dance floor. Despite the spectacle, no one really took notice; only a few sweeping glances here and there. They were all too busy getting their groove on themselves to pay that much attention to a feisty couple.

Malik hated to admit how much he was enjoying himself.

All the worries of his mundane life at home seemed to fly

right out the window. The little cutie in front of him was hot. Not just hot. He knew the way she squirmed her little body all over him, rubbed her clit on his thigh, made sure to rub her own thigh on his dick, which he knew she could feel was almost at full mass, and let him rub his hands all over her chest that he couldn't seem to peel his eyes away from, that she was a true freak at heart.

After a few more dance moves, she chanted in his ear over deafening thumps of bass, "Buy me a drink," mid-sway to the beat.

Malik gave her a lust-driven nod.

She interlaced her fingers into his, drug him off towards the bar, and muscled her way through the crowded dance floor with Malik in tow. Malik paid little attention to the way she parted the crowd like a female pit-bull to a dark corner of the bar, more concerned at the way her fat ass switched with each step.

Just that easy, he had her.

Just that easy, he was in trouble.

$$ $$ $$

"Four shots of Patron," she hollered out to the bartender.

"Four shots?" Malik thought, *"I thought you said* a *drink, meaning* one*? And Patron?"*

Malik tapped his pockets. It's not like he couldn't cover the tab, he just didn't *want* to. He didn't come out for all of that. What the fuck was he doing anyways? By the time he could process everything, the bartender slid those four shots across the counter.

"Enjoy yourself, cutie," the female said sensing his reluctance. She handed two shots to Malik and retrieved the other two. She raised her shot in wassail fashion, they clinked glasses, and knocked them back. "What's your name?" she asked with a raised voice in Malik's ear over the thumping music, and fast blinking lights.

"Abdullah," Malik returned without hesitation in her ear; there was no way she was getting his *real* name out of him. "You?"

"Sandra." The way she hesitated, looked away, and knocked back that second shot right after, Malik could tell she gave him an alias as well. "Come out to the clubs much?"

"Naw. This is actually the first time in about ten years. Other obligations." Malik wiggled his wedding ring at her.

"You're married?" she asked with wide eyes. Malik nodded. "Is she here?"

Malik hit her with a twisted look. "What do you think?"

"Does she know you're here?"

"Nope," Malik said as if it was nothing.

She smiled wickedly. "Neither does my husband."

It took for her to flash the huge rock on her ring finger for Malik to finally notice it. Malik eyed her in an entirely different light. Countless thoughts began to invade his mind. The way she was dressed. Letting a complete stranger grind all over her, feel her up at will, acting like she was so loose and fast in public. What would her husband think if he could see her now?

Shit!

What would *his wife* think?

"Why'd you come out tonight?" Her question snapped Malik out of his mild daydream.

"To do something different. Take a break. Change it up a little something. What about you?"

"I always come out to the clubs. Being married don't mean my life has to come to an end. I like to come out, drink, dance, party, have a good time. He doesn't. He's boooooring. He doesn't like to have fun with me anymore. Me..." she smiled that wicked smile of hers again, "...I still loooove to have fun." A wet tongue danced across her top lip, she peered up at Malik through squinted, lust-filled eyes. "Do you want to have some fun with me tonight?"

She shimmied her short self up to sit on a high bar stool, leaned back against the counter facing the crowd, and pulled Malik between her thighs by his belt. There was no denying it: Malik loved the attention that little cutie showered him with, especially since his wife was being a little distant with him lately.

"Not *too* much fun. I do love my wife," Malik confessed, not with very much conviction.

She spread her legs wider at the slight sense of resistance she felt coming from his end to pull him in even closer, purred, "I love my husband too. He is my entire world, and I would never think of leaving him for anybody. But love has nothing to do with what's about to go down right now."

She stared up into Malik's eyes the whole time. From the bottom of his, he could see her hand reaching out to him. He felt her petite hand seeking, searching out to embrace. She found her destination, cupped her hand over his dick. From their time on the dance floor, grinding and feeling all over her, it's not as if his erection ever fully went down in the first place. With her squeezing and caressing him over his jeans, her determination, she quickly raised him back up to a flesh rock.

A sense of nervousness washed over Malik.

The game sure changed since the last time he used to club hop, and being in the presence of that little aggressive vixen revealed just how much he was really out of the loop. Malik knocked back his second shot. He tried to silence that angel of guilt screaming at his conscience while she steadily fumbled with both hands on his waist. Sandra had him harder than he'd been in years. A dick pulsing, throbbing, beating on those *True Religions* so strong he had no choice but to accept the carnal sin he was living in.

He could see she found fascination in it. The way she rubbed all over it, squeezed him as if she took pride in her accomplishment, and tried to stiffen him all the more, he knew she was hot. So hot that she began to unbuckle his jeans, and zip down his zipper. Malik instinctively glanced around over both shoulders.

"Are you *crazy*? What are you...what are you doing?" Malik gasped nervously.

They were in a tight corner of the club, she had her back pressed in a crease of a wall and the bar, but there were still dozens of people around them, literally inches away. Huge flashing disco balls and multi-colored lights spinning on metal fixtures above them left them practically invisible to anyone who wasn't directly on them.

"What does it look like? I'm having fun," Sandra replied.

She reached into the slit of his boxers, fished out his dick; seven inches of rock hard flesh easily broke free. Malik wedged himself in between her thighs even closer, more in line with trying to conceal his exposed erection from the three females less than a foot away from them at the bar, than from any ill intentions.

Who was he kidding?

He would have closed the distance closer than two souls could connect even if those females *weren't* there.

Their eyes remained locked. Malik's breathing increased.

Sandra didn't give a fuck about their surroundings, and made no attempt to conceal what was going down. She remained fixed into his eyes, and steadily guided his flesh stick closer; her entire body slid lower in that bar stool, until her ass practically hung off the edge of her seat. Malik knew things had gone too far to turn back. He was gonna fuck her. Hell yeah, he was gonna fuck her. Break her little thick ass off something serious, right then, right there, with no one being the wiser.

One hand lifted her heavy thigh to prop it even wider on the footrest, the other slipped in between her open invitation to find her warmth.

"What's this, no panties?"

$$ $$ $$

Sandra smirked devilishly at him when he first discovered her secret of going commando. Two fingers explored, searched blindly in secret amidst the chaos surrounding them. He found a small landing strip of soft pubic hair above her sensitivity. A middle finger sliced her fleshy petals open.

Damn!

That girl was soaked, practically dripping. Had liquid flesh running all down in between her inner thighs.

A true to life freak!

Malik didn't penetrate her with them. Naw. He was experienced enough to know the clit, and about an inch under the hood, was where it was at. He collected a nice scoop of her nectar, coated the tips of two fingers, and deliberately tickled her tiny climatic button. Her mouth hung agape, unrestrained moans were muffled, lost in the atmosphere of deafening music. Her eyes lowered to lust-filled slits, sliced so thin in lust Malik would have thought she was half-Asian, or smoked a half-ounce of sour diesel to the head the way her body reacted to him.

"This what your lil freaky ass came out for tonight?" Malik whispered in her ear, licking and nibbling on her earlobe. He was hunched over her, his hand deep between her thighs, moving like a piston, stroking, caressing, finger fucking her like crazy.

"Hell...fucking yeah!" she breathed from deep in her chest, grinding her crotch against his busy fingers. "Baby, I came out to find a hitter just...like...you."

Malik knew he had her open. Even his wife couldn't deny how talented he was with his fingers. He knew how to be delicate yet firm, knew how to strum and play on her flesh like the strings on a musical instrument. In the excitement of it all, it only took a couple of minutes for Malik to feel her body tighten, tense up, then release.

She cocked her legs obscenely wide, threw one hand on the back of his, squeezed his arm, and mouthed out a throaty, "Yeah…yeah…don't stop! *Don't…fucking…stop!* Here it…ohhh, that feels *soooo* fucking good," into the club's ether.

Her orgasm poured out of her flesh faucet like warm water to coat his fingers.

The music was deafening, but Malik still had to take a quick peek around them, search to see if those three females on his back heard her cries of passion. One of the females on their side did. A dark skinned woman who failed miserably to hide her fascination at that couple squeezed in the corner. She passed subtle glances in curiosity, kept returning, and nursed on her drink through a straw, although that watered down spirit became the last of her concerns.

Things had clearly gone too far for Malik to give a fuck. Knowing that female on their side was being nosy as hell, Malik still wedged himself in closer, got deeper between her thighs, and positioned himself in the ideal spot to slide his dick right up in her. A few in and out pumps, a better position, angled even closer, a few more, pleasurable grunts, and Malik got it perfect – he buried himself up in her till his balls smacked her ass.

"Oh my God! No they're *not* doing what I *think* they're doing," came the not so startled reaction from the female on their side.

She nudged her other two girls, and gave them excited head gestures to the haps. Three spectators made no further qualms of their interest – they all stared in amazement, and intrigue, at that stocky, brown-skinned brother pumping away, digging all up in that petite brown-skinned girl, going to work on her.

A petite powerhouse who took it like a champ.

Malik was really trying to put her ass through it too. He had his hands cupped up under her thighs, held a tight grip, and yanked her back on him with each thrust forward to rattle the barstool underneath her, giving her everything he had.

"Eeewww, that bitch is *out there*. She truly letting him fuck her, *right here*, in front of *everybody*."

"Those motherfuckas are *crazy*."

"That hoe is the *poster child* for THOT's the world over. Shit, but they need to add two new letters, GF, and I don't mean girlfriend. More like, **T**hat **H**oe **O**ver **T**here...**G**etting **F**ucked!"

"Damn! He bout to break the seat from the way he fucking her."

"You gotta give it to her though, cause that lil bitch is *taking* that dick! Umm hummm. Represent gurl. Make your sistas proud!"

Malik heard every excited utterance those females prattled on their side. Their dismay, their aversion, their excitement. Yet, no matter how despairingly they spoke of that spontaneous, feisty couple, he noticed how they weren't so offended to walk away. In fact, the thought of them eyeing his every move aroused Malik even more. He could see their voyeuristic endeavors had the same effect on Sandra as well.

"Damn, this chick look sexy as fuck taking it," Malik thought, analyzing her the whole time.

They were right.

She took dick like a champ. A petite, certified pro.

A little freak that never stopped being greedy for more.

Malik wanted to kiss her. Tongue her little sexy ass down with those huge, lip-gloss coated lips she had. That was his thing – kissing. He couldn't. That would have been too intimate. There was no romance between them. That mystery girl went out that night searching for a good, hard, *impersonal* fuck, and Malik planned to give her just that.

He struggled to last longer, savor the moment, extend that secret slice of stolen existence between them, stretch a memory sure to be stored in his mental rolodex for future reference, but when that little freak lewdly flicked her tongue out at him, and mouthed behind panted breaths, "That's...it, baby. Oh yeah, give it...to me. Come on, *give* me that dick – *harder!* Break this...fucking...pussy off! Make this...pussy feel... sooo good," Malik let her have it – he buried himself in her to the hilt, and flooded her womb with everything he had.

"Oh...FUCK!" Malik cursed ecstatically.

Three healthy squirts of cum shot from the head of his dick deep in her womb, the barrage of a billion babies sprayed every inch of her inner walls like gunshots.

"Fuck! Damn it!" Malik cursed again, that time under his breath the second he returned to earth from the haze of ecstasy clouding his head for the last forty-five minutes.

"What in the hell did I just do? Every drop up in this freak?"

He knew he should have pulled out, retreated, buss that shit in between her thighs, on the face of the pussy, on the seat, shit, on the club floor.

At least *some* of it.

Anywhere but *in* the pussy.

He did pull out after a quick pang of guilt from soaking in her warm insides, and fixed himself back up. Sandra attempted to clean up any evidence of their misdeeds as well; a few damp napkins from under ice melted glasses at the bar were used to wipe up the moisture between her thighs. She hopped down off the bar stool like nothing happened, wiggled down the sides of her tight one piece that rode up almost to the top of her waist, and smiled at him so bright she was practically glowing.

"Now *that* was fun!" she chanted, like the end of experiencing her first roller coaster ride. "I also think that entitles me to another drink."

Malik didn't find humor in her enthusiasm. The deed was done as far as he was concerned.

And another drink? *After* he already blew her back out?

Ha! Yeah right! She must have lost her fucking mind.

"You're right, that was fun. Best time I've had in years. Thumbs up on having some blazing ass fucking pussy. With that being said, good looking out for the nut, you can hold on to it for as long as you like, keep that pussy tight, have a great life, and…oh yeah, deuces!" Malik chanted, exploding two fingers up to flash the peace sign to her. A smile, a quick wink, those were the last things Malik had for her before he turned his back on her to disappear into the crowd.

He had his fun for the night, but now it was time to head on home.

$$ $$ $$

"Naw, not that one. Honey dip was right though. With them big ass lips, that chick look like she got a mean suck game. Could suck a damn golf ball through a garden hose in one deep breath. I'm talking bout that other little baddy. The one that had on all white – leather mini-skirt, white fishnet stocking, white leather boots that came all the way up to her thighs."

"Oh, you talking bout the one cliqued up with the chick who looked a little like Serena Williams? Brown-skinned cutie with the ass almost as fat as hers too? Well, naaaaw. She ain't fucking with Serena's ass, but her shit was still fat as a motherfucka!"

A group of four brothers broke out in laughter.

Malik heard every word of that rowdy group, a pack of brothers his age, who didn't act their age, who stood in front of a line of urinals relieving themselves. They were going back and forth about their objects of fascination. He was in one of the individual stalls with the door locked, listening as an irrelevant spectator. With his jeans halfway down his knees, he used a few damp towelettes to wipe up all of Sandra's flavor from his faded erection, and did a quick, time-pressed cleanup of the mess between his thighs.

"Damn, did that chick get wet."

That was all *his* work.

The thought of what he'd done tickled an unbelievable smirk out of him. He blew that chick back out something serious, tore her little ass up, and made her buss off at least three times from the way she was crying out; the wet spot staining his boxers, and zipper around his jeans, being clear evidence of that.

It had been ages since he had a good, hard, passionate fuck like that. A few children and a sense of familial obligations sure had a way of dimming the raw passion which shone so brightly when he first crossed paths with his wife. Now their entire lives revolved around schedules; even when they got together sexually.

"You think them baddies wanna smash tonight?"

"All fucking day, my boy! Fuck you think they came out to the club for, just to look cute? Them baddies trying to get wild tonight. And you already know we better be the heads to snatch them up to get wild with."

They roughhoused amongst each other as they constructed fantasies of lust in their heads. Malik muffled a light chuckle. While those brothers schemed on what they hoped the night would play out for them, Malik took pleasure in the fact that he was ahead of the game – the deed for him was done right there in the tight corner of that nightclub.

Even in his younger days, as wild and adventurous as he and Tanisha thought they were, they never did something as spontaneous and brazen as that. She'd always been the more traditional type. Whatever the case, it was over. Now all that was left for him to do was head on home to his lovely, faithful, beautiful...

"There you are. I was looking for you."

Malik emerged from the bathroom, thinking about his wife, to encounter Sandra leaned up against the wall, feet from the men's room. The first sight of her standing there waiting for him took him by surprise.

"What are you doing?"

"I was looking for you, to have some more...*fun.*" She pushed herself from the wall, and reached out to embrace him.

"We *had* our fun. I told you, I'm married. *You're* married. That was it. I'm calling it a night," Malik said bluntly. He coldly put a stop to her advances, and brushed her hands away. "Listen, don't get me wrong. I had a good time with you tonight, a *real* good time. Best time in *years*. Quiet as kept, you're just my type – a lil freak, and girl, you's a lil freak if I ever seen one, with a lil tight ass body, that got some good, *good* ass, *tight* ass, *wet* ass pussy. Seriously, your pussy was fucking phenomenal! Shit *still* got my dick stuck with the smiley face. But this was a one-time thing, a memory that I can flash back to. Nothing more. It was fun while it lasted, but it could only last for this one night. You take care of yourself."

She was given a more sincere once over, and a smile, before Malik rounded her to walk off.

"Ok, Mr. No Fun. I understand," she called out, "but I really need you to do me one last favor. I need you to give me a ride home. When I was having...*fun* with you, my ride left me. And I know you're not the type of guy who would just leave a girl you just had so much fun with stranded here, would you?"

Innocent flirty eyes came along with her soft request. She reached for Malik's hand.

Malik shied away again, snapped, "Who told you that? Yes I am! I'm leaving your ass right here. You can't find another ride? Somebody else to take you home, to have *fun* with?" subtly gesturing to the slew of other brothers flooding the tight corridor, some who had no qualms gawking, making eyes at her.

"No, sorry. You're the only guy I decided I wanted to 'fuck for fun' tonight. So it's either you, or I'm on my own, stranded."

Malik sighed.

An intentional gaze was thrown down at his watch; closing in on quarter to two in the morning.

Malik sighed again, huffed, "Look, I'll give you a ride, but that's it. I'm serious. Can you feel me on that?"

She smiled the same wicked smile she hit him with since they first made acquaintances.

"Sure. Just a ride. I promise, I'll be a good girl." She rose two fingers in the air; an honorary salute. "Scout's honor."

$$ $$ $$

A couple of glances were thrown at Sandra in his passenger seat. Malik drove in silence feeling a good buzz from the exhaustion of seminal fluids, along with the few shots of liquor coursing through his system. A track from the Game's *'Documentary 4.5'* album bumped quietly on all sides in the tight cabin of his *Chrysler 300*.

Sandra seemed to be enjoying it. She sat on the edge of the passenger seat, the sun visor folded down, the mirror flapped open, toying with her hair and make-up. Bangs were tweaked, individual curls coiled around a manicured finger, a fresh coat of lip-gloss applied before she playfully blew an approving kiss at her reflection.

"So, what's she like," Sandra posed, turning to him with her new face on.

Malik barely heard her; he was zoned out with a light head nod to the beat.

"Say it again."

"Your wife. Tell me about her. What's she like?"

Malik sliced her with the corner of his eyes, uttered, "I'm not doing that. I don't want to talk about my wife."

"Why not?"

"Because."

Sandra ignored the center armrest between them, she shimmied herself closer. "Is she cute?" Her petite hand found Malik's thigh. She gave it a firm squeeze, gazed up at him innocently. He brushed it away.

"She is. She can be sexy as fuck when she wanna be."

"Sexier than me?" Sandra slapped her hand right back on his thigh.

"Yep!"

Sandra giggled at his blunt reply. "Really? How about the sex? Is she freaky?"

"Did you not just hear me? I thought I just told you I didn't want to talk about my wife."

"Just answer the question. Is she freaky?" Sandra repeated. She got nothing out of him, not even a telling expression; he just stared off blankly, continued to drive. "Being you won't answer me, I'm just gonna assume that she isn't. So I can see she is nothing like me."

"Yeah, you got that right," Malik was quick to say.

"Why isn't she like me? Hmmm…let's see. Is it because she would never let you do to her what I let you do to me? Let you fuck the shit out of her right there in the middle of a jam-packed nightclub."

As if her hand had a homing device embedded in his leg, she casually worked it up his thigh until her nimble fingers groped at the bulge in his jeans; she could feel him growing.

"Hell naw! She would *never* do no freaky shit like that." Malik tried to brush her hand away for a second time; it was hardly worth the effort. "My wife don't get down like that."

"Why?" Sandra asked sexily.

"Because. She just don't do shit like…I don't know. She just wouldn't."

"Would you *want* her to?" Sandra reached over Malik for the lever on his side of the seat, she reclined it back to give her better access.

"Naw. I'm good with what I got at home. I like that I got a good girl."

The corner of Sandra's lip curled into a wicked smile. "Then yeah, you wouldn't like me, cause I'm far from being a *good* girl." She managed to free that stiff piece of flesh from his jeans despite the slight resistance he put up. Yet, instead of being content with fishing him out through the slit of his boxers, she said in a demanding tone, "Sit up," and snatched his jeans down his waist past his knees.

"Yo, you buggin for real."

Malik tried to concentrate on the road with his jeans halfway down his thighs, drive within the white divider lines while that little vixen made it her mission to squeeze him up nice and stiff. It was becoming increasingly difficult by the second. Almost impossible. Especially when she dove her head in his lap and wrapped her lips around him.

"What is you...you...are you cra...oohhhh shit," Malik stuttered before he melted into an ecstatic sigh. He involuntarily clutched the steering wheel over her head, grasped it in a white-knuckle grip.

The wet mouth sucking him so passionately felt exquisite.

She polished the tip, licked deliberate circles around the head with her soft tongue, and pulled him greedily into her hungry mouth. She was right. That little vixen bobbing her head up and down in his lap, slathering all over his stiff dick with a satisfying moan in the center lane of that well lit road without a shred of shame, was nothing like the traditional, conservative wife he had at home.

He viewed Sandra in an entirely different light. She was something different, foreign. A one-time fling he could do anything he wanted to. *Anything.*

Fuck it.

Malik made up his mind. He was going to slut her out. Treat her like a true freak, do the unthinkable, then go home to something respectable. One of his hands released a tight grip on the steering wheel. He found the back of her head.

"Yeah, you got that shit. Handle that pipe. Han-dle!"

Malik didn't need any assistance to guide her head up and down the length of him, and fill her mouth with his dick. He still did it anyway. She was sucking the shit out of his black flesh stick, working him over so beautifully, bowing down and blessing him with a passionate suck, even taking it *all the way* down her throat.

Gag reflexes gone.

"Don't...stop, boo. Keep going...keep...sucking that shit," Malik growled, showing aggression, his breathing labored. Her sucking lips, wet tongue, and coaxing hand worked him over in perfect harmony.

That petite, chocolate cutie could suck some dick, and Malik knew at any moment, from the rate she was going, that he would be sure to fill her cheeks with more nuts than a chipmunk stocking up for a long winter, before, "Naw! Naw...yo, what the fuck is you doing? Keep going," Malik panted. It became obvious she could sense the inevitable as well; she sucked her lips up off his dick with a pop, released her hand, and sat back in her seat.

"You said your wife ain't freaky, but I am. And this," she shook her head disapprovingly, and cleaned the corners of her lips of saliva with her thumbs, "This just ain't freaky enough for me." Sandra pouted like a spoiled little brat until a thought hit her. "But I think I know something that is."

She peeled the straps of her tight dress over both shoulders; her healthy bra covered chest popped free. She quickly shimmied out of her tight ensemble, and tossed it with a flick in the back seat.

"Are you fucking crazy? Put your clothes back on," Malik said, but couldn't help but to chuckle at her audacity. He could barely keep his eyes on the road when she reached around to unclip her bra. In seconds, aside from those four-inch stilettos coiling black leather straps around her ankles up to her calves, she was naked as the day she was born, butt ass, in her birthday suit, right there in his passenger seat.

"Kinda. But trust me, I can get even crazier."

She didn't leave much room for Malik to protest before she crawled over the armrest into his lap.

$$ $$ $$

"What is you...yo, you buggin for real. I can't...you bout to have me wrap this shit around a pole! I'm serious. I can't see the road. We're...we're gonna crash," Malik cried, trying to peek over her petite but thick frame blocking his immediate view.

"Just relax. Here, I'll drive this thing," Sandra gave him back, positioned herself over his lap, took the steering wheel, "you just drive *me.*"

Malik knew it was a lost cause, he couldn't resist. Not the way that little vixen grabbed the steering wheel with both hands, arched her back so lewdly over him, and wiggled her fat ass which blossomed open like a flower over his waist.

There wasn't a chance in hell Malik could see shit on the road in front of him, only that she cut the steering wheel for them to turn up on the expressway, nor did he care. The relatively slim waist and firm bubble he palmed in a tight grip before him became his sole focus of attention. Two hands easily sliced her fleshy ass cheeks in half. An erection that stood up stiff in his lap was swiped a few times between her soaking wet pussy lips.

"That's it, baby. There you go, take care of it. Go...faster!" Sandra chanted thickly, rolling her ass in teasing circles above him, anxious for entry.

"Digging up in her, or hitting the gas?" Malik thought. He wasn't quite sure.

Fuck it!

He did both.

He began to gradually ease her down onto his lap – up, down a little, up again, down a little more on his stiffness – steadily working himself up in her tight wetness, while at the same time gradually accelerating the gas.

"That's it. Uummm...huummm," Sandra hummed from deep in her chest, "Go. Faster. Faster!"

Her hips came alive. Sandra crouched forward; her face came inches from the steering wheel that she handled like a *NASCAR* driver. It wasn't intentional, not even thought out – Malik leaned on the gas even more. There weren't that many cars out on the road that night after two in the morning, but the few that were keeping pace with them began to whip by to disappear in his rear-view.

"Go, baby. Go. Faster! Go!" Sandra demanded excitedly.

She began to bounce wildly in his lap, moaned out freely in a liberated cry of exhilaration, and dipped in and out of the few lanes of traffic. Malik held a vice grip-like clamp onto her waist, and *'drove'* her energized round ass with short, jabs-like thrusts. He dug up in her with determination from underneath. The gas pedal kissed the floor.

Malik couldn't determine how fast they were going. He only knew they were easily flying down the Interstate nearing the hundred mile per hour mark. That petite fireball slamming herself up and down in his lap as if she was possessed became his only concern.

Faster.

The engine began to squeal, the pressure from the motor reaching its peak.

Faster.

Faster!

"Oh, shit!"

Sandra quickly yanked the steering wheel sharply to the right. Lost in the throes of impaling herself with that thick dick underneath her, she came seconds away from barreling head-on into the back end of an eighteen-wheeler at over one hundred and twenty miles per hour.

French Montana's 'Go', and an impending orgasm, had her in a zone – she dipped around that tractor trailer channeling the essence of *Danika Patrick* in full control to resume the snapping pop of her hips in a pulse-driven, sex-fueled, reverse cowgirl.

Faster.

Faster.

Malik felt that distinct tingling sensation building up in his loins, his body grew hot, he got light-headed.

Faster.

The shrill pierce of three hundred and eighty iron horses under the hood were drowned out by Sandra squealing an ecstatic, "Oh, there it is! That's it, baby. Don't stop…ohhhh, I'm cumming! *Don't… fucking…stop!*" in the tight cabin; a warm burst of liquid spilled out from between her thighs to puddle Malik's lap.

Faster.

That extra wet signal of her reaching her peak, and squirming like a whore in heat in his lap, did it for him.

"Ohhhh shit…*yeah*! I feel it. Give it *all* to me, baby!" Sandra shrieked pleasurably the second she felt his orgasm squirting in torrents to fill her up. She didn't stop riding him, nor did Malik stop impaling her with dick. The thrill of breaking practically every motor vehicle law ever written, while at the same time simultaneously experiencing the best orgasm of his life, kept him going.

More, faster, more.

The sensitivity that normally forced a break out of him after an orgasm became lost in the throes of excitement. He wanted to fuck that little chocolate brown cutie like she couldn't believe – so he did. Surprisingly, he couldn't hold out much longer – it only took another record-breaking five minutes of recovery time for him to feel his third orgasm of the night squirting out of him deep in her belly.

Malik almost passed out from the sensation.

All the energy of his being poured out of him in synch with him filling her womb. His foot fell off the pedal, he fell back slumped in his seat, deflated. Within a couple of miles, as if his vehicle ran out of gas, they gradually slowed with Sandra firmly in his lap steering the car onto the emergency lane on the side of the highway. She finally crawled from over him, and reached into the back seat for her dress.

"Now *that* was what I call fun," Sandra sighed slightly winded; she stepped back into her dress with an indelible smile. "So, whaddya think? Was *Sandra* wild enough for you? Or next weekend do you want to make acquaintances with *Veronica?*"

Malik peered over in complete admiration at his wife, Tanisha, in the passenger seat. He couldn't believe how convincing she became in her role-playing routine. How his previously conservative wife transformed her into the shrewd, sexually insatiable vixen she made herself up to be from the onset of their 'chance encounter' at the club.

She peeled off her wig to expose a clean set of cornrows; baby hairs were pressed down on the sides. That was the woman he knew, the image of the wife he married. He basked in an afterglow of satisfaction at the thought of everything that went down that night.

"Baby..." Malik leaned over the armrest, and did what he wanted to do all night, but couldn't if he wanted to remain in character – passionately suck on her tongue and bottom lip – then cupped her head to whisper in her ear, "...I don't know if I can handle another episode with Sandra, let alone this mysterious Veronica. But I was never one to run from a challenge. Next weekend, bring her on."

Third Interview

"Well, well, well. What do you know? Right on time today."

Dr. Black reclined heavily into a plush leather office chair behind an immaculate wooden desk with a polished countertop.

"So, what do you think?"

A bookmark was placed in a copy of Nathanial Brandon's *'The Six Pillars of Self Esteem'*, and placed on the center of his desk, before Dr. Black gestured to a completely furnished office with the wave of an open palm.

"Looks good, doesn't it? I wish I could take credit for even a single picture on the wall, but I can't. Kiara. She always had an eye for interior design. Just one of her many other talents. Where is she? She had to run a few errands. I concluded my scheduled meetings for today, outside of our interview, so she took off to handle some things. I swear I don't know what I would do without her. That woman...well, no need to go into all of that right now. So, what did you make of it? No. Not of the new office. I mean of the second couple, Malik and Tanisha."

Dr. Black's laughs heartily.

"They're...*adventurous*, wouldn't you say? Role playing, voyeurism. They're into their thing something serious, got their own little thing going on."

The thumb drive was handed back over.

"How many times did you watch this? Three, four, ten? Should I wash my hands? Naw, I'm just joking. I'm just proud of them. They came a long way since I had my first session with them. When they first came to see me, you would have been surprised to hear that they'd been married for over fifteen years. It became a mission in itself to pull them out of their shells. To teach them that their sex lives was a normal expression of their total personality. Role-playing. Swinging. Voyeurism. Multi-person marriages. Couples are doing it all today behind closed doors, mostly on the low, to make their relationships work.

"Malik and Tanisha, while they haven't explored those unique lifestyles, yet, they have been exploring the notion of role-playing, as they demonstrated on that drive. Before I continue, let me clarify something here. It isn't all about sex. Fucking, and sucking, and licking, and satisfying the flesh is good. *Real* good. You know I love it. Yet, sex isn't the end all to all problems. The thing is, most of the couples who seek my counsel seem to be having that particular problem: how to spice up their marriage.

"In my experience, the two major factors which seem to be at the core of relationship problems are *fidelity/intimacy* and *money*. Of course, there are a plethora of other things that can hinder the growth and development of a relationship, but I only tackle issues of intimacy and communication.

"How some relationships start out on a bad note when people get together solely because they experience a strong sexual attraction for each other – she's beautiful with a fat ass, and a total freak in the bedroom; he's fine as hell with a six-pack, packing ten-inches, and got a lot of money – then confuse this lust for love because of those strong feelings, sometimes ignoring the fact that they have little to any values or interests in common.

"You'd be surprised at the amount of couples who have little, to no genuine admiration for their significant other. Yet, who became bound to each other because they fell into a habit or routine, have incompatible personalities, and basically have little or no authentic interests in each other outside of the fact that one or both people involved are hooked to the other person's loving. Relationships like these, as you could imagine, are doomed from the start. They just can't see it yet. The lure of good sex, and that mind-blowing orgasm, is shining so bright that it keeps them blinded in the dark. Drink?"

A few tumblers and a bottle of *Remy Martin* were removed from a brass wet bar in the corner.

"Yeah, I've interviewed a good majority of young couples who go through such problems. Think about when you were younger. How many of us had the wisdom and foresight to see past a strong sense of stunning beauty? Shit, when I was in my late teens, early twenties, there were three things I looked for in a young woman: a pretty face, a curvy body, and a sense of attraction strong enough that we couldn't remain in each other's presence, for any period of time, without tearing each other's clothes off."

A half-filled tumbler on ice was handed over to the journalist.

"When individuals mature, notice how I didn't equate age with maturity, some will begin to see past that. Most will begin to look for something meaningful, real. Not just lust. Love. But in order to truly love an individual, one would have to see that person for who they really are, not the front or mask they put on to impress the other with.

"*Denzel Washington* and *Angela Basseting* themselves through their relationship wouldn't be their true self, just the person they're *pretending* to be. Actors. That front-a-role, subliminal, pseudo-image bullshit I spoke about in an earlier session. We don't play those games here. We get to the heart and matter of who a person really is.

"To do this requires one key factor: the ability to see that person with reasonable clarity. Sometimes couples, in their strong desires, tend to idealize or glamorize their partners, misperceive them, exaggerate their virtues, and blind themselves to their shortcomings. That's no good. What they need to do is see the good, and the bad, the weaknesses, and strengths, in each other in order for true love to grow.

"When I began my counseling sessions with Malik and Tanisha, I followed the traditional route of screening them with questions. I tried to figure out clinical diagnoses on them, to fit them into a pretty little box, that I could tie up neatly, with a pretty little bow. PTSD. Depression. Narcissistic personality disorder. Midlife crisis.

"It wasn't until I rewired my train of thought, and began to build with my new clients, that I began to enlighten them on concepts like *Individualism* – the supremacy of an individual's rights; that he or she is an end to him or herself, not a means to the end of others, and that the proper goal in life is self-realization and self-fulfillment. Do the math to that – *self-realization:* to understand self, and *self-fulfillment:* to satisfy oneself fully."

$$ $$ $$

"Many don't have those fundamentals prior to entering a session: to know that they should think and judge independently, respecting nothing more on this physical plane than the sovereignty of his or her mind. This realization doesn't normally come to fruition until that person does some independent soul searching, seeking, and wanting more out of life; what I went through in that prison cell. Not really looking for more *materially*, but more *spiritually, psychologically, emotionally, intellectually,* and yeah, a freer version of themselves *sexually*.

"In order to do that, they had to realize that the starting point begins with the ideal that he, or she, must be selfish.

Selfish in the pursuit of self. And there's nothing wrong with that once one *over*-stands this concept. A concept that doesn't intrude, or deprive others, but a selfishness that is actually healthy. One should be selfish in the pursuit of maintaining their health, preserving their sanity, pursuing happiness, or fighting for their next...*inhale...exhale*...breath. You feel me?

"This principle needs to be fully embraced, not just by my clients, but all people, cause the bottom line is people who do not experience that selfish love for self will have little capacity to experience, or more importantly, accept the love of others. The same with people who are devoid of self-respect; in all likelihood, they will have no respect for others, regardless of any love they may think they have.

"The questions I pose along this train of thought is: could love alone guarantee that Malik and Tanisha will be able to create a fulfilling and satisfying relationship? Could love promise that Salim and Naomi will act mature in all situations, or project wisdom? Can love teach them communication skills, or techniques on conflict resolution, or the ability to integrate love into other spheres of their lives? Of course not. This takes conscious thought, rational thinking, intelligence."

Dr. Black took a sip on his tumbler.

"Malik and Tanisha, and every other couple on this planet, will continue to grow and evolve, individually, and as couples. Their needs, their goals, will grow and evolve right along with them. Within this journey of growth and evolution sometimes new goals and desires emerge that will cause a subtle or major division within their relationship, and there's nothing wrong with that. That's just a part of the process, the journey. That's just a part of life. Sometimes that division might rise to the level where they become two different entities, on two different courses, and have to go their separate ways.

"There's nothing necessarily wrong with that either. If something like that was to unfold, they could look at that time spent together as something that brought them beautiful memories and life experience. Still images in their journey of life one was glad to have lived. The only time something like that could become a cancer is if those individuals realize that their relationship no longer benefits either of them, that they've grown apart, yet, they fight to hold on to something that shouldn't be held on to. They don't possess the wisdom to know when to simply let it go.

"Malik and Tanisha were seriously struggling with their relationship for months, almost a year. They were close to calling it quits. They were arguing all of the time, fighting, luckily not physically. But the verbal was just as destructive, if not worse than the physical. They were becoming toxic to not only themselves, but to their children as well, who was forced to witness it all.

"They questioned why they were even holding on to their relationship. Was it for the kids? The sanctity of their marriage vows? The comfort of companionship? They didn't know. They were at a point where it didn't look like their relationship could be salvaged. They decided to take a break, get separated. Some may ask: how would they be able to determine if their relationship was worth salvaging, or if they were, as I mentioned earlier, fighting to hold on to something that should no longer be held on to?

"That's the question of the century. The answer: *wisdom*. Or another simple conclusion: *is the relationship still productive?* Is it growing, or is their growth being stunted? Let's take it back to the basics again: love. Emotional love, by definition, is an intense affection for another person based on personal or familial ties; a strong affection or attachment to another person based on regard or shared experiences or interests.

"To break that down – love is an emotional response to something we highly value. To experience a supreme sense of peace in the existence of the loved object; peace within their presence, peace in building with them, peace in interacting with them. To love is to find peace in the being whom one loves, experience pleasure in that being's presence, find gratification and fulfillment being in contact with that being.

"With that love follows emotion. And just like all emotions, love gives rise to evaluation and action tendencies. The first thing I enlighten my client's to is they have to recognize emotions for what they really are: *value responses*. Automatic psychological responses of what we perceive as the helpful or harmful relationship of some aspect of reality to ourselves. Malik and Tanisha were responding in an adverse way to each other when they were arguing and beefing, considering the other being an adversary to their happiness.

"*Over*-standing this on that level, if one were to consider any emotional response, from fear, to love, to anger, one can notice that implicit in every response is a dual value judgment. The duality being pronounced is 'helpful' or 'harmful', and also 'to what extent'. There are also varying degrees of emotions according to their content and intensity. When one dissects love in this context, love could be considered the highest, the most intense expression of the assessment 'beneficial for me', advantageous to my life, when you put in perspective what the loved object is.

"When one has an emotional response towards something, there is an impetus to perform some action related to that particular emotion. Fear is an emotional response to that which threatens his or her values; one's first instinct, their knee-jerk reaction, is to avoid or distance themselves from the feared object.

"Love, the complete opposite: to achieve some form of contact with the loved being, some form of interaction or involvement. If you do the math to both of these polar opposites, you will see that although we may fear something, it is not always beneficial to avoid it. Just like everything we love, we shouldn't necessarily rush to have some form of interaction with it.

"One of the values of passionate love that Tanisha learned

is to embrace it as an outlet. It gave her a channel for that flow of energy, a source of inspiration, a gift of her existence, a confirmation of the value of her life. Some couples lose that along the way before they come to grips and find it again. Some might never find it at all, no matter how you try to open their third eye. Fortunately, my clients have.

"Do you know how? By learning to stand before a psychological mirror and visualizing themselves as an object in reality, conceptualizing the physical entity before them that is their true self. There is a value in being able to see ourselves for who we truly are, and not only being able to say, 'I see me', but also accepting that 'that's me'. The manifestation of this value is called *objectivity*."

$$ $$ $$

"When I began my sessions with Malik, and we traveled on this topic, the issue came up about if there was a direct sense in which he could experience this? Was there a mirror in which he could perceive his psychological self, outside of self? No doubt.

"That mirror could be experienced by looking into the eyes of Tanisha, his significant other, another consciousness. The principle of psychological visibility. A visibility that could be detected through Tanisha's personalities; her personality expressed through her behavior, through the things she said, and did, and through the ways she said and did them. Through this expression, Malik became an object of perception to not only Tanisha, but others as well.

"When Malik responded to Tanisha, to her view of him and her behavior, her perception was in turn expressed through her behavior, by the way she looked at him, by the way she spoke to him, by the way she responded to him, and so forth. If her view of him was consistent with his deepest vision of who he felt himself to be, and if her view was communicated by her behavior, he would feel perceived, feel psychologically visible. *'She can understand me, she can relate'*. Tanisha became his psychological mirror.

"This isn't the only way. When one encounters a person who think as they do, who notices the things they notice, who value the things they value, who tend to respond to different situations as they do, not only do they experience a strong sense of affinity with such a person, but they can also experience themselves through the perception of that person. Some may view someone like that as their soulmate.

"That's what Tanisha needed to experience to the most intense degree with Malik to feel fully visible. That in loving him, she encountered herself. That Malik, ideally, reacted to her, in effect, how he would react to himself in the person of another; that he perceived himself through Tanisha's reaction.

"In doing this, that visibility brought about self-discovery. And a consistent experience of visibility in their relationship unquestionably introduced contact with new aspects of who they were. When that visibility progressed in Malik and Tanisha's relationship over time, and especially when it maintained itself across a significant period of time, one of the most intriguing aspects that they learned about each other was how they expanded the awareness of self, how the other brought out deeper aspects of self.

"Tanisha's desire for love from Malik was inseparable from her desire to be visible to him. If he would have made a claim to love her, but when he began to express what he found as lovable characteristics she didn't think she possessed, didn't necessarily admire, and definitely couldn't relate to, she surely wouldn't feel that he loved her for her, or truly understood her.

"She didn't want Malik to love her blindly, not when his claim came with an edict that he loved her for who she was. She wanted the love that he had for her to be for specific reasons;

because of who she was. She knew if Malik made a declaration of love to her for reasons that didn't reflect her self-perceptions, values, or standards, if he didn't love her for who she truly was, she wouldn't feel satisfied, she wouldn't feel truly loved, cause she wouldn't feel like she was actually seen by him, visible; she wouldn't feel respected, or felt Malik was responding to her for who she truly was.

"This is only one of the principles that I travel with my client's on – that to feel understood is the essence of the principle visibility. The desire for two people to enter into a sexual union, as well as a psychological marriage of the minds, is one of the defining characteristics of two souls wishing to unite. I'm not talking about the one who uses sex as a form of recreation, or as a pacifier to suppress emotional issues, but as a celebration of their union.

"Sex, and the profound importance of it in our lives, lies in the extreme pleasure it offers to man. And pleasure, for man and woman, extends far beyond the luxury of physical satisfaction it provides, but becomes an intense psychological need.

"Pleasure, and not just sexual, is a metaphysical connection to life, the reward and consequence of successful action. Just as pain indicates the opposite: it represents a symbol of weakness, of failure, of destruction. Measuring these two opposites in this light, within the experience of pleasure, implicitly, one has the feeling and thought of, *'I am the sole controller of my existence. I am experiencing the ultimate satisfaction to reality right now'*. Just as the experience of pain manifests the opposite: *'I'm feeling hopeless, inefficient'*, and implicitly, *'I am not in control'*.

"During one of my later counseling sessions with Malik, and our discussions on pleasure, he became enlightened, had a eureka moment, and explained his ideas of pleasure beyond the physical to...(Dr. Black gazed at the *Tag Heuer* on wrist)...well, what do you know. That's our time. If we keep this up, the way I'm dropping this heavy mental on you, you'll be versed just about as deep as most of my client's. Speaking of clients, here."

Another thumb-drive was handed over.

"I'm feeling our little ritual of leaving you with visuals of these forms of sexual sciences. Peep the technique of these two. Next week, same time. We'll reconvene, and discuss the tools that make these unions work. I'll see you then. Peace."

Case File #31 - Victor & Zakia

Zakia knew it was going to be a long day.

For the past two months, together with her partner, Andre, they'd been going over and making sure all of the appropriate preparations were made to ensure everything went down smoothly. Their 'members only' on-line clothing company, *Modelme.com,* had been engaged in strict negotiations; they were vying to secure a contract with a big client to possibly enter into a partnership with him.

Although the numbers had been pretty good since the inception of their company over two and a half years prior – their staff swelled from a mere three employees to an astronomical thirty-seven, most within the last year alone, their bottom line took on a steady nine percent increase annually, she even had plans to open a second office and branch within the next year – Zakia knew this particular client would really do it for her.

As always, Zakia was one of the first to arrive well before the six am hour. She slammed the trunk on her kitted out *BMW X5* after snatching out her burgundy leather attaché case, and a brown cardboard box filled with some new designs. Zakia walked light on her toes, her strong, powerful gait leading her, a mid-length cream trench coat floating gracefully behind her.

Each step managed to tickle a perverse smirk out of her as she made her way to the front entrance.

There was rarely a morning when Zakia didn't slow her pace to steal a quick peek at her appearance in the gold tinted reflection of the windows enveloping the whole building. That morning was no different.

The hairstyle wasn't the same, although she couldn't deviate too much from that; her finger-thick, auburn dreads, long enough to touch the center of her back, were twisted up in cornrow-meshed braids, and wrapped in a stylishly tight bun, held by two black chopsticks.

Form fitted, purple, designer *Reem Acra* blazer, white dress shirt, more buttons undone up top than usual, highlighting much more cleavage on her 36C's than previous times, a matching skin tight, knee-high skirt. That was definitely out of the ordinary for her. Form-fitted slacks were her trademark. That morning, for her own furtive reasons, the skirt had to do.

Not bad.

It really highlighted the slimness of her waist, and ballooned her hips out in true hourglass fashion. She didn't even have to get a peek behind her to sense how the tight material accentuated every curve of her thick, but firm, forty-two inch round ass; six years of religious training at *Fitness Planet* really did her body justice. A dichotomy came with the appearance, especially since the notion of hot sex dripped from her being like five hundred pounds of flesh after an hour in a sauna.

A part of Zakia didn't like that, despised it.

She was an exceptionally attractive, strong black woman, built like the lead video vixen in a rap video. She was all too aware of the stigma attached to women in an economic world predominantly dominated by middle-aged white males, which is one of the reasons why, despite being proud of her shapely physique, she made it a point to tone down any sexual overtones in her appearance when she entered the workplace.

The last thing she wanted to be brought up on in the court

of public opinion were charges of not being able to cut it in her field, and resorting to the safety net of her sexuality to make it. The gender card. The race card. Affirmative Action. No one who experienced her business acumen *personally* could bring her up on such charges.

She was known as a shrewd, ruthless businesswoman from anyone who had the experience of witnessing her business suave. But for those who didn't know her, she wanted all first impressions and judgments of capability to be based on her mental, not her physical. And on such a morning, Zakia knew she was going to need every modicum of her keen business suave if she was going to see things through to the end.

"Good morning, Mrs. Thornton," the receptionist at the front desk greeted; she presented Zakia with an *Ipad* from the side of her computer.

"Hey." Zakia placed the box on the edge of her desk, attaché case on the floor, and received the *Ipad*, "Andre should be sitting in on the meeting with us this morning. We should be starting at around nine." Zakia swept her fingers over the face, opened a few files to pull up certain reports, checked her itinerary.

Her receptionist stared at Zakia oddly. She held one eyebrow subtly arched, observed her keenly, and watched her every move. From the time she'd been working there, she'd never witnessed Mrs. Thornton that chipper so early in the day. Really any part of the day. Around the office, Zakia was known as the 'Ice Queen' for her no nonsense attitude. The aura she basked in that morning was surely unusual.

"The conference room has been set up as you ordered. Would you like your regular French vanilla latte?" her receptionist questioned, trying her best to mask intrigue.

"That would be great. Thank you." Zakia handed her back the *Ipad*.

"I'll have it in your office immed..."

"Ah, thank you," Zakia spit curtly, "I'd appreciate that."

Her receptionist winced slightly from her sharp reply, and

eyed her even more strangely as Zakia scooped up the box and attaché case, and bustled off to her office.

$$ $$ $$

Zakia sat at the helm of a massive circular conference table with Andre, her partner, slash co-founder, slash Chief Creative Officer, sitting diplomatically by her side. The client who they were to conduct negotiations with arrived right on time, as scheduled.

He sat with his silent partner, a finely polished Latino man in his late twenties, halfway around the table. From the moment she arrived, Zakia couldn't deny the odd stares she received from her employees. Zakia surely wasn't her usual self. She'd been practically glowing the whole morning.

She could even sense the few glances being thrown at her from the eyes circling the huge conference table. Zakia tried to ignore it, bit the corner of her bottom lip, crossed her legs under the table, and toyed with her *Ipad* in front of her to prep herself for her presentation.

"You ready?" Zakia's partner whispered discreetly; he snapped her out of her blissfully ambiguous trance.

"Ah, yeah. Of course." Zakia cleared her throat, shook her head, cleared her thoughts. "Good morning to each of you, Andre, my staff. I would like to express an especially warm welcome to Mr. Davidson and his associate for joining us this morning. As each of you are aware of..." Zakia opened scripturally, and for the first time all morning took on the staunch demeanor she was known for taking, "...I'll get straight to the point here..."

Zakia went on to elaborate, in explicit detail, the crux of the offer their company presented. She held in her hand a small device that controlled an overhead projector directed at a clear white wall, flashing through an array of slides to assist her in her presentation.

Zakia strolled in a methodic pace around the table a few times, controlled the room, directed them to pie charts and bar graphs on display, and held them entranced with her every word. Only those intimately familiar with her conference room guerrilla style tactics could detect the eccentricities in her character that morning; her potential clients remained oblivious.

"And with that, I'll open the floor to any questions." Zakia clicked off the projection screen and raised the dimmed lights with her small multi-remote. She returned to stand at her leather chair at the head of the table.

"Yes, you mentioned the incorporation of furniture on this site. Would the inclusion of such sales take place immediately?"

Zakia took a deep breath. She closed her eyes, and secretly pushed another button on the remote concealed in her hand.

"Th...the inclusion of furniture, which we see our biggest competitor have already been selling themselves, will contribute tremendously..." Zakia paused, took another deep breath, rocked subtly from side to side, gathered herself, finally said as if it was forced, "...to our company. This is something that has been researched and tested. Tried and proven." A few supporting nods were given amongst her staff; Zakia's client's weren't so quick to agree.

"Research? According to *our* research, there are other studies which suggest otherwise," a doubtful voice spoke in opposition, "But we needn't get into some long drawn out debate about numbers, now. What concerns me is the methods in which you plan to include the furniture you just mentioned, what appears to be your selling point this morning. An asset that you feel the need to include immediately. I'm curious as to..." Mr. Davidson paused when he noticed Zakia's eyes rolling lightly behind half closed eyes. Her Gucci tipped fingernails applied pressure to the top of her seat, she squirmed a little more.

"Mrs. Thornton, are you...are you ok?" one of her

coworker's asked. The show of concern had all eyes in the room, some who drifted off mentally at the mundane of such meetings, on Zakia.

"I'm...I'm fine. I just got a little light-headed," Zakia sighed, having a hard time remaining still. Her partner took notice.

"What Mrs. Thornton is trying to say is..." Zakia's partner, Andre, stood to his feet by her side to take over, "This addition is good for business. Great. I stand by her decision, one hundred percent. To include furniture on our website immediately, will not only boost our bottom line by..." from the bottom of his eyes he caught Zakia squeezing the head of her chair even tighter, white knuckles, heard her breathing slow to a light pant. "Why don't you let me finish up the rest of this." He placed a comforting hand on her shoulder. "Go get some air. You look a little flushed."

All eyes in the room, like they were watching the climax of their favorite movie unfold in the flesh, were glued to Zakia's every move with unbelieving eyes. Never had they seen her take on such a seemingly impassioned state, all without any obvious provocation. She had a hard time remaining still, swayed a few times in place, appeared to be on the verge of collapsing, yet the whole time held an almost indistinguishable smirk on her lips.

"Ladies, gentlemen," she finally gathered herself, turned to her client's, "I really do apologize. It must have been...been something I ate. I'm really sorry. Please, excuse me," Zakia said impulsively.

In haste, she dropped her small device, quickly crouched down to retrieve it, and scurried out of the office to the ladies room.

$$ $$ $$

There were only a few occasions in Zakia's adult life where embarrassment unraveled her to such a state where shame steered her away from even gazing at her own reflection. Just a few hours earlier, she experienced just one of those rare moments. What was even more troubling was such a pivotal moment occurred at a time when she had a crucial meeting with a prospective client.

Never mind the fact that they did indeed secure the contract; Andre related how although *he* closed the deal, it was *her presentation* that they were the most impressed with. The fervor in her voice, the glow of her aura which radiated from her being to such a degree that it could actually be felt in the room, the passion and elegance in her tone, despite the few slights of concern, convinced them to sign on to the full stipulations of her proposal.

That wasn't the point.

The point is she failed in her attempt to fully see it through to the end, that a chink in her armor became exposed at her haste departure from negotiations so close to closing the deal. That she became disorientated, when she convinced herself her ecstatic state of mind accompanying her through the course of her presentation would actually *enhance* the flow of her pitch, instead of the opposite, *derail her.*

Even worse, she would have to convey this failure to her husband, Victor. Convey this after she assured him, quite arrogantly, that she could do it. For close to an hour the night before, they discussed the meeting in depth in their bedroom.

"I got all the confidence in the world you could close the deal without *any impediments. I just don't think you can do it under...certain conditions,"* Victor said, rummaging through one of the double doors of an expensive white armoire with silver accents.

"Care to make it interesting?" Zakia challenged.

She made her cocky stance leaned forward in front of a mirrored dresser. Transparent, pink silk negligee, white paisley bra, matching white paisley boyshort panties all up in her, inches of ass cheeks spilling out. She twisted each individual dread at the root, applied dabs of beeswax.

"*Don't I always?*" Victor moved articles around, rustled items aside, his eyes lit up. "*Ah, here we go.*"

He fished out an object hanging on the back door, held it up dramatically in the crux of his index finger. Zakia continued her twisting, inspecting each dread from the root down to the tips, refreshing her African pride without much mental effort. She sliced her gaze back at him through the reflection, spotted his weapon of choice. A twinkle flickered in her eyes, fascination with just a hint of fear.

"*I'll give you one opportunity to back down. Cop a plea, save face, and I'll let you live. If not, trust me, shit will get ugly.*"

Victor did give her an opportunity to back out.

Well, not really.

Cop a plea? Save face? He'll let her *live, or shit will get ugly?*

Coming at her like that, punking her, that was a challenge if she ever seen one. How could she back down to that? She couldn't. Such was the ebb and flow of their relationship. And Zakia knew she would be damned if she would start backing down from his challenges, ever, even at the risk of securing one of her biggest client's to date.

The more Zakia thought about it, the more the challenge took on such a dangerously alluring appeal: obtain one of the biggest client's she ever faced encumbered with the hurdle Victor presented. Secure the client, *and* beat Victor at his own game, all in one fell swoop. A double-edged sword. One she could wield to her advantage if she succeeded; or go down in a massive flame of glory if she failed.

The challenge became too tempting for Zakia to resist.

"*You should have never opened your mouth. You're on! Let's see how ugly shit can get.*"

She took the bait, and like a marlin that got caught out in the high seas – hook, line and sinker – Zakia knew she had to serve up what her hands called for.

Time to pay her dues.

$$ $$ $$

Zakia rolled her Beamer to a stop in her driveway.

Victor was already there; his *SLK 350* evidence of that.

Instead of carrying a downtrodden air of defeat, Zakia walked lightly, and held her head up high. She dropped her trench and attaché case on the seat of a chair in the foyer, tossed the blazer mindlessly over the back of the couch in the living room, and headed straight to the kitchen. A drink was definitely in order. Scotch, no rocks. Zakia poured herself a healthy portion in a crystal tumbler.

"So, what's the verdict?"

Zakia didn't get the chance to swallow her first mouthful before she heard his voice coming from above her. A glance over her shoulder, she lifted her eyes to Victor. He walked smoothly across the open second floor, ran his hand across the polished wooden banister, took the spiral staircase, each step taken methodically. He wore a massive, plush, dark blue robe with gold stitching, and black house slippers. A slight smirk floated across Zakia's lips hidden sneakily behind the tumbler. She returned to her drink, and kept her back to him, almost as if to refuse him any satisfaction so early upon her arrival.

He made it to her in no time; his methodic pace permitted him to inspect her keenly from behind. Even after almost a decade of marriage, Zakia still managed to ignite certain things in him whenever she dressed like that. Business attire always did it for him; one of his many fetishes. He was sure it had something to do with the power associated with it. Then of course, there was also that back shot on Zakia, her bubble in those tight skirts; they resembled two basketballs stuffed in cotton.

Victor rounded their imported, black marble kitchen island,

got a good look at her face, her eyes. He needed to see her eyes. In the past, they made a game of it. They would sit Indian-style in the middle of their living room floor, facing each other, without words, without moving, just looking, absorbing the being of the other, allowing impressions to form, allowing fantasies concerning the other to develop without censorship, trying to read what the other was thinking; how much they could see into each other's minds.

Victor studied her that evening with the same objective.

He removed the drink from her hand, almost snatched it away, spilled a few drops on the counter, his attempts to rattle her, expose her, staring intently into the dark brown windows to her soul. Didn't quite get the reaction he intended, or hoped for. No matter. He waved the tumbler under his nose, inspected its texture, and casually raised it to his lips. He refused to even blink as he tried to mentally strip away any 'tells' she tried to hide behind to mask her false bravado.

Oh, Zakia was good, *real* good. An Asiatic empress who donned the ultimate poker face; empty, stoic, expressionless. Still, didn't matter. Victor knew he was better. It took time to dissect her mental, extract fragments of her psyche, couple that distinct twinkle in her eye with her subtle body language – one of her *tells* she never knew she exposed – to tell him everything he needed to know.

"No comment? You really want to do this the hard way? Ok, suit yourself, soldier. I guess there's only one way to find out. Time to get this beautiful, ugly."

$$ \$\$\ \$\$\ \$\$ $$

Victor knocked back the rest of her drink, and placed the empty tumbler on the counter in front of her. No more of an inspection was needed. Off to the living room he went. He returned moments later to witness Zakia pouring herself a refill. He dropped her handbag dramatically on the counter, and rifled through it. Cell phone. Items of make-up. D&G wallet. One at a time, Victor placed them on the counter.

"Bingo!" He lit up when he finally retrieved his item of interest. Zakia remained silent, nursed a few sips, cut occasional glances at him through squinted eyes. "From the looks of this, it looks like you may have actually gone through with it."

Victor caressed the device between his fingers. It resembled a small car remote starter, only more advanced. Zakia was leaned over the counter, propped on her elbows, her fingers circled around a crystal tumbler filled with three fingers as if it was a steamy mug of cocoa on a cold winter day. She remained still, unmoved physically and emotionally. She followed him with a slice of her eyes when he circled her again. Followed him till she could see him no more when he took her back

He was out of range, but with Zakia arched over like that, her ass thrust out in such a salacious pose, it wasn't too hard for her to guess where his focus of attention landed. What she knew made him weak. A soft hand ran down the small of her back, it quickly grew firm. Zakia's style of dress held her belt buckle on her side. Victor tugged at it, unfastened it, pulled it off with one smooth motion through the hoops.

"Did you go through with it?" Victor's voice grew rich in aggression.

Zakia didn't answer him, didn't say a word. Victor peeled down the zipper on the side of her dress. The white dress shirt tucked neatly inside was yanked from her waist. Victor disheveled her clothing, did as he pleased, and slid his index finger in what appeared to be the strap of her G-string high on her waist.

"I see you wore it. The question is…" Victor circled his arm around her to wave the remote in her face, "…were you brave enough to turn it on?"

Zakia's breathing grew shallow, a slight twinge of butterflies fluttered in her stomach, she squirmed nervously in a sexual sway that only her husband would have been able to detect. He removed the two black chopsticks pinning Zakia's dreads up in a bun; her finger-thick locks fell loosely down to the center of her back.

"Take those off – now!" Victor ordered.

Her thin belt dangled menacingly in his hand, within the other, he ran his fingers across the remote. A brief stint of hesitation on Zakia's end, less than three seconds, and Victor whipped the belt through the air, and brought it down in a firm slap against the side of her right thigh. Zakia still took her time; she finally wiggled her skintight skirt down over her thick thighs. She did it on her time, became defiant, rebellious; it fell into a clump around her ankles.

"What else?" Victor posed mysteriously.

Zakia sighed heavily, sucked her teeth, and dramatically rolled her eyes. She proceeded down each button of her expensive white dress shirt, and moved at a snail's pace, the whole time staring at Victor with her lip snarled, her demeanor that a spoiled teenager being reprimanded by a stern parent. The folds were sliced open, teasingly, taunting him, then coldly brushed from over her shoulders; it fell into a pile on the kitchen floor over her skirt.

Zakia stepped out of them, and kicked those garments away from her with an insolent flick of her foot. Light jewels with a heavy price tag – four karats on her earrings, thin necklace with a dog tag diamond medallion; another three karats, ten-karat princess cut diamond wedding ring with yellow canaries, two tennis bracelets – she stood proud in five-inch, red bottom stilettos, virtually nude in the center of their kitchen, bursting out the seams of a purple lace paisley bra which meshed perfectly with her creamy, milk chocolate skin.

From first appearance, she appeared to be wearing a simple black G-string.

It wasn't.

It was actually a toy they purchased together a few weeks prior perusing a sex store online; a leather G-string that attached a small, curvy-headed vibrator in the crotch, in the shape of a 'C', about the size of a four-inch fat shrimp.

The device, when inserted, was angled perfectly to stimulate her g-spot; a mimic of two fingers under her hood, a consistent, curling 'come-here' motion. Another three prongs, in the shape of a triangle, on the inner surface of the crotch were strategically placed to vibrate over her clit. It was powered by a small battery, and could be activated on voice command, or manually on various speeds from a remote control – the very remote Victor wielded in his possession like a weapon.

"I didn't think you'd do it. Wear this..." Victor hooked a single finger in the elastic strap, pulled it back as far as it permitted, and released it to snap back to bite into her waist; Zakia flinched, and gasped a sexy moan, when it stung her naked flesh, "...to such an important meeting. What was our secret word again? Hmmmmm, now just what was it?"

Victor lifted his head to the ceiling, pondered the thought. After a moment, he lowered his gaze conveniently on the remote.

"That's it – *immediately.*"

A press of a button detonated the contraption on its lightest setting; it sent shivers down Zakia's spine.

She gasped out another tiny moan, contained her breathing, eked out, "But I *did* do it, proved you wrong, *and* I got the contract," without the slightest of conviction. Her voice was quite the opposite of her regular tone; passive and weak. Victor reacted in the next breath – he filled his hand with a fistful of her dreads, and snatched her close.

"Did I say you can speak?" Victor twisted her neck, forced her to face him. He eased her ear close, mere inches from his lips. "The deal was you had to wear this thing for the whole day, more specifically, throughout the whole meeting. And every time you heard the word *'immediate'*, or any derivative of it, you had to turn up the setting," Victor hissed in her ear.

Zakia shivered from the dual sensation. Her eyes were sliced low in lust, a perverse snarl curled the corner of her top lip into an arrogant snarl. Although Victor only set the vibration on its lowest setting, one out of a scale of ten, it still tickled Zakia oh so lovely in all the right places.

"And you lied. *You* didn't close the deal, *Andre* did. How do I know this? It's because he called earlier to send his congratulations."

Busted!

$$ $$ $$

Victor sucked her earlobe into his mouth as he called her out on her lie. He bit it lightly, sucked on it to soften the sting, then bit it again harder, sucked it again, hard and soft, gave her only a prelude to her punishment. He turned up the vibration on the device a notch higher; two. Zakia's moans progressed, her hands tightened into fists, she instinctively kicked out her legs a little wider.

"What was the bet? Do I need to remind you?" Victor's tone grew harsh. Despite holding a relatively tight clutch on the back of Zakia's dreads, she managed to shake out a slight nod. "The bet was if you lose, you would have to be disciplined. Should I discipline you now?"

From Zakia's end, he got another light nod, that time more animated with a soft, "Do as you wish. I fear nothing. Especially not from...*you*." She arched her back deeper, almost tauntingly, steadied herself, braced the edge of the kitchen island for support, and prepared herself to take his discipline.

The belt Victor wielded was thin, maybe two inches thick,

made of leather, the letters *CK* stitched in black thread repeatedly across the entire length of it. Not very menacing at first sight, but sure to pack a mean and powerful sting if handled properly. He drug it lightly from the top of her back down the crevice of her spine; Zakia shivered again. It was subtle, but her ass began to roll in tight lewd circles. The belt kissed her naked skin across both cheeks. The blow came so light she didn't even flinch. Victor did it again.

Still no response.

"I thought you said I lost the bet, and you were gonna discipline me," Zakia taunted with squinted eyes sliced over her shoulder back at him. "I'm supposed to fear *that?* Fucking pathetic."

A snarl curled the corner of Victor's top lip. "Oh, you wanna get cute?"

The belt was abandoned all together. A smooth hand caressed over Zakia's naked flesh. Rubbed in admiration, palmed lightly, Victor pinpointed a specific target on the center of her right ass cheek, wound up, and brought his hand down with a firm…SMACK! The distinct sound of flesh against flesh echoed throughout the whole kitchen.

He did it again – SMACK – that time just slightly harder.

That got a flinch out of Zakia, accompanied with a pleasurable hum. She closed her eyes dreamily, bit her bottom lip, and hissed defiantly, "That's it? This is what you call me *losing*? That's all you got?"

Victor cranked up the volume on the vibrator, jumped it to four. He activated the clit-simulator, and delivered a few more sharp stings across her ass. He concentrated on a specific spot, the *same* spot, over and over on both cheeks. Victor didn't reach ten spanks on that ass – it began to leave his hand hot – before Zakia began to shudder underneath him.

Humility quickly became her.

Let her live?

Hell fucking naw!

Her arrogance warranted his form of punishment.

He turned up the setting even higher – five...six...seven – loud enough to finally hear its muffled, distinct buzz where he stood; it sounded like a cell phone ringing between her thighs. He continued to pummel relentless, well-timed spanks on that ass; enough to jiggle her fleshy, forty-something inch cheeks, and rattle her entire physique with each echoing clap.

The throaty moan that poured from Zakia's lungs vibrated off the kitchen walls, it resonated throughout the whole first floor. A moan Victor was quite familiar with.

"Ffffuck you! Shhhit! Ffffuck...you!" Zakia hissed behind gritted teeth. "You can't...you'll never... I'll never submit...to you. Ohhh, fuck! You...you mother*fucker!* That...fucking thing...is fucking...killing my... fucking clit! Agghhhh...FUCK!"

Zakia broke, tried to conceal her first loss, a crack in her climatic dam, but became exposed when Victor glanced between her legs to witness clear streams of her orgasm rolling in beads like tears of joy to glaze her inner thighs; droplets of her nectar puddled the white linoleum between her heels.

"Naw, fuck *you*, my beautiful, arrogant, headstrong queen. And you don't think so? Alright, let's see."

Zakia braced herself for the impact, gripped the edge of the counter, tighter, with everything she had, white knuckles. She shook violently, her entire body trembled. She took those stinging spanks on that ass, one after the other after the other, and tried to shift away to avoid him hitting the same spot, but couldn't. She took it on the same spot, over and over and over, that device hammering her g-spot, nonstop, those prongs buzzing ferociously on her clit, fucking punishing all of her senses at once.

She withstood the extent of his pleasurable torture, took it, five minutes...ten...fifteen, handled everything he dished out. She refused to submit, bit her bottom lip almost to the point of drawing blood, squirmed her ass in tight little circles, arched her back deeper, egged him on even in her weakness, and goaded him for more, her legs wobbling to the point of almost buckling out from underneath her.

Victor witnessed her agony, her sweet suffering, a woman struggling on the brink, chuckled, then prattled, "Ahhh, dis one is strong like bull," in a Michael Blackson inspired African accent.

Zakia stood strong, panted, slapped the face of the kitchen counter with an open palm, once... twice...three times, whimpered, tears in the corners of her eyes, took it, fought it like a champ, refused to lose. Victor cranked up the volume – eight...nine...ten – tested the device at its peak setting, the clit stimulator as well. *Knew* that would do the trick.

It didn't.

Shit!

He couldn't believe it.

Close to twenty minutes, straight, with vicious spanks on that ass, the device at its absolute peak, left his wife practically standing in a puddle of cum. An African queen still going strong. A woman with an unbreakable will.

He cursed under his breath, *"Who the hell is she, the black Wonder Woman?"*

He got angry, continued to spank her, what appeared to be an act of clear aggression. Still no submission on her end. When all else failed, Victor took it to the extremes – he sneakily wet his finger in saliva, slid it behind her, and slipped that single digit between her cheeks to rub a wet finger in circles on her back door. When he got it nice and wet, he applied pressure, and wormed it into the first knuckle... second, until buried it all the way into the hilt.

Zakia's eye popped open, she lost her breath, came, *hard*, actually squirted in orgasm, for the third time, and finally lost that fight, crying, "Eieee...eieee...Eiffel Tower! Eiffel Tower? Fucking Eiffel Tower!" in concession, inching her ass away from the invasion.

That was their signal, their code word.

Victor removed his single finger from wiggling in her forbidden warmth, immediately killed the power on the remote, ceased his spanking that he administered as if she really was a bad girl, and actually caught Zakia before she collapsed. She panted heavily, completely out of breath. When she finally regained control, she peeled that device, which had been lodged in her for the last ten hours, down around her thighs like panties, and dropped it to the floor as if she was actually scared of it.

Unlike Zakia, Victor wasn't so intimidated by the furtive, erotic play piece Zakia disregarded where she stood. Victor hooked his index finger in the string of his weapon of choice, that black leather contraption on the kitchen tiles in a clear puddle of her liquid pleasure, and lifted it prevailingly with a perverse smile; it was saturated, literally dripping in Zakia's sex.

"Hey, tough guy..." Victor called out; Zakia snatched up her dress shirt, shrugged it over her shoulders, swiped up the rest of her clothing scattered across the kitchen floor, and peered over her shoulder back at him, still slightly winded, "...you have to go to the bank next week to refinance the mortgage on the house, don't you? What do you say, run it back? Double or nothing."

Zakia squinted playfully, subtly shook her head. She couldn't help but to crack a jilted smirk.

Not much thought was given.

She swiped up the tumbler on the counter, knocked back the rest of the glass in one shot, and blurted, "You're on! Cause I got just the right plan to put your slick ass back in place," then strutted away with a prevailing switch of her hips.

Fourth Interview

"What the deal, what the deal? I'm glad you made it in today. One thing no one could ever accuse you of is not being consistent. What is this, the third, fourth interview? They're really starting to stack up a little something, huh? I would think by now you're starting to *'do the one'* to my psychology, piecing together how I dissect the wisdom I impart on my clients to keep them going.

"You look a little confused. Don't really know what to think anymore, do you? Recap. Your publication hears rumors of some exclusive new sex therapist that has this impressively successful track record of spicing up couples lives, giving them deep jewels, so they send you out to interview me. Then when we first meet, I was in the process of...clearing up a few issues.

"We meet at a later date, set the tone off right – I bless you with a few exclusive *Case Files* showcasing my...eh, client's methods at work. Now as you sit here before me today, donned in my casual attire, you experience vestiges bleeding through, an echo of the man I used to be in a former life. Now you're beginning to question yourself – just who is this Dr. Anonymous Black individual? We'll get into that later. Right now I'm more concerned about that last *Case File*, Victor and Zakia."

The journalist removed the flash drive from his satchel, placed it on the edge of Dr. Black's desk.

"They are unique, aren't they? I like them. The one I'm most proud of is Zakia. When I conducted my first interview with her, the first thing that came to mind was the stereotypical acronym – **S.W.A.**: *Sista With* an *Attitude*. Many sistas who are really headstrong get that, from first impression.

"I can't speak for all of them, but with Zakia, I came to find out she's just a very dominant woman. She was quick to point out how this dominance intimidated the majority of men she encountered. The funny thing is, when she met Victor, someone who was as equally dominant as her, most who knew them thought it was going to be a recipe for disaster, a powder keg waiting to explode.

"What some predicted to be a very short-term relationship, with the possibility of the police being called in to settle a domestic dispute, blossomed into a twelve-year marriage that's still going strong. Little did most know, all Zakia longed for was someone who was not only *not* intimidated by her aggressive stance, but could match her aggressiveness with his own. Zakia isn't alone. That style of woman isn't uncommon, especially amongst the business world.

"Sistas being confronted with a masculine economic society, a society in which they could either sink or swim in, most don't see failure as an option, so they go hard. They get just as grimy and ruthless as their male counterparts, sometimes harder, knowing passivity could be taken as a sign of weakness.

"Don't let her be as beautiful as *Beyoncé* with a body equivalent to *Ki Toy* to match. Then she might be charged behind judging eyes and unspoken thoughts of only excelling solely on her looks. Forget the college degrees. Screw that she graduated at the top of her class. Fuck the fact that she was miles ahead of her peers at every juncture. Naw, that's 'affirmative action' hard at work, or she got there because she was pretty. Some would even accuse her with getting on her knees, and getting her lips wet, or bending over to get that position. Faced with such an onslaught of opposition, most of my sistas grow hard, build up thick skin.

"Zakia was no different. A mid-thirties, good looking black woman with a physique similar to *Lira Galore*, venturing into one of the most brutal, competitive industries out there – the clothing game – built her up to be a meat eater. She was aggressive in her professional, business world, so it wasn't too unusual for that same aggression to spill over into her personal, and even her sexual world. What was unique with Victor is he never viewed her powerful stance as a challenge to his manhood, as most *insecure* men would.

"He embraced that power in her, what he related to as the same power he had within himself, and made her feel comfortable to express it. He didn't make her feel like it was the womanly thing to do to tone it down, or be more feminine. He encouraged that strength, cultivated it. With the freedom to be who she was *naturally* in his presence – feminine dominance – she eventually excelled in her career, and found the utmost pleasure in her life. A pleasure that coincidentally spilled over into their bedroom.

"You see, I traveled with them, Victor and Zakia, in fact, all of my client's, about the issue of pleasure. How pleasure, in everyday life, including in the bedroom, presents two experiences vital to our growth and development: that *life* in itself is a value, and *we* are a value. Let's go deeper: connect pleasure with the act of sex.

"Sex is unique amongst the other forms of pleasure because it integrates the body, *and* the mind. Perceptions, emotions, values, and thoughts are all made manifest through the act of sex. Sex offers someone the most intense form of experiencing their total being, of experiencing their deepest, and most intense sense of self.

"Volumes can be revealed about an individual once you learn their sexual psychology. Does everyone who engage in sex experience the depth of it on this level, or fully *over*-stand the significance of it in revealing their thoughts? Of course not. But Victor and Zakia have. They achieved complete harmony in who they are, who they *really* are.

"Zakia evolved into a highly aggressive woman, but deep down, her desire outside of conquering was to be conquered. To be dominated, as she dominates in other facets of her life. Victor offered her that, without any pangs of shame or guilt. He allowed Zakia to feel comfortable enough to use her own body as a direct immediate source of pleasure, a vehicle of pleasure, and she allowed him to do the same.

"Sex, within the sphere of their lives, became the ultimate act of self-assertion, and Victor and Zakia's acts of self-assertion took on the form of *S&M*. In this form, they both found pleasure in expressing themselves. Found their sex most intense when it was equally an expression of love for self, of life, and for each other – wearing black leather, and exerting their will on the other. In this sense, they experience a unique and intense form of self-awareness, both by the act of sex itself, and by their verbal, emotional and physical interaction with each other.

"I won't pretend this deep connection occurred overnight. Victor and Zakia were fortunate though. They both enjoyed a strong spiritual, physical, and emotional affinity for each other, along with another important component – complimentary sexual personalities. The result was a sense of visibility, of the deepest possible experience of self, of being spiritual, as well as physically naked in front of each other, and glorifying in the act.

"Without this experience, without this feeling of being physically, spiritually, sexually and emotionally connected, there would have been a sense of sexual alienation, or at best, physical frustration. I'm sure all of us experienced this at one time or another in our lives: You got your eye on that significant other, looks right, body right, then when you engage in the act of sex something is just 'off'. Something's wrong. You can't seem to connect.

"Coin flip. The other side to that. The side that when one connects with that other, both of their physicals flow like poetry in motion. They knew how to push all of the right buttons, had all of the right moves, knew how to say and do all of the right things, and left the other so depleted of orgasmic fluids they rendered them dehydrated.

"Yeah, you have. The smirk on your face says it all. This connection of physical and mental goes by many names. Some call it an energy, a vibe, a frequency, a connection. In a nutshell, simply put, their complimentary sexual personalities were harmoniously in sync."

$$ $$ $$

"This is the highest and most intimate tribute one can offer another – that they value the individual for the person of who they are, and their significant other values them in the same capacity. That it is the *person*, not simply because she is pretty, got sex appeal, got a phenomenal body, he got money, handsome, a big dick, but them as a person that is the source of their pleasure. To be seen as more than just a body that offers a good fuck, and satisfies selfish needs. To feel, and sense, in their heart: *because of who I am, my total being, I am able to make this person feel what they are feeling.*

"You've seen and heard it before. A brother continually frequents the nightclubs, picks up women who have the looks and bodies equal to video vixens, lures them back to his lair, and engages in the most obscene form of hood Kama Sutra with them. Yet, for some odd reason, he always feels empty, dissatisfied, disconnected after exhausting all seminal fluids. Why? Because although the act of conquering that new conquest may be physically nourishing, an ego boost, there is no satisfaction to the soul.

"It's shallow, no real feeling attached. An empty fuck with absolutely no emotional investment. The same applies for a woman who mistakenly believes she will fill that void in her life, or find that special someone, by filling her mouth, or thighs, with rock hard erections. And even if she did find some weak-minded brother who she ensnared with her sexual prowess, on a deeper level, she will see the truth of reality for what it really was – she got a weak-minded brother pussy-whipped.

"He wouldn't really care about her desires, her wishes, her aspirations. Only how well she will use her mouth on him, or another opportunity to sink up in that silky wet flesh between her thighs. And their relationship will only last as long as she accommodates him sexually, only as long as she continues to open her mouth and her thighs for him, because it was never really about her, only the release she offered him.

"Do the math: if sex is an act of self-celebration, the freedom to be spontaneous, emotionally open and uninhibited, then the person one would most desire is the person whom one feels the freest to be who they are, the person they would regard as their appropriate psychological mirror; the person who reflects their deepest view of themselves, and of life.

"Victor and Zakia learned to encounter passionate love, and even tapped into their primitive instincts of raw sex. This enlarged, and deepened, the aura of desired contact between them. Their desire was to explore each other through all of their senses: touch, taste, sound, sight and smell. The fantasies and fulfillments of Zakia, became the intense, personal interest of Victor, and vice versa.

"They enjoy, and share, feelings and emotions at greater length, depth and regularity than many other couples in other relationships. It's as if they became one person. Their most diverse traits, characteristics, and activities providing a spiritual, intellectual, physical, emotional, and sexual charge to the other.

"This is the significance of the first client I allowed you to view, specifically Naomi, obtaining such a stimulating sexual charge out of inviting another woman into her bed for Salim. This is why the second couple, Malik and Tanisha, can find such pleasure acting as if they were complete strangers, and acting out their role-playing routines. Why Victor and Zakia enjoy the switching of power they play back and forth between each other in their roles of dominance.

"At the outset of all of my sessions, I screen my client's by posing some basics questions: *To what degree are they aware of themselves as sexual entities? How do they perceive sex and its significance in their lives? How do they feel about their own bodies? Not just how they look physically, but do they visualize their bodies as something to value, are they comfortable in their own skin, do they see themselves as vehicles of pleasure? How do they view the same sex, the opposite? How do they view the body of the opposite sex? What do they most enjoy, visually, in the opposite sex? What is their most pleasurable encounters in sex, honestly? What was their level and ability to act on those desires and express themselves freely in their encounters?*

"When Zakia began to reflect, dig deep, and soul search to find the answers to such questions, that's when she began to really define her underlying sexual psychology. Began to overstand that within the act of sex, probably more than in any other sphere of her life, the total of her personality tended to find its full expression."

$$ \$\$\ \$\$\ \$\$ $$

"Analyzing it from this perspective, one could even argue to experience the optimal of visibility and self-objectification required her to interact with a counterpart, in her case, Victor. Think of the wisdom of God *'making man in Our image, according to*

Our likeness', pronouncing it is not good for man to be alone, and designing for him his mate, taken from the rib of man, hence – bone of my bone, and flesh of my flesh. Woman.

"A union in which the two shall become one. Masculine and feminine balanced in one physical, in harmony. There is so much symbolism within this wisdom. Even if one isn't religious, one can *over*-stand why someone like Zakia, a woman, can embrace and exert her masculine side; it is scientifically proven that male and female embryos have the same external anatomy for the first few weeks, and their internal reproductive organs have not yet differentiated. Embryos at this time are described as being 'sexually indifferent'.

"On a physical and emotional level, we all carry within us male and female aspects, but within man, the male principle ordinarily predominates; in woman, the female principle. To piggyback on the issue of first encounters, I've had discussions with client's who wanted insight about the concept of *'love at first sight'.* Personally, I over-stand that fascination, attraction, intrigue, and even passion may be experienced 'at first sight', but not love. Love, on that level, requires knowledge, and knowledge requires time.

"When someone professes to experience 'love at first sight', it could be perceived as that, in retrospect, not taking into consideration that the powerful emotional response they experienced 'at first sight' could have just been validated, and confirmed, by later experiences in such a way that love does when it eventually evolves.

"Zakia disclosed when she first encountered Victor, the genuine affinity she felt for him. It was like a melody, music she could sense in his presence. A melody that was in complete harmony within herself. The way Victor experienced himself, the energy within him, the concentrated power, his happiness, his outlook and approach on life allowed her body and emotions to respond faster than her thoughts could shape words. The sense of life Zakia experienced, the emotional form in which she experienced her deepest view of existence, her relationship to this existence, is rarely communicated by the act of mere words.

"When their relationship progressed, knowledge of their union began to be made manifest in more recognizable forms. An affinity was discovered by them learning each other's values, or disvalues. By observing each other's manner of moving, talking, conveying emotion, reacting to events. How they interacted with themselves and others. By the things said, and the things they learned didn't have to be said. By the explanations given, and the ones that weren't. By their unspoken signs of mutual understanding.

"Within the course of building with my clients, an *overstanding* unfolds that the love of their mate, when it's at its purest form, should be a testament of them being admired and loved for the things they wish to be admired and loved for. Equally important, in a way, and from a perspective, that is in accord with their own view of life. In order for Victor and Zakia's relationship to continue to thrive and flourish beyond that initial affinity, that 'love at first sight', there had to be a foundation of basic similarities. A mutuality that crossed the spectrum of mental, physical, and emotional.

"But the complete picture of two souls uniting in love isn't only experienced with an actual mirror-image of ourselves. One of the beauties about relationships is the excitement, and importance, of the complimentary differences they share.

"When Zakia encountered Victor, learned that he adopted an outlook on life that she immediately recognized, that mirrored survival skills similar to her own, who learned to cope and adapt to situations that resembled the traits she acquired all of her life, there was a shock in recognition, a sense of a profound bond that occurred instantaneously. She felt, without question, that Victor had to be her soul mate.

"But no two people are identical. No two people experience reality in an identical manner, not even identical twins. No two hold the capacity for the same potential, experience all identical experiences, and because of that, they are inherently different. Yet, when Victor began to experience their differences as complimentary, it not only stimulated his relationship with Zakia, but their relationship became challenging, exciting, a dynamic force that enhanced feelings of aliveness, growth, and expansion between them.

"My clients have expressed, in so many words, how they experience in their significant other an embodiment of a part of themselves that has been struggling to emerge. Coincidentally, their mate would normally see a similar possibility in them, which would result in an explosion of love, a sense of exciting aliveness, which only grows through contact, involvement, interaction.

"Victor and Zakia experienced this. Malik and Tanisha, Salim and Naomi, and many other clients. Gaining deeper insight into their relationship should force them to pose a series of questions to self: what were the things within themselves that their significant other awakened within them? What is their experience in their relationship with that person in contrast to others? What are the feelings most alive in the presence of their significant other? When they honestly answer those questions, that's when they'll come to *over*-stand some of the most important reasons why they fell in love with that particular person."

$$ $$ $$

"For couples like Victor and Zakia, Malik and Tanisha, Salim and Naomi, who are truly in love, and have been together for many years, they may continue to discover new reasons for being in love with their significant other, reasons that were intuitively or subconsciously grasped very early, 'at first sight', but over time manifested itself from feelings into words.

"Not that Victor, or Tanisha, or Salim needed to name all of the reasons they were together, or that it was even relevant to do so, but that when they did discover this revelation, if they wanted to explore it, it could be beneficial to ask their significant other: in what ways were they alike? In what ways were they different?

"Keep this in mind: all of the high science that I'm dropping on you could only apply to individuals who are mature, looking to enhance a *mature* love, because there is such a thing as an *immature* love. A love, that despite age, cannot fully unfold due to an individual's arrested development *emotionally*, *psychologically*, and enter into their relationships with the mentality of children waiting; waiting to be validated as a person, waiting for unconditional love without reciprocation, waiting for confirmation that they are beautiful, intelligent, relevant. Waiting to be rescued.

"I've encountered clients like this before. Individuals with questionable self-esteem. One's who governed their lives around the desire to be pleased, to be liked by others, at all costs, usually to the detriment of themselves. Individuals who seek to be taken care of. Or, on the flip side, those who actively try to control the other, dominate, manipulate, coerce to satisfy their needs, because they don't trust anyone to see them for who they truly are, and give their genuine love in return.

"Individuals who have no confidence in themselves, who believe without the masks, the façade, the front-a-role portrayal, the manipulation, that they just aren't good enough. One's who live out the helpless and dependent role, others, controlling and overprotective. Within these two opposites remain the fact that they both live with a sense of inadequacy, an emotional deficiency, and they continually seek out a significant someone else they feel can correct it.

"They never will, so their search will continue. And it continued on in several of my client's until counseling taught them to transfer the source of their approval from others, to self.

Prior to this discovery of others to self, their sole existence was to feed off of others like an emotional leech, perceiving others not as equals with wants, desires, and needs much like themselves, but as sources of gratification to be used and manipulated to satisfy their own selfish needs.

"Two quick examples of *Case Files*. The first: a woman. Antoinette. Thirty-six, but because she refused to abandon the ways of her youth, was still immature at that age, hadn't fully developed psychologically, and came to view herself as unloved, not enough, rejected, so she dealt solely with players who were emotionally detached from their own emotions. She ensnares a drug dealing hustler, deals with him simply because he looks good physically, got the money, style, status, potent sex game, all of that. Because she can't see deeper than the surface – his perception of her – she doesn't understand why he's cold to her, unemotional, unable, or unwilling to show her any real love, so the hunt will begin.

"In time, flaws from previous relationships will visit her like ghosts from the past. She attempts to ignore it, suppress it. She can't understand, or explain, why she finds herself so compulsively drawn to him. For this particular gangsta, she has to have him. She'll break him out of his player ways, find a way to inspire in him all the responses she felt eluded her, what she failed to receive in her past relationships with the other thugs.

"What she doesn't appreciate is unless other factors change to generate a positive shift in her psychology, that brother is useless to her. Outside of him punishing, and putting those extra miles on that precious passage between her thighs, or providing her with mouthfuls of his natural protein, he would only be stimulating to her in the unconscious soap opera she doesn't even recognize she is starring in, and only so long as he plays her hot and cold, loving and distant, caring and uncaring.

"Because if he was to flip the script, and invest in her fully, he would no longer project the image of that elusive gangsta that was previously unattainable to her. He would immediately fall out of the role she cast him in, the script he was supposed to act out. So at the same time that this Antoinette woman cries for love, she takes careful steps to maintain the distance between them to prevent him from giving her the very things she asks for.

"If this gangsta somehow, as a result of her efforts, pushed the issue and tried to convince her he is exactly what she needs by showering her with his individual, undivided love and attention, Antoinette would most likely get disorientated, withdraw, fall out of infatuation with him. Her reason being, her rationale: *'He ain't a gangsta no more. He got weak, turned into a sucker, soft, pussy whipped, lost his touch with his inner thug, and that's why I ain't feeling him no more'.* Mental turmoil. A conflicting dichotomy in the mind that is impossible for both extremes to coexist.

"Flip side: the other side of the same coin – that gangsta thug. A brother that's so immature that he holds the notion that no woman, none of them, can be trusted based on his past experiences, so he erects emotional walls to never let any of 'them' in, while at the same time, deep down, really wants to find a woman to love and call his own. One of Salim's defects in character prior to counseling. So what this individual does as a result is..."

Dr. Black peers up at Kiara entering the office, jacket on, another thrown over her forearm.

"You have business you have to tend to. Your engagement," Kiara says firmly.

"Well, who am I to argue? Duty calls. I apologize. We'll continue this at a later date. Here..."

Another thumb drive slid across the desk.

"I'm sure you're acquiring a particular taste for the couples in these videos. There are, in fact, some scientific lessons to be learned from them. See if you can to pick up the similarities, and their underlying differences. Do the math to them. Tell me what you think. Until next time. Peace."

Case File #17 - Salim & Naomi

From the recliner in the corner of his bedroom, Salim had the perfect angle to watch Naomi's every move.

He sat with his legs crossed, left index finger on his temple, resembled the *Malcom X* portrait. Resembled it, but contradicted righteousness from what he held in his other hand – a burning blunt married between two fingers; a trail of squiggly smoke danced chaotically from the tip, a third of it consumed.

His focus intent, eyes intoxicated slits, a perfect combination of *Kush* and lust.

Naomi entered from the bathroom moments earlier, wrapped in only a towel. She headed straight for the closet. She paid little attention to her significant other camouflaged discreetly in the cut, although a sweeping glance to her side let Salim know she acknowledged his presence. She cracked a half smile. Salim didn't. He was too lost in thought. Lost on her whole aura, and what they established over the years, for him to take notice of the energy she projected towards him.

They'd been together for over a decade, but Naomi still had the power to incite certain feelings within him from just a visual. It had always been like that. But with time, it evolved to a level of perfect emotional harmony. Like every relationship, they'd been through their fair share of ups and downs. The true test came at the hands of the mother of his first two children.

He had two kids by her, both boys; fifteen and seventeen. He'd been through hell with her, not that she was the sole reason for the madness they called their relationship. Salim was knee deep in the streets, closing in on his upper thighs, working his way up to a full brick of *fish scale* at the time. A construction worker by day, by nightfall, laying the groundwork to become one of the city's biggest heroin suppliers.

He barely wanted to deal with her on a level outside of the bedroom – or the reclined passenger seat of his Lexus, or in hotels rooms, or that one time he crushed her in the bathroom at his boy's house party – let alone start something serious with her. But once she had Salim, Jr., a small part of him figured he'd try out the whole 'wifey/relationship' thing.

Not one hundred percent commitment or anything like that, but claim her, make her his woman, instead of just the 'sexy redbone with the fat ass' he was fucking. A mere year and a half after getting an apartment with her, and sexing her virtually every single day, unprotected, led to his second son. That didn't mean there weren't other little flings on the side – by his recollection, easily a dozen, three of them being her own girls – but they were just that, side flings. She was wifey. A wifey who knew he was cheating, not nearly to the extent of how he got down, but cheating nonetheless.

This led to endless fights.

Less than two years after tackling the family thing, he fumbled, moved out. He took back to the streets with a vengeance, a kilo of heroin flipped to two in no time, grinded nonstop, and crushed everything with a cute face and a fat ass even harder from what he felt was lost time he needed to catch up on.

Within the midst of it all, Salim met Naomi. What he

initially intended to be the *'just friends with benefits'* package – because after dealing with his children's mother for those few years, he had no intention of jumping right back into something serious again – didn't work out that way.

Naomi started to grow on him.

He found himself spending more and more time with her. The few trips to the city to re-up on his drug packs, helping him to bag up, nursing him back to health after he got shot, taking the wheel as the get-away driver when he sought revenge in a drive-by.

Naomi, his new *Wisdom*, his new wifey, she was ride or die.

Then the court cases came.

All of the other females in his life left him for dead, especially after they heard what he was facing; fourteen to thirty-three years for attempted murder and carrying a concealed weapon. Before the fangs of a prison system swallowed him inside its belly, knowing he was facing numbers that could be branded on the back of a football jersey, Salim proposed to Naomi. Not one hundred percent on the up and up, more in line with trying to take advantage of the conjugal visits he schemed to get while on the inside.

Yet, something happened as he awaited trial for those charges. Stuck in a prison cell for twenty-two and two, faced with spending a little over three decades of his life behind bars, forced Salim to do some serious soul searching. He evaluated his life. Twenty-five. Two kids. No career. No real prospects. Countless failed relationships, mainly because he kept them all at a distance.

The revelation: Naomi.

She was a queen, loyal, committed. Always had his back, rode with him to the end, even trooped it out with him through those charges. Then the time came for them to travel mentally in letters. With her, he took it deeper than anyone he ever conversed with in his life, which led them to see just how much they had in common.

If anyone deserved to be given a chance at something real, it was her. Salim made up his mind to do just that. Fortunate for him, he beat the attempted murder charge; copped out to a lower charge, third degree aggravated assault; time served after four years and some change.

When he first came home, with the allure of beating those charges hyping his release, he fell victim. The threesome his man treated him with at his 'coming home' party, the few times he went to see his sons and stayed the night with their mother. The old flings resurfacing anxious to sample some fresh prison dick. Within a month of that crap, he shaped up to keep it one hundred, and give his all to Naomi.

That's when the problems began with his son's mother all over again.

$$ $$ $$

How could he love her? How could he choose that side bitch, Naomi, over her? They had kids together, a family, history. They were supposed to have a future together. Not commit, and have some beautiful future, with some side bitch.

Salim stood firm. Naomi was the one, especially after they had their first child together, a baby girl, his first girl, Aisha. The mother of his two sons wouldn't go away so easily. That's when his kids were used as weapons, pawns to push in her twisted game. Child support called on the daily as an attempt to cripple him. Even the unthinkable – she started sleeping with one of his closest friends, *former* friend, with rumors of their scandalous episodes floating around in cyberspace; videos in which she allowed him to violate her in every way, just for spite.

Through it all, Naomi stood by his side, had his back.

All of those trials and tribulations led to a deeper bond,

especially after she received her BA in Business Management, and pushed him to get his own degree. She believed in him, which led Salim to believe more in himself, outside of his survival skills in the streets. Five years later, Salim owned one of the top promotions companies in his state, all with the help of Naomi.

A few unruly ashes were tapped in an ashtray on a nightstand. Salim raised the blunt back to his lips, his every move deliberate. A heavy cloud of the most powerful piff on the market fogged his features, soon obliterated by a thin trail of white smoke blown so smoothly from his lips. Bloodshot eyes locked onto Naomi. She moved with the same grace as her unknowing counterpart.

The plush white towel wrapped around her body was thrown on the edge of the bed indifferently. A visual of her nude body from behind creased a slight snarl on the corner of Salim's lip. He was a full-fledged ass man, and Naomi, his wife, sure had one. One of the best he ever had the pleasure of *visualizing* with his very own eyes. Unquestionably the best he ever had the pleasure of *playing in*.

So round, like a perfect half-moon, attached to a set of powerfully thick thighs and a slim waist. Naomi made sure to keep it that way, especially after their daughter, by hitting the gym three to four times a week to keep her figure in tiptop shape. She rifled through one of the top drawers, fished out a sky blue G-string, and a matching bra.

"I want us to go out tonight," Salim said as if the thought just came to mind.

Naomi wiggled those panties up over her dark chocolate thighs, jiggled her ass a little to squeeze the material up in her, sighed, "Go out where?" peeling off the silk head wrap tying her hair down; it was wrapped in a tight beehive, a wave brush laid down a few unruly strands.

"To get something to eat."

Naomi tied her hair back down, turned around to spot the look Salim gave her, said, "Sa, it's late. I just put Sha to bed. If you want something to eat, I can make you something real quick. Or better yet, let's just order in." Naomi crossed the room, spotted the blunt between his fingers. "Yo ass just got the munchies." She plucked it from his fingers, and took a few tokes herself. Maybe not the best decision; a few pulls could put her in the same position of being infected with the munchies herself.

"Get dressed. We're going out to eat. TGIF. Naw, Applebee's."

"Sa, look at the time," Naomi gestured to a digital clock on the nightstand, "it's after ten."

She slid under the sheets on her side of their king-sized. Salim ignored her, walked over to the closet, plucked out a miniskirt, a half-shirt, and Naomi's pink and white *Air Max's*.

"I'm bout to call my sister, tell her to babysit for a couple of hours."

"Sa, for real, go without me," Naomi whined, "Just make sure you bring me something back."

She snuggled herself up under the sheets tighter, made herself comfortable. Salim reached for the phone. When the call connected, when Naomi heard him talking to his sister, she sighed heavily. The covers were thrown off her body with a pouty huff.

"I swear, sometimes I feel like punching you right in your face!" Naomi cursed, slicing him razor thin with a playful roll of her eyes.

$$ $$ $$

After a huge meal, something Naomi knew in the next couple of days she would live to regret, Salim managed to pull her out of her insipid shell. *Applebee's* had a uniquely distinct way of doing that. By the time they moved on to dessert – with several Long Island Ice Teas downed in between – Naomi melted off her previous frost to be feeling no pain.

"Where are you going?" Salim noticed how Naomi drove past the street they would normally make a right on to get home; the street slowly vanished in the back window. "You know my sister got her college classes tomorrow, and said she was only going to watch Aisha for a couple of hours. She's sitting in the crib waiting on..."

"Negro, will you shut up," Naomi sighed, "I just wanna get a couple more drinks. You're the one that wanted to get me up out of my nice comfortable bed to go out. So now we're out. Just a couple more drinks at a bar, maybe a game of pool. Don't worry, we'll be back before twelve, or one. No later than two."

Salim opened his mouth, only for Naomi to give him the hand, and continue on course with her midweek entertainment. Salim shook his head with a lighthearted huff under his breath. Maybe that was his fault. Not maybe. He did get her up out the comfort of their bed to insist they go out to eat. What type of equality would it have been to shut her down now that she was on a roll?

She increased the volume on the stereo.

Rick Ross' *'Blowin' Money Fast'*.

"...I think I'm Big Meech, ungh!...Larry Hoover, whippin' work...hallelujah!..."

A deep rumble of bass vibrated from the trunk to resonate throughout the cabin. Naomi, in sync with the Teflon don, quoted the song, verse for verse, as if he wrote those lyrics specifically for her.

The apparel she wore – white, fitted, *NY Yankees* hat two sizes too big, tipped to the side over her left eye, underneath a white do-rag, the tail tied up in a loose knot, loosely strung *Nikes*, tight jean mini-skirt, pink hoody – she played up the persona of a *'Street Queen'* to perfection.

"*This chick really think she gangsta,*" Salim thought.

He sat in silence, enjoying the sights and sounds of his wife spitting lyrics, 'gangsta leaning' with a smooth nod in the driver's seat, to whipping his head out the passenger window when a familiar visual caught the corner of his eye.

"Turn around," Salim blurted.

"What? What happened?"

"Turn around. The bar we're going to is right over there."

Naomi didn't question it. A drink was a drink no matter where she got it from. She hugged a quick U-turn at the next intersection, headed back in the direction where they just came from. Before she got within a block of where Salim instructed her to go, she could see what his sights were set on. The car rolled at about ten miles per hour as Naomi approached a huge, flashing, neon blue sign: *Seduction*.

The caricature of an extremely voluptuous woman in the same neon blue flashed off and on in five stages – back arched, progressing to her whipping her hair back wildly, breasts pointed to the sky. Underneath this prominent display, there were several eye-catching advertisements: nude, lap dances, private shows. Naomi turned up into the parking lot.

"Why'd you come up in here? I was talking about that *other* bar across the street," Salim said sincerely. Naomi turned to him, noticed the hint of a smirk behind the stone face exterior he tried to maintain.

"Yeah, I know," she squinted at him, and twisted up the corner of her top lip, "Put it all on me." Naomi parked in the closest space she could find. "This is all me. You had nothing to do with this."

They tumbled through the dual front doors of that strip club like a couple of rowdy teenagers – Salim pinching her ass, Naomi jumping from his playful ribbing, giggling, shoving away his light carousing. It wasn't until they made it through a small sea of scattered tables, and took their first sight at the front stage, that they calmed down.

Salim had been there before, almost two years prior. The place changed, made some new upgrades. Even in the dimly lit atmosphere, he could make them out; newly lighted mirrored stages, ceilings, new poles, sounds, big screens. On that Tuesday night, there weren't that many patrons, mostly males at the bar, some lined attentively around a t-shaped stage; at least another three couples amongst them.

Salim and Naomi paid little attention to them, more concerned with a buxom blonde built like a brick shithouse in the middle of her routine. Conquering just one of four stages, she gyrated her body under flashing strobe lights to the sounds of Big Sean and Nicki Minaj's *'Dance A$$'*.

Salim cut a glance at Naomi on his side, read her, noticed how that female left her just as entranced as him. The blonde was a dead set knockoff to the voracious vixen *Coco*. Luxurious, natural blonde hair, tracks added, two feet long from her scalp, braided in two pigtails with cute little baby blue bows at the tips. Baby blue, thigh-high fishnets. Six-inch white stilettos. Topless, bottomless, titties, ass, and pussy out on full display. She danced on the center stage, spaciously sandwiched by two other girls on each side; one Spanish, one Asian.

No one would have even known they were there.

'Coco' was immaculate. A trillion degree sun amongst cold, dead stars.

She hijacked the attention of nearly every eye in the room. Her physical, her aura, her movements, poetry in motion. She swayed in perfect synch to the beat, popped her ass oh so seductively at just the right moment, and had enough sex appeal to distribute healthy servings to each girl there, *and* have some left over for at least three more.

Salim and Naomi navigated themselves through the dimly lit, smoke-filled, sexually charged atmosphere, found the perfect location, and sat tableside with the perfect view to soak in her hypnotic performance. What might have been foreign to another pair came quite natural to them. They both had uniquely similar tastes, and set their sights on feeding them.

"Shit! That vanilla bitch is built like a fucking Mack truck," Naomi said thickly, glued to the blonde's every move. "Her body is out of this world." She kept a furtive eye on her husband, and watched his that were locked like heat-seeking missiles on the blonde. "Look at you. Damn motherfucka, blink! And close your mouth," Naomi laughed. "You love that shit, huh?"

Salim snapped out of his lust-induced trance, slurred, "White girl is thick as a motherfucka. Stacked up in all the right places. Shit, she close to battling it out with *you* up in this piece."

He tried his best to suppress a smirk, knew his snide remark would get a good charge out of Naomi. It took a few seconds… five…for his little…four…comment to…three…hit…two…home…

"Oh, it's like that?" Naomi finally peeled her attention away from that Caucasian seductress before them, and gave it all to her husband on her side. "You think that *fake shit* right there, is fucking with this *real shit* right here? That that little *plastic surgery, cosmetically-constructed*, Barbie doll can hang with all of this *natural, back to Africa shit* right here?"

Naomi didn't hesitate.

She rose from the table, the zipper on the front of her hoody came down. Salim tried to concentrate on the blonde on stage, but couldn't deny the little strip tease his wife performed for him less than a foot away.

He wasn't the only one.

By the time Naomi stripped that hoody from her back, swung it like a lasso a few times above her head, and kicked her thick, chocolate thigh over Salim's waist to sit on his lap, face forward, she attracted the attention of at least a third of the patrons there; Cardi-B & Megan thee Stallion's *'WAP'* took over to grumble through the speakers.

"You really think Miss blonde Barbie doll over there can knock *me* out of the box? Negro please." Naomi squirmed, danced, and twerked on Salim's lap to the beat. She leaned over into his ear, sucked on his earlobe, and whispered, "That bitch can't handle all ten inches like I can. You still ain't learn that yet?"

Naomi moaned, purred, simulated sex noises in his ear, and sighed like she had the 'D' deep up in her at that very moment, "Ain't no other bitch *ffffucking* with me. You know that, boo. You ever had another bitch...ummmm, *suck* on that *black candy stick* like me? Or, ummmm...*swallow* all of that *Egyptian sweetness* like I love to swallow? Or, have another bitch...ummmm, *take* all that dick, soooo deep, like I can take it, all up in her?"

Naomi purred every word, and taunted him with a slithering tongue in his ear. His jeans tightened underneath her in seconds. The bulge of his erection pushed up a powerful tent, strained for release. Salim instantly forgot all about the blonde, or any other scantily clad or nude woman vying for attention around him, solely focused on the show Naomi performed for him.

She spun her fitted hat backwards, nodded to the beat. Her hands fell to her chest. She hit Salim with a seductive look through lust-slit eyes, began to boldly rub her breasts. Salim reached out to embrace her fleshy thighs. Coarse hands caressed baby smooth, milk chocolate skin. Fingers kneaded, explored, worked around her slim waist to embrace her huge ass.

"Um, don't touch me." Naomi smacked his hands away. "Why are you even watching me? Watch *that* bitch. After all, she is battling it out with me up in this piece, remember?" Naomi reminded. She got a wicked kick out of torturing him like that.

"Battle with me? Please!" Naomi thought.

She did tricks on his lap that even had the other girls impressed; she spotted them passing subtle glances at her, curling their lips, rolling their eyes in envy. By the time she spun around, bent over with her hands on her knees, and performed a breathtaking twerk routine, one of the bouncers walked over.

The Anonymous Black Files

$$ $$ $$

"Chocolate deluxe, you *can't* be serious. You can't do it all like that up in here. You don't see what you're doing? You got most of these motherfuckas up in here watching *you* instead of the other working girls," the bouncer said, gesturing to the audience she attracted. "Look at them. These motherfuckas just waiting to make it rain, *for you*. I don't know how long I can hold them back, *or* the ladies in here. Shit, every girl that work in here wanna *kill* your ass right now." He couldn't help but to chuckle at that.

"Soldier," he turned to Salim, "I don't wanna have to throw you, or your beautiful black queen out, but she gots to calm all of that shit down, or talk to management, get on that payroll, something. Cause with those looks, those moves, that face, and that body, she sure enough got a bright future ahead of her, and *behind* her," he ended, with a purposeful glimpse at Naomi's huge ass.

The bouncer gave them a look that spoke of his hands being tied; a well-dressed gentleman at the bar, who appeared to be the owner, watched him and that couple's every move. Naomi trapped the tip of her index finger between her teeth, became an innocent schoolgirl, and continued to defiantly twerk and bounce in the most obscene manner all over Salim's lap like the bouncer's words had no effect.

She popped her ass on his erection, simulated sex with their clothes on, imaginary fucked him reverse cowgirl, until the bouncer had enough. He shook his head after a clearly prolonged moment of enjoying her moves himself, and reached for Naomi's arm, but immediately stopped short. He turned to Salim, and retreated when he noticed his features darkening, noticed him on the verge of attack at the mere suggestion of another man attempting to touch his wife.

"Ok, ok, ok, Debo," Naomi raised one hand to the bouncer, placed the other on Salim's chest, calmed her husband. "I'll be a good little girl." She hit him with innocent, doe eyes, which strangely enough, were not so innocent at all, and added, "Only if you tell Miss Blondie to come over here when she's done." The bouncer studied her with unsure eyes, her husband with death in his, hesitated. "I just want to talk to her, ask her a question. Damn, I ain't gonna hurt her. Well, unless she wants me to."

The bouncer smirked, nodded, more out of respect for her husband, saluted the general, and walked away.

Naomi crawled from over Salim's lap, and snatched up her hoody that landed a few feet away. By the time she situated herself back in her seat, the blonde finished her set. The bouncer held true to his word; from across the room, they could see him whispering something in her ear, pointing them out.

"Give me some money," Naomi said urgently. Salim lifted a single eyebrow at her. "Hurry up. Take some money out for her. Speak the language that she understands."

Naomi didn't give Salim much time to respond before she was digging at his pockets. She helped herself to his knot of bills, peeled off a twenty, and waved it with an exaggerated flip of her wrist in the air at the blonde. The greenback caught Coco's eye like a beacon; a language she understood.

"Something is really wrong with you, you do know that right?" Salim said amused, watching Naomi doing her best to grab the blonde's attention. He knew when his wifey was *'turn't up'* like that, on a mission, it was almost impossible to turn down, and derail her.

"Shut up. So you can have *your* fun, looking at all this tits and ass jiggling around here, but I can't have *mine*?" Naomi said rhetorically. "Speaking of fun, go get us something to drink. A bottle of..."

Naomi turned to her side at the approach of a petite,

brown-skinned female boldly invading their personal space. White, pleather, thigh-high boots. A microscopic G-string. Star-glitter pasties barely concealed her nipples on her firm C-cup.

"I saw you two over here earlier, you dancing. You guys look like so much fun, and I was wondering if you two wanted some company." They barely heard her soft voice over the thumping music, but did notice the mischievous glint in her eyes that she mainly kept on Naomi. Salim smirked, and stepped off; he left them both at that table, alone.

"We are. Fun that is. What do you have in mind, cutie?" Naomi asked enthusiastically. The girl was cute, but there was no mistaking where Naomi's attention was directed. She made sure to keep her eyes on the blonde, a signal that conveyed she was their first choice.

"I was thinking maybe I could dance for the both of you, one song a piece. After that, I'll give your sexy ass a lap dance for free," the stripper said, soaking in what she viewed as a chocolate object of feminine perfection in her eyes.

When the blonde noticed one of the other girls at the club zeroing in on that dark-skinned couple who beckoned her earlier, and knew there was a strong possibility at losing *her* money, she snatched up at least three hundred dollars in small bills from her set, and rushed over in their direction.

"You could, cause you are a lil sexy ass chocolate drop, but you're not," Naomi said flatly. "Different tastes for different nights. Chocolate, butter pecan, Asian cuisine. Tonight I'm in the mood for a little vanilla in my cocoa." She brushed that brown-skinned stripper aside who dropped her warm smile, and shrunk a few inches in defeat at the diss.

"You were asking about me?" the blonde said to Naomi, more to announce her presence to the competition. She had singles, tens, and even some twenties stuffed down four garter belts on her knees and naked thighs; easily over two hundred, including the two fistfuls of dollars she clutched in both hands.

Clearly a hot commodity.

"I was. My husband and I noticed you, and we like you."

Naomi soaked in that blonde up close, and was even more impressed than before. Despite the dark room, smoky atmosphere, and fast blinking lights, Naomi could see that the blonde had an immaculate shape. Silky flawless skin. D-cup that stood out stiff behind nipples the size of dimes; definite implants. An incredibly slim waist, extremely flat stomach, pierced belly button, coke bottle hips, muscled thighs, firm calves, huge, round, ass-shot inflated ass, one hundred and sixty pounds of some powerful blonde pussy, all held up in some six-inch, white and clear fishbowl heels.

There was only one tattoo on her whole body – a small pair of cherries on a stem, right next to a tiny upside down triangle of blonde pubic hair – as if anything further would tarnish a completed work of feminine art. To top it off, 'Coco' had the most piercing shade of light grey eyes Naomi had ever seen on another human being; eyes so exotic they were more fitting for a cat. Naomi literally felt her mouthwatering at the visual before her.

"Damn! You are fucking sexy as hell," Naomi said thickly. "You were exactly why I decided to come here. I was hoping you could dance for me, with your beautiful self. Oh, and my husband too."

Naomi rose from her seat to slide up next to the blonde. With those heels, the blonde had the advantage; almost a half-foot over Naomi. That still didn't stop Naomi from embracing her wrist, and easing that blonde close on the aggressive like some average street thug.

"Thank you," the blonde sighed behind an innocent blush, "and dance for you? From what I just saw a few minutes ago, I should be asking you to teach me some of those moves." She licked her lips deliciously at Naomi, while at the same time, took inventory herself of that extremely dark chocolate powerhouse of a vixen sweating her with eyes that screamed the feelings were mutual.

"How about this," the blonde leaned over suggestively into Naomi's ear, brushed her huge breasts against Naomi's shoulder, taunted her with those flesh globular headlights, purred, "let me go put these tips away, and we can hang out in one of the VIP rooms. Fifteen minutes. I'll meet you back there, ok?" The blonde hit Naomi with an inviting smile. When she got a wicked smile out of Naomi in return, she hit her with a quick wink, and made her way through that dusky setting towards the back.

"Don't tell me your crazy ass scared her away," Salim said, approaching Naomi toting two bottles of *Nuvo*, noticing her glued on the blonde walking away. They both couldn't seem to peel their eyes from the way the blonde's fleshy ass swayed in cadence with each step, like a slow moving see-saw lava lamp rolling with the wave, until she disappeared from view.

"Little ole me?" Naomi held her bottom lip pouted out. She finally gave her husband her undivided. Well, more to the two pink bottles of bubbly dangling from his hands; she relieved him of one, and chugged a hearty mouthful. "Never. In fact, in fifteen minutes, we're gonna put your lil smart ass to the test. Time to find out if you still think Miss Barbie can knock me out of the box."

$$ $$ $$

With a third of a bottle in Salim's system, and another third in Naomi's, they were both floating on cloud nine. The bass thumping like therapy in the main room was muffled – sounded like Drake, something off that *'Visions'* album – but it still traveled through every morsel of their being, along with the energy of fruity flavored liquor coursing through their system like liquid crack.

The VIP room wasn't all the club hyped it up to be. Nothing but a tight back room, with dark, wood grain walls, one completely mirrored taking up one side of the whole room, a brass pole affixed to the center adjacent a plush leather, eight-foot couch, and a questionably clean matching recliner off to the corner that was clearly tucked in the shadows for nefarious reasons.

They'd only been in that back room for a little over ten minutes, but alcohol, high-strung hormones, a sexually charged atmosphere, and their mutual desires led to the obvious – they couldn't keep their hands off each other.

Naomi sat face forward, straddled across Salim's lap on the center couch cushion. Her tight mini-skirt was hiked up around her waist, rolled up around her slim midsection like a belt, every inch of her fleshy ass exposed, that G-string all up in her, lost in her nature. Salim's hands were all over her, palming her rich, dark chocolate flesh in firm grips.

She ground herself lewdly on his lap, massaged his crotch with hers. She sucked Salim's tongue softly, savored his saliva, sucked him deep in her mouth, and gave that little wet part of him head. She moved to the beat, couldn't keep still, and mewled out a sexy, whimpering moan with both hands embracing the sides of Salim's head.

"My...queen, let's get...let's get right," Salim panted between excited breaths. Naomi hardly let him up for air; she dove her tongue into his mouth, feasted on him, sucked on his bottom lip. "Sit up. Let me take my shit out...slide it up in you."

"Un ung," Naomi hummed with her mouth still on his, subtly shaking her head no. She peeled it away only long enough to twist his ear inches from her wet lips, and purr, "Ummmm, not gonna happen. I don't even think I'm gonna let you fuck me tonight. You'll be lucky if I even let you *taste* my pussy. You've been a bad boy, so no goodies for you tonight. In fact, no, I changed my mind. That's all you're gonna get tonight. You licking my pussy, *eating me*, while at the same time, *eating your own words*, thinking about that Dallas cheerleader that you claim is close to battling it out with..."

They both turned at the implosion of music pouring into the tight room when the door sliced open. They froze, deer caught in the headlights, both stuck on the blonde peeking her head around the corner.

"Is it safe?" she inquired, interrupting that feisty, married couple mauling each other on that plush sofa. She quickly stepped in, and closed the door behind her; she made sure she blocked that nosey bouncer's view who he stood just a few feet away on the other side of that door, on post.

"For now." Naomi had to forcefully peel herself from over Salim's lap, and playfully slap his hands a few times from his determination to keep her close. "But I won't make you any promises."

Naomi floated across the room over to the blonde, gently embraced her hand, and led her over to the couch. From the main room, the blonde slipped on a white G-string, and a matching bikini top that was so tiny she might as well still be wearing nothing at all. Her make-up was reapplied to perfection. She looked like an actual Barbie doll, in the flesh, down to the hair she let down, no longer in two braids.

"Drink?" Naomi posed, more as a statement than a question.

"Maybe just a sip." She raised the fresh bottle to her lips that Naomi handed her. She took a few light sips, only for Naomi to help her out by tilting her head back with the bottle.

"Don't be shy. Get your drink on," Naomi said, giddy as a schoolgirl. The gesture forced the blonde to down a few large mouthfuls; drops of it spilled down the corners of her mouth, beads showered her neck, and rolled down into her cleavage like alcohol rain. "That's what I'm talking about. Yeah, I want to have some fun with you tonight." Naomi's speech became slurred, her body swayed freely, a corollary of hard liquor and dark thoughts conquering her senses.

"I'm Naomi, and this is my husband, Salim. What's your name, beautiful?"

The blonde could see that the milk chocolaty, midnight black female before her with the infectious aura, pretty white smile, fitted hat, do-rag, Nikes, and gangsta swag was clearly buzzed, if not bordering on the edge of a full-on drunken stupor. The sight of it amused her.

"Persia. Do you guys come to the club often?"

"No. But now that I know you're here, maybe we will," Naomi said shamelessly flirting. "When I first saw you, I knew I wanted to spend some one-on-one time with you. See some things for myself, and prove some things to others." Naomi eyed her from head to toe. "No doubt about it – you are one badass motherfucking bitch."

Naomi returned to her seat on the couch, snuggled up next to Salim, and nestled herself into her husband's loving embrace. Tucked away in the VIP, with that attractive, black couple sitting as anxious spectators on the couch, the blonde didn't have to be told what time it was – she switched into seduction mode, got her mind right, began her routine.

Her hips came to life. She moved in perfect synch to the muffled beat in the main room, and to the beat in her head. Her perfectly manicured, French-tipped fingers circled gracefully around to grab the pole. She danced around it, made that prop her bitch, seduced it, and ricocheted the same seduction that beautiful African American couple radiated onto her, hotter than the sun.

She left Salim and Naomi completely mesmerized.

The way she backed up on that pole, swallowed it between her fleshy ass cheeks, literally make it disappear, how she clapped all fifty inches of it up and down all over the length of it, from a standing, bent over position, all the way down to the floor, as if she was using the material between her crotch to polish the brass, or massage her clit with the ceiling high fixture, how she climbed mid-range, dangle upside down, only to scissor her powerful thighs around it to perform tricks five feet from the floor, upside-down, was bar none.

She did it all. All of her tricks on full display.

Once she knew she had them nice and primed – she finished her impressive pole routine to stand before them less than a foot away, looked them both directly in their eyes, smirked, gave them her back, peered over her shoulder, winked, innocently trapped the tip on her index finger between her lips, smiled again, bent over suggestively lewd, and performed the grand finale, down on her hands and knees, slowly twerking her massive ass in circles, side to side, up and down, culminating each cheek on command, left cheek, right cheek, left...left, right...right, transformed her body into a flesh vibrator – she returned upright in her position of dominance to peer down on them.

"Who's first?" she asked, cutting confident eyes between them.

"Her," Salim said without hesitation. He turned to Naomi to see her staring back at him; a mischievous smirk floated across her lips. "I just want to watch, see y'all battle this out."

The blonde smiled herself, oblivious to that couple's secret experiment, accepting that invitation as her husband's chivalrous gesture to be a voyeur with his wife and another woman. The blonde used two fingers to tug at the micro-thin, spaghetti string strap of her bikini top around her neck; it rolled away from her milky skin. The string behind her back came next. Each gesture played out smooth, deliberate, and sensual, to produce the desired effect.

Her G-string, just as tiny, nothing but strings and a triangle crotch the size of a bookmark, was peeled down in slow increments over her curvy waist, thighs, calves, everything done with grace and finesse. She danced herself over in a few steps to straddle Naomi's lap. All it took was a few moves to get a reaction out of Naomi.

"No, no. No touching," came her soft, sexy warning. "*I can touch, if I like, but you can't.*"

The caveat came a little too late – Naomi already filled her hands to cop a good feel on those huge breasts jiggling in her face. The blonde took pleasure teasing her, she was shameless with it. She allowed that chocolate vixen that she tormented to explore those money makers before she removed, and lower Naomi's hands, several times, to keep them at bay.

Hands that instantly made their way back to her chest, felt up, and explored every time the urge hit her. Hands that had to constantly be removed, time and again, to keep them within club standards after Naomi freely felt up. Hands that the blonde finally agreed could remain on her thighs and ass. She thrust her huge breasts in Naomi's face, shrunk away, leaned back, giggled, and laughed after Naomi flicked her tongue out to swipe it across those pea-sized nipples – they grew hard and firm as a result – and resisted the urge to reciprocate from the way Naomi licked her lips and blew kisses at her.

The blonde was having so much fun, playing with, and teasing the wife of that couple, getting herself equally, and undeniably hot in the process, that she didn't even notice her husband on their side peeling off his jeans till they were down around his ankles.

It caught the blonde completely by surprise when she took in that first clear visual of his thick, veiny, jet-black, ten inches standing proudly erect from his waist. A distraction that diverted her attention to a second, more nefarious surprise when Naomi casually slithered her hand up between her wide spread thighs, and tickled her silky, wet petals.

At first touch, Naomi could feel that that blonde was soaked, literally dripping.

"*Fucking tease,*" Naomi thought, with a wicked smirk, and an arch of a single eyebrow.

Naomi knew how to play that game too – well. She tickled that blonde's velvety pussy lips, targeted her erogenous zones with two fingers, until her mouth fell agape, and left her eyes rolling hazily in her head.

She panted a pathetic, "You...you got's...to chill. Gurl, you can't be...you're not...supposed to be... be...oohhhhh...that feels so...so good. But...but, you're not...supposed to be...doing that," failing to convince anyone that she really wanted Naomi to stop.

Naomi looked up into that blonde's face, her sheer ecstasy, her bliss. Her top lip snarled. Naomi knew she was fucking her up. Two talented fingers, and an experienced thumb, on just the right spot, the other hand squeezing and spreading her left ass cheek to hold her open from behind, Naomi knew it would only be a matter of time before the blonde melted like white chocolate under a hot lamp under her touch.

$$ $$ $$

"Oohhh...chill...hold up. Oh...noooo. Damn, bitch, you bout to...to make me...oh shit! If you keep ...doing that...you're gonna make me...make me fucking cum."

The blonde's whole body tightened like the tips of Naomi's fingers sent a jolt of electricity through her. She sunk her nails into Naomi's shoulders, squeezed her tightly, braced herself, and let out a throaty sigh when that burst of warm liquid spilled from her center.

Naomi turned to Salim, gestured to her husband like her handiwork was child's play, and said quite causally, "How bout it? Think that dick can turn this bitch out as fast as I just did?" sure of herself when she knew she had that blonde under her complete control. Salim didn't answer her. He simply stared at them both with lust-filled eyes, watching his wife at work, turning that blonde out.

"How about you, Barbie? You wanna get on that right there?" Naomi posed to the blonde.

Her head was thrown back to the ceiling, she panted excited, shallow breaths. It took a moment to clear the clouds of a post climatic haze fogging her senses to slice her eyes down on it. The sheer sight of such a strong piece of black virile flesh conjured up in her the most primal of desires.

Salim sat back proudly, confident, cocky, literally, showcasing the pride of his African manhood. It stood up proud, almost a foot from his waist, hard as a flesh rock, and thick as a cucumber. The blonde parted her mouth like she was on the verge of saying something, but nothing came out. Nothing more than a few weak moans behind excited breaths; Naomi didn't stop her busy fingers for a second.

The blonde didn't have to say a word, not for Naomi to hear the fascination spoken in those light grey windows to her soul. The look in the blonde's eyes alone, the way she stared hungrily at that throbbing piece of flesh between her man's thighs, was one of the main reasons Naomi loved entertaining the inclusion of another woman.

"Cat got your tongue? Ok. You snooze, you lose." Naomi shrugged, she removed her wet fingers from in between the blonde's thighs. "I'll show you how to take care of that right there. Your ass gotta be this fat, thighs this thick, and pussy this tight and deep to climb up on that ride anyway."

Naomi eased that blonde up off her lap after she sensed how she really didn't want to move, or peel her eyes from her man's manhood, and stood before them. The few articles of clothes Naomi wore fell to the floor in seconds. Naomi stood completely nude in new Nikes hidden away in that VIP, proud, just as proud as her man. The twinkle in the blonde's eyes as she soaked in all of that chocolate flesh reflected how she was definitely impressed. A look down at Salim's dick to see him harder than he'd ever been told Naomi she crushed her in competition.

"Barbie's battling it out with me, huh?" Naomi posed rhetorically, standing side by side with the blonde.

To Salim's left – the naked blonde, her milky white flesh, and curvy features, propped up in heels.

Pan to his right – Naomi a half-foot shorter, still with her fitted hat on, backwards, her midnight chocolate flesh, curves much more defined and firmer than her lighter skinned counterpart, ass naked with an unbelievable aura of sex appeal and confidence.

Salim was left speechless.

Naomi wasn't.

"Tell me when I'm done if she's still battling it out with me, smart ass."

As if they were acting out a script – which in actuality was a spur of the moment affair – Naomi turned to give Salim her arched back, propped her hands on her knees, twerked smoothly, danced as if rhythm was injected into her intravenously from birth, and positioned herself to hover inches over his waist.

Reverse cowgirl.

He was familiar, knew the drill, loved it when his wife blessed him with it.

"Take mental notes. Peep the technique. Trust me, Persia, I promise you, you'll want to use this move one day," Naomi said to the blonde.

Salim anxiously reached for her. He guided her waist to him, gripped two palms full of those fleshy cheeks he fell in love with at first sight, ass cheeks that couldn't stop swirling in rhythmic circles, couldn't stop twerking, and eased her thick frame down on him to nestle himself in an incredibly wet, incredibly tight, incredibly warm snug home in her womb. A throaty moan poured out of Naomi's lungs behind a wicked smile.

"The trick...to mastering...this technique right here is...control. *Complete* control. No matter...how much...he tries to...no!" Naomi spit harshly, cutting her 'reverse cowgirl class' short to peer over her shoulder back at Salim. "What are you doing? *Don't* move. We're...*entertaining* our guest right now."

Her harsh scold, and flinch that signaled the cease of that tight, wet pussy keeping him nice and warm, calmed Salim; he ceased screwing it up in her, and simply sat back to enjoy the ride. Naomi playfully rolled her eyes at him.

"Back to what I was saying," Naomi returned to address the blonde, her body came back to life, "Control. This is *our* motherfucking position. *Boss Bitch* shit. A bitch that know how to get *her shit off*, first, take a motherfucka down, make him *your* bitch, take control. Boss bitch all over this fucking dick. You see, ninety-nine percent of these...brothers, especially these...big dick ass Negros, hitters that *know* they packing heavy weight, don't have the...discipline to...just sit back...and enjoy the...sensation of some warm...wet...tight...juicy...delicious pussy...swallowing them in *sooooo*...fucking deep. They just gotta try to take control... and dig it all up in you, especially...when it starts to get goo...good."

Naomi closed her eyes. The rhythm, the sensation, the feel of melting her wet flesh into her husband's rock hard flesh took over, controlled her, while she struggled to hold true to her own edict, and remained in control herself.

"Because...hitting all this dick...from this angle..." she worked her hips up and down, swirled in a circle, up and down, swirled in a circle, up and down, swirled in a circle in perfect harmony with an ecstatic wave consuming her, in perfect synch with muffled music, five minutes, straight, adding minutes, "...being able to...control right where it...goes. How much...or how deep...sliding it...all over..." Naomi's voice cracked, her body trembled, lip twitched, "...all over this fucking clit...beating on this clit...to also hit...to massage...to stimulate your g-spot ...will be sure to...to... to...oh *yeeeeeah*...that's it...that's it *right there*, daddy!"

The Anonymous Black Files

A sharp burst of warmth Salim knew all too well showered over him.

Naomi didn't stop bouncing and dancing all over that flesh stick.

She handled him as if she was test-driving a Bugatti on a racetrack. She shifted through every single gear, tested the shocks, the speed, the handle, ripped through the transmission, zero to two hundred in under five minutes, until she maxed out, full throttle, and fully worked that earth shattering orgasm out of herself.

"There. You see. *Our* ride," Naomi pronounced victoriously, breathing lightly, glowing in a light sheen of ecstatic sweat. "Are you ready?"

She nestled herself comfortably in Salim's lap to thoroughly swallow his thick, ten inches deep in her belly. Did that mainly to show that 'opposite of her' in every way how it was supposed to be done. How a strong black sista knew how to take down, control, and handle a strong black dick.

"Did you take notes? Think you can handle it? Because I'm warning you, you see it. My hitter packing a fifty caliber, loaded with hollow tips, and know how to break some shit off proper. He knows how to 'body a bitch'. Leave a bitch laid out like a crime scene on a king-sized. Make a bitch rethink, reanalyze, and question her whole sex game. Fuck around and make a bitch have to take it back to the drawing board."

The blonde bit the corner of her bottom lip innocently, cut a few nervous glances back at the bouncer guarded door and club full of unknowing patrons on the other side, then subtly, almost timidly, nodded. Naomi cracked her notorious textbook smile.

"Got her!"

"Just like I told you..." Naomi instructed, lifting all the way up with a slight moan; she stepped aside to display Salim's thickness drenched in her essence, and reached into his pocket for a *Magnum* condom, "...control. Don't worry, I'll coach you through it. Cause trust me, once you get it right, baby girl, once you learn how to boss bitch control some big shit like this, you'll learn how to give yourself, and him, more thrills than any ride Six Flags ever built!"

Case File #19 – Salim & Naomi, to be continued in:

The Anonymous Black Files 1.2: ***The Interviews***

Fifth Interview

"My brother. I was just thinking about you. I had a session with another couple earlier, and you came to mind when we touched on this very interesting topic, one of my favorites actually. What was that? Oh, the last tape. Salim and Naomi. Yeah, they know how to chop it up nicely, don't they? They're different. I like them. Some would say they know how to have fun, *their version* of fun, make the most out of life, and the relationship they have.

"They only found that kind of harmony within each other once they figured out one of the major keys to their happiness, why they learned to mesh so well together: they both see each other clearly. That *visibility concept* I was talking to you about. That same *sense of life*. They're on the same wavelength, and both have the same sense of vision of how they view sex – as somewhat of a sport. Amusement. A playful competition where it's sort of them against the world.

"What they have is very unique. Yes, extremely unorthodox, but unique. I've interviewed other couples who tried to experiment on their level, threesomes, and it proved to be a disaster. At the same time, if Salim and Naomi tried to follow the mold of another couple, that other couple's methods may not have worked for them either. That's the beauty, but also, the extreme difficulty of why most people can't seem to remain in long-term relationships.

"No same sense of life. No visibility. No complimentary differences. Rewind: the other couple in my previous session. Well, before I continue, let me premise this by highlighting one thing about these principles that I'm dropping on you. If you haven't noticed it by now, they all have an underlying theme. They're all tied together. They're all interconnected, sort of like how different musical instruments all flow together on one track. A concept that flows right along with that *rhythm and energy* within self.

"This is one principle that doesn't get much recognition, yet it is extremely vital that couples have it, despite so few people recognizing, or even understanding it. To break it down in layman's terms, or what I call, 'doing the one' to, this rhythm and energy concept pertains to the differences between individuals and their biological rhythm, and natural energy levels. These principles have been studied so thoroughly that even biologists acknowledge that every person possess an inherent biological rhythm. Listen close, do you hear it?"

Dr. Black raps in a rhythmic thump on the arm of the recliner with an open palm and fist, nods his head to the beat.

"Naw, I'm messing with you. Not that type of rhythm, but it's close. I'm talking about what scientists describe as a biological rhythm that shows up in patterns of speech, how individuals have distinct movements, how they respond emotionally, what some psychologists would describe as temperament.

"From now on, try to pay attention to how some are naturally, and inherently, more energetic than others. Physically, emotionally, and more intellectual than others. They think, move, react, and feel faster or slower than others. I'll break down both aspects of it. Build/Destroy.

"First, let's *destroy* the *negative* aspects of this rhythm and energy phenomenon, then we'll *build* on the *positive* aspects of it. Walk with me on this. Two separate *Case Files*. In the first, there's an instant attraction, physically. They converse, begin to dissect each other's psyche, find themselves dancing on the edge of something deep, and real, based on many affinities and complimentary differences. Yet, there's this subtle, almost indescribable mysterious friction between them. They can't explain it, can't put it into words.

"The more they travel mentally, physically, the more they experience this unexplainable irritation between them, an irritation that becomes too difficult to account for, to overcome, so they are forced to accept the undeniable conclusion that they are out of sync with each other. This could account for an example of incompatible differences in their biological rhythm and inherent energy levels.

"The one whose rhythm and energy is naturally faster may feel frustratingly impatient with the one who is slower. The one who is naturally slower, more lax, may feel chronically pressured to speed up to keep up. It's as if they're experiencing a different reality with the one they're seeking to be in sync with.

"What becomes a tragedy, is in an attempt to correct the differences they're experiencing, the faster of the two may respond even faster, the slower of the two becoming even slower, both trying to force the one they seek to connect with to adjust to his or her own natural state of being, completely unaware that what they are seeking to attempt is close to impossible.

"They make several attempts, but nothing seems to work. They don't *over*-stand this phenomenon. In the end, they'll create reasons to justify why they couldn't seem to make it work. If they have to, they'll *invent* faults that the other *must* have had, and justify the apparent breakdown in something that began so beautiful on these 'faults' that they just couldn't seem to get past, all the while remaining completely oblivious to the deeper science behind their incompatibility; what I've personally experienced in other couples, but that's for a later date.

"Moving forward. Now that we've destroyed, let's *build* on the *positive* aspect of this phenomenon. The same scenario as the first: two individuals meet, form an instant attraction, find themselves on the verge of establishing something deep, yet instead of experiencing this unexplainable irritation, that friction, they feel completely in synch, in harmony, a sense of rightness about their relationship, an unspeakable knowing of each other in a very special sense.

"Remember this...(Dr. Black raps lightly on the arm of recliner again, nods to the beat)...you feel that? Now you. Join in. Think of it as Double Dutch. When you feel the right opening, hop in. Come on, trust me on this."

Another set of hands join in the rhythm, they pound out a beat in perfect harmony.

"You feel what I'm talking about? The couple that has this rhythm within themselves would experience this on a subliminal level. Their basic affinities and complimentary differences well synchronized with their biological rhythm and inherent energy levels. When all of these factors are manifest, the result is a sense of harmony, a resonance between them, as if they were moving with the same silent music on the melodious track of life.

"Once Salim started to do the math to this, paired this in conjunction with the other qualities he shared in common with Naomi, then he began to over-stand why he felt a more compelling attraction to her – over virtually every other woman before her. Why he enjoyed a love relationship with her in which they explored so many areas untapped, or even thought of, in other relationships. Simply put: they are harmoniously compatible, without being emotionally undercut by that subtle irritating friction I spoke of earlier."

$$ $$ $$

"Imagine when a couple finds something like this: this beautiful union of love, basic affinities, and complimentary differences, all flowing in harmony with their biological rhythm and inherent energy levels. When they have this, they create their own little private world.

"Salim and Naomi. Malik and Tanisha. Victor and Zakia. Two individual selves, two unique personalities, two different senses of life, two individual islands of consciousness that found each other, and developed a new world between each other that they will both inhabit as long as they continue to build on their relationship.

"These are the worlds they created for each other. Worlds of silent understandings and unspoken words, of graceful glances that speak volumes, and witty shorthanded signals that are uniquely understood. Each of my clients who related their blessing of falling in love more than once has expressed that each relationship had its own music, its own emotional highs and lows, its own unique style, its own world.

"They began to view this world as an emotional support system, an endless source of nourishment and energy, something sustainable apart from the outside world. When Salim and Naomi first met, at that first moment of contact, it was like a metaphorical Big Bang – the creation of their new worlds began. Then as time progressed, as the depth of their relationship evolved, they evolved right along with it to create an entirely new entity, something the likes neither of them has ever encountered.

"When Salim and Naomi fell in love, and fully decided to link themselves in commitment to each other, they unknowingly embarked on one of the most formidable undertakings man had the daunting task to embark on, especially in this day and age of low tolerance, lack of compromise, and instant gratification – how to make their relationship work.

"Of all the crucial issues it would take for Salim and Naomi to make it, of all the factors that are vital to ensure Malik and

Tanisha have a healthy relationship, of all the principles that need to be applied to the fruitful development in Victor and Zakia's relationship, none is more vital for each to possess a healthy dose of self-esteem. Without it, it would be next to impossible for either of their relationships to survive.

"It sounds cliché, but the truth of the matter is if we don't have love for ourselves, there is no way we can have love for someone else. Why? Because if we cannot love ourselves, it would be almost impossible for us to believe that we are fully loved by someone else. Impossible to accept love. Impossible to receive love. Being no matter what their significant other will do to show signs of professing their love, it will not come off as convincing, being the individual will not believe they are loveable.

"Let me shine light on this. I've had couples who didn't *overstand* the significance of how self-esteem played an integral part of, not only their relationship, but their whole life. First, let's begin with what self-esteem is.

"Self-esteem encompasses two things, both aspects are interrelated: *a sense of personal efficacy,* meaning the power or capacity to produce a desired effect, and *a sense of personal worth.* It is the integrated sum of self-confidence and self-respect. The belief that one is competent for this existence. Not only competent, but worthy of it. Self-esteem is to have confidence that you can meet all of the requirements of life, and like a track star, jump over each hurdle we are confronted with daily.

"Think about if an individual didn't have this. If an individual felt inadequate to face the challenges of life, if they lacked self-trust, trust in their own mind to meet life's challenges. No doubt one would conclude that this individual had a deficiency in some form or fashion, right?

"If they lacked a basic sense of self-respect, a sense of being worthy of happiness, love, respect, fulfillment, the right to assert their legitimate needs and wants, one could easily surmise that they lack the capacity to demand this from others. But this is exactly what they will need in order to possess a healthy self-esteem – a sense of self-worth.

"Many of my clients, prior to exploring this issue, never took the time to sit down and reflect, in explicit terms, how they were entitled to be happy. How they were entitled to the assertion of their own wants and needs. How the satisfaction of their innermost desires was their natural birthright. When I counseled them on how to go about this, this led them to a deeper understanding of their love, and a greater exploration of their sexuality.

"By no means does this mean they are perfect, or that their self-esteem is complete. There is no such thing as an individual possessing complete self-esteem, or someone completely devoid of it. Self-esteem exists along a continuum, and can be measured in matters of degrees. It would be impossible to encounter an individual without a shred of self-esteem, or, on the flip side, an individual so full of self-esteem that it would be spilling out of their ears, and they would require no further room for growth.

"The thing with self-esteem, which some may not fully appreciate, is it affects practically every aspect of our lives. Low self-esteem, and its direct correlation to relationships, plays such an integral role that Tanisha's level of self-esteem actually determined the choice of person she fell in love with, and her conduct in that relationship.

"Once one does the science to self-esteem, one will see how someone like Victor, with a similar self-esteem, would gravitate towards someone like Zakia. How Naomi gravitated towards Salim, Malik to Tanisha. How high self-esteem gravitates to high self-esteem, medium to medium, low to low. How this is a result of them feeling most comfortable expressing themselves with those whose ideals resemble their own.

"The way I'm defining this attraction, this gravitation, I'm not speaking solely of the fleeting sexual response one would feel at first glance, but the kind of attachment that can be better described when one seeks to define love. I've counseled clients, where after only a few sessions, I've come to conclude that deep in their psyche, they unknowingly accepted that they are not enough. That they are not loveable as they are. That it isn't natural, or normal, for others to love them.

"Yet, if you were to ask them, without fail, they would righteously, and defensively, profess: *"That's stupid. Of course I want to be loved,* deserve *to be loved. Who* wouldn't *want to be loved?"* Little do they realize, those deeper, negative feelings are still lingering inside, simmering like good stew, waiting to sabotage their very efforts to achieve it. And only when they become fully conscious of their self-sabotaging beliefs will they be able to change their behavior."

$$ $$ $$

"People act on the image they see themselves in, and their actions produce results that continue to support their self-concept. Positive self-concept, positive results. Negative self-concept, well, you know. Straight disaster.

"One of the first critical steps in sustaining a happy, romantic relationship is the ability to embrace the love for yourself, and the naturalness of being loved by someone else. Love yourself, *truly* love yourself, and then you'll wholly, and genuinely, be able to allow, and accept, the love of others. If not, if an individual unconsciously view themselves as unlovable, to try to teach them how to solve their relationship problems by learning communication skills, or an advanced style of Kama Sutra, or methods of mental jujitsu, will all be done in vain.

"That's the problem with so many couples going to just any couples counseling now. They're going on the assumption that one or both of them are already open to the concept of love.

But what if they aren't? I gotta bring this to a close, but before I close this session, I gotta travel back to the topic I was discussing with the couple I was telling you about, the one where you came to mind. The topic of autonomy; the concept of self-direction and self-regulation.

"This session wouldn't be complete without me shining light on the subject, being autonomy and self-esteem go hand in hand. I love 'doing the one' to if an individual is autonomous, considering once I *over*-stood this principle, it helped to enlighten me to just another aspect of their mentality.

"As you witnessed, I have several clients, but Zakia is someone that I would classify as the epitome of a woman who is autonomous. A woman who understands that others don't solely exist to satisfy her wants and needs like some emotional leech.

"In fact, even prior to entering our sessions, she was on the opposite side of the spectrum, not relying on the love and devotion of others, but taking the responsibility of being happy on herself. Imagine how many people out there would be happier if they just adopted that philosophy? Zakia was truly autonomous because she didn't walk her day-to-day life continually questioning if her self-esteem was in jeopardy.

"She learned early on that the source of her approval concerning her self-esteem wasn't *external*, but resided from within. *Internal.* Wasn't at the mercy of every individual she encountered to make her self-esteem determination. Others who were weaker in this regard cannot accept the rejection, or acceptance, of that pretty woman, the denial, or approval, of the cute brother with the nice body, as just that − a single encounter. They would take that as a measure of their *entire* self-worth.

"To be truly autonomous is to have respect for another's choice to pursue their own destiny. To respect their moments of solitude. To accept their preoccupation with other matters outside of the relationship that have absolutely nothing to do with their partner, because their level of self-esteem isn't determined by how much attention their significant other will pay them. Career development, personal unfolding, spiritual enlightenment, all matters that don't necessarily have to involve their partner.

"But that's cool. On several occasions, that's needed. Space apart. Correction. Not only *needed*, I would go so far as to say that it is *mandatory*. To allow your partner that space, that freedom, that time alone. Just imagine how much more refreshing this relationship will be when they do find the time again to unite? Not only will the degree of their associations flow much deeper, but they will appreciate each other all the more, being their aloneness enhanced their love with a unique intensity.

"Sort of like fasting. Have you ever fasted? No. Well, when you first fast, say with food, for the first couple of hours, days, your body will respond to such a denial. You will see clearly how dependent you've become on indulging in fleeting *wants*, instead of satisfying any urgent pressing *needs*. Now imagine when you do eat. A three-course dinner, dessert. Your appreciation for your favorite dish will be savored all the more. Now apply this same concept to relationships.

"When you give your partner space, time to breathe, moments of solitude, you won't be so easily overwhelmed by the reality that such aloneness does exist. And within this aloneness, you will get a deeper *over*-standing of self, and who you really are. A deeper *over*-standing of your partner. See them for who they really are, and come to make peace with it. Sometimes it takes for you to *not* see a person for you to see them for who they really are.

"Because without it, without those times of solitude, without those moments of insightful soul searching, if this individual constantly avoids this aloneness, seeking to deny its existence by constantly seeking affection and attention from their partner, this relationship will ultimately evolve into a form of unhealthy dependence. Something that stifles and suffocates. Something that becomes clingy, instead of embracing. Something that pollutes the air, instead of becoming fresh oxygen to allow them to...(*inhale... exhale...*)...breathe.

"This is the type of equilibrium that must exist, along with a realistic view of who they, and their partners, really are. We traveled on this earlier, how Salim and Naomi maintain realistic views of each other, their fantasies and desires, along with Victor and Zakia, Malik and Tanisha.

"In order for them to truly grow as couples, they need to embrace each other for who they really are, virtues and shortcomings, in a realistic light. If not, they are doomed to be expecting a manufactured fantasy of their partner, which would result in resentment when that person didn't live up to this expectation. They may even feel betrayed, hurt, or deceived by their partner's actions, when in reality, if they would have simply dissected this person's psychology in a realistic light, they would have known that this person was acting completely in character.

"This is what I traveled with Salim and Naomi about. This is the realistic view Victor and Zakia have of each other. This is the examination of self Malik and Tanisha has taken. This is why they work. There is no denying the reality of who they really are. They..."

Three large gentlemen in suits and dark sunglasses storm the office. They all arrive with hard features, evil scowls. Intimidating presences envelop the room like a black cloud.

"Um, I seem to have some...uninvited guests. I'm sure you can see your way out. Here's the next case study. I'll see you next Thursday. Hopefully. Peace."

Case File #25 - Malik & Tanisha

A perverse smirk continued to crease the corner of Malik's top lip.

He stood in front of their mirrored dresser in their bedroom, struggling, fighting the urge to slice his eyes up to his reflection, knowing just a visual of himself, and the thoughts that tickled him so deliciously, would render any attempt to wipe it away futile.

Instead of warring against the inevitable, Malik continued on with the task at hand – rummaging through one of the top drawers, plucking out individual articles, and stuffing them in a bag he sat on top. He was so lost in thought he barely heard Tanisha when she entered the room.

"Where's the kids?" Tanisha asked.

She carried in with her a few unopened items: lotion, baby oil, deodorant. They were neatly placed alongside various other toiletries across the dresser. She got no response from Malik. After situating the items in a nice, neat line along the back (she was a stickler for order) she glanced over her shoulder back at him; he continued on with the packing of his black duffel bag.

"What are you doing? Where are you going?"

Malik could almost predict her movements down to a ten-minute window whenever she headed out to the store on a Saturday morning, like clockwork. Not the whole monthly stock up thing, not on that day, just a few knickknacks, leaving him the perfect window of opportunity to get the kids out of the house.

"Where are *we* going? You'll see. As for the kids, I hustled them up together, and got them over to my mother's..." Malik zipped two of the compartments closed, "...for the entire weekend." He didn't have to stop what he was doing to sense how the latter part of his answer stopped Tanisha dead in her tracks.

"The weekend? For the *entire* weekend?" Tanisha returned, her voice got lighter and more energetic with each word.

"Yup." Malik put the finishing touches on the bag. "Wanna know why?"

"Who the hell cares! You got us the whole weekend without them. However you did it, and for whatever reasons, big up to you," Tanisha cheered, all smiles.

She gave him a high-five. A faded grey Nike *'Just Do It'* t-shirt was peeled from over her head, and tossed on the corner of a small foot stand by the closet.

"But since you obviously put some effort into whatever you got up your sleeve, so much so that you gotta pack a bag for it, just what do you got going on in that creative little mind of yours?"

The thought of what Malik had planned for them on that sunny, weekend afternoon didn't appear to hold her as much as the three wigs displayed on their own headstands on one of the larger dressers. Malik followed her with his eyes as she approached them, one in particular, in only her bra and a pair of snug, grey sweatpants.

On her five foot few inch frame, they were practically at eye level. A few unruly splints on the third one, a short bob, got her attention. For one hundred and twenty dollars, she thought her eyes were playing tricks on her. They *better* be. She removed it from its stand, inspected it closer.

"One of the things we talked about before. I figured instead of us continuing to talk about it, we just do it."

"Which is?" Tanisha asked, clearly paying more attention to the wig than him.

"Which is something you're just gonna have to wait to see for yourself." The strap of the duffel bag was slung over his shoulder. "So get dressed. Nothing too fancy, something comfortable, and let's get the fuck up outta here," Malik ended, giving her a nice, firm, playful slap on the ass.

$$ $$ $$

Malik made it his mission to keep under wraps whatever he had planned for them.

From the time they rolled out of their driveway, and for the whole two hours they'd been floating down the highway, Malik was doing an excellent job of remaining tightlipped about their afternoon…well, at the time, evolving into their early evening escapade.

"Are we going out of state? Am I underdressed? Should I have packed an overnight bag?" Tanisha popped questions like shots in the air, her signal flares; they all fell back down to earth like slowly dying flames to fall on deaf ears. Malik gave her nothing.

Her next attempt: the bag Malik packed.

When Tanisha tried to reach for it, figuring if she couldn't get anything out of him, her investigative tactics would give her some clue from the contents of the bag, he coldly shut that down too.

"Damn nosey. Just sit your impatient ass back and relax. Here, you want to do something? Enjoy." Malik pushed a brown paper bag at her.

A six-pack of strawberry-mango wine coolers.

The sight of the strawberry-flavored bubbly washed all of Tanisha's concerns away. *Fuck it.* No matter. It was a beautiful, sunny, eighty-six degree, lightly breezy summer day. Tanisha sat back, nursed the first bottle, absorbed the scenery, figuring whatever he had in store for them, she was going to enjoy it.

Close to three hours and five wine coolers later, Tanisha sat up a bubbly bundle of energy in the passenger seat when Malik pulled off the interstate. She had a really nice buzz going on, and took in with anxious eyes the wooden plague of what looked like a huge state park.

Nature's Escape.

"The kids are that bad that you don't even want to take them to the park no more?" Tanisha said with a light chuckle.

The first thing that came to mind: a family outing at the beach several years prior. Nine-year old Jayden threw a mean temper tantrum most of the day, courtesy of his younger brother reveling in the torment he could see his harassment incited in him. At the time, Tanisha was too preoccupied with the baby, two-year-old Shadrika, to tend to the nonsense. Handling the boys, that became Malik's job.

"Damn near..." Malik returned, "...but that ain't why they couldn't come. This right here, this is our day. A day for grown up's. A day just for us. Trust, the shit I got planned, the kids can't be around for that."

His tone, demeanor, the mysterious look Malik wore all morning like a mask throughout most of the drive, gave Tanisha a nice, little, tingly feeling inside. Not just from the visual of her man looking so sexy, so handsome, so confident, or the magnetic energy radiating from his being less than three feet away from her that drew her in like gravity, but more in line with the unfolding evolution of what she knew to be her husband.

For the past year and some change, he'd really been a bundle of surprises when it came down to springing things up on her in an attempt to spice up their marriage. First, it was the adult videos – a progression from couples, to threesomes (Tanisha secretly loved those the most, for her own little furtive reasons), to hardcore, full-blown gang bang orgies – to a plethora of spicy toys, to their latest adventures in role-playing.

Tanisha was more than enthused to jump on board; after a decade and a half of marriage, they were both in desperate need of a pick-me-up to add a little spice in their love life. The whole role-playing routine became a phoenix rising from the ashes to revitalize the monotony of their slow dying marriage. Who could have imagined taking on the persona of any femme fatale her freaky little mind could think of would stimulate her with such an exciting sexual charge?

Reenacting those videos awakened a side of her that remained dormant, and became the perfect ingredient to revitalize her imagination. That made her a match for Malik, equaled the playing field, being he was usually the initiator of their newfound sexual adventures, springing, and executing, ideas on her faster than she could keep up with.

At least he used to be.

The nightclub, the façade of being strangers equally complicit in a spontaneous affair on their significant others – all Tanisha's work. The persona of a seemingly insatiable character on a threesome video – a petite, brown-skinned vixen, fat ass, big chest, a little hefty, quite like herself – planted a perverse seed in her psyche to emulate that fantasy in the flesh.

Welcome to the birth of *Sandra*.

Tanisha loved playing the role, the role of what she felt *reversed* the rules of engagement between the sexes: a sexually uninhibited female taking on an uncaring masculine persona indifferent to societal standards.

The idea of getting thoroughly fucked like that, right there in the tight corner of that nightclub, knowing full well the numerous unbelieving eyes who took in the spectacle of what they thought were two total strangers, and that little pint-sized, bombshell with her legs spread wide on that barstool taking all that dick with no shame, and loving every second of it, almost pushed Tanisha to orgasm the moment he entered her.

Then there was the drive home.

Tanisha had every intention of continuing to play out the role of the adulteress, lean over, drop her head in his lap as he drove, and suck his dick to climax, even swallow his cum to really play up the persona, only to be overcome with a spontaneous urge to drive *him* all the way home – literally. Yeah, that whole night, the meeting at that nightclub – all Tanisha's work. The brainchild of what her creative little mind put together.

Yes it was.

The spontaneity of it all drove Malik wild. She knew it would.

It also drove him to the subsequent – to try to outdo her. Which is why when Tanisha spotted them rolling up into a row of hotels structured in a retro, log cabin design, neatly shrouded in the concealment of acres of greenery, she knew it was time to get her mind right.

$$ $$ $$

"This is it, momma."

Malik snatched up that black duffel bag from the back seat, and was out the door before Tanisha could get a word out. Tanisha casually rose from the passenger seat, removed her large round sunglasses. She found herself enamored by the scenery. Perfectly manicured foliage, neatly trimmed grass, a rainbow of flowers lined the walkway to the main building, birds singing in a cacophony of songs on such a beautiful summer day.

Three couples traversed the grounds; all in their mid to

late thirties, early forties. A light breeze danced over Tanisha's skin, tickled the naked flesh between her thighs, and kicked out the truffle on the back of her flowered sundress. She shivered pleasurably, found herself growing hot at the warm sun enriching her brown skin, the wine coolers she knocked back on the drive there, and the lure of what Malik had planned for them. Tanisha interlaced her fingers into Malik's, and eased him close by her side; they walked side by side to the main building.

"Well, good afternoon," the receptionist said quite bubbly at the main desk. A young brunette, easily in her early twenties, held Tanisha and Malik with a penetrating smile. "Is this your first time at *Nature's Escape?*"

"Well, yessirre bob it is," Malik said just as quirky and chipper as her, showing all teeth. Tanisha involuntarily choked out a sharp chuckle. Only she could detect the way Malik mocked the young brunette and her cheery demeanor sitting at full attention behind the desk; she twisted her features oddly at Tanisha's reaction. Malik handed over his license.

"Oh, Ok. Let's see here," just as fast the brunette's bubbly self returned. "Here you are. Looks like you guys have reservations for the Candy suite." The brunette handed Malik a plastic key card along with his license. "It's a really nice room. Great view. By the way, if you guys missed the easel, don't forget about our annual couples meet. It starts at six in building four. I hope you guys can make it."

They didn't make it ten feet away before the brunette added, "I really love seeing beautiful couples such as yourself frequenting our quaint little outing. I think you'll make such a nice addition to our loving family."

Tanisha lifted an inquisitive eye, thought, *"Couples such as yourself?"*

It took the receptionist to say such a thing for it to finally dawn on Tanisha. Compared to nearly every other individual they encountered, there was one unique underlying difference between them, herself, and her husband – they were the only black couple there.

One Spanish couple disappeared into a similar building, definite professional types, and they were way out there somewhere in the middle of the woods – not the first choice on the list of where most in their tight circle would disappear off to – but still, no other *black people* as far as the eye could see.

That didn't mean there weren't any other black people there. It's just that if they were, Tanisha hadn't seen any – yet. Nor did she necessarily care about them, or any other couple for that matter.

Her only concern at the time: Malik.

The three hours they drove, which strangely flew by in no time, along with the videos she watched on the way there (that sneaky motherfucka filled the videos in his car full of nothing but stripper showdowns, twerk competitions, and porn), left Tanisha fiending to get to their room. Malik inserted the key card in the door, and barely turned the knob, before Tanisha shoved him in.

"Damn, momma," Malik said with a smile, struggling to keep his footing, "Look at you. Ready to get that shit on and poppin' already." The momentum of Tanisha's shove forced him to plop on the edge of a full-sized bed in the center of the room. Tanisha was all over him; kissing, groping, mauling. She tore at the buckle on his stonewashed, slim fit jeans.

"What do we got, about thirty-six hours before we have to leave this little private get-away and return back to our regular world? Shieet! I'm trying to make the best of *all* this time."

She anxiously fished into the slit of his boxers, and caught his semi-stiff erection. Just the sight of his dick moved Tanisha to smoothly lower herself to her knees between Malik's thighs at the foot of the bed; his veiny, seven inches standing up stiff, pulled her in like a magnet to metal.

Her gaze was locked, eyes sliced low in lust, she licked her lips deliciously. With Malik propped up on his elbows, he watched every second of her light brown face lowering over him till the view of what he was so determined to see – his rock hard erection being polished between her thick, wet, lip-gloss coated lips – became slightly overshadowed by a wavy swirl design of cornrows decorated over Tanisha's scalp.

"Lean that shit back, baby. Yeah, hold your head back," Malik breathed, lightly caressing the back of her head.

"Now which one of us look anxious?" Tanisha sighed, rubbing all over his thick shaft to squeeze him up nice and stiff. "You wanna see that shit, huh? You wanna watch me? *See* what's making you *feel* so good?" Tanisha purred slyly, licking all over the head of his dick like her favorite lollipop. She thoroughly polished the head, spit shined him, before exaggerating the parting of her lips to take him into her greedy mouth.

"Shit, you already know," Malik sighed, which came out more like a growl. "You know I love watching how my wifey handle that. That's *my* work right there. I schooled your lil freaky ass enough with that 'brain' to teach you how to become a scholar."

Tanisha blushed with him still in her mouth, her eyes twinkled, she removed him long enough from her lips to purr, "Listen at you..." then quickly returned to give him a few soft licks, some more delicate sucks on the head, "...trying to take credit for all the hard work *I* put in."

She held his rock hard flesh in complete admiration, licked a deliberate trail from his balls, up the underside of his shaft to the tip, then lowered her mouth over him to take him in a third, a little more, she filled her mouth halfway, staring at him directly in his eyes the whole time. She polished that dick in her mouth with a sneaky look in her eyes, sucked, and slobbered all over him, studying him to gauge his every reaction, then slowly sucked her lips from him with a pop.

"I got that good brain, huh?" she boasted with an exaggerated lick on the tip, "studied real long," another lick, "never missed a class," slid her hand up and down his saliva-slicked shaft, "I even stayed after class with the professor for that...*extra credit.*"

She hit him with several trademark tricks she learned over the years, little tips which she knew her husband loved so much. Malik squirmed delectably under her touch.

It only took five minutes, and Tanisha unleashing a trick he never experienced before, to leave Malik panting, "Damn, who the fuck was *that?*"

Tanisha winked at him with him still in her mouth. She worked him over a little more, hit him with the trick again, and smoothly sucked her lips up to the tip, slurring, "Sandra." She immediately took him back in her mouth, paid complete homage to his ebony tool, coated him in a light film of saliva, ran her hand over him gently, delicately, rhythmic strokes, and bathed him between her lips.

"But I think...wait a minute. I think...I think I hear someone else." Tanisha listened in the quiet room as if someone else was speaking to her. "Yeah, I think I hear...*Veronica* calling. Oh yeah, that's her. She says she wants to come out and play. And you know Veronica. She likes to get a little..." Tanisha nibbled on the head of his dick, "...kinky."

A devilish smirk floated across Malik's lip at the thought of Tanisha channeling the persona of one of her most dominant personalities – Veronica – someone who he knew to be one of her raunchiest characters to date; it ran a shiver down his spine.

"Focus. Think of something else. Focus!" Malik thought.

He had to focus on something, anything, redirect his thoughts. If not, if he kept staring down at that alter ego Sandra...wait, no Veronica, well, whoever the fuck she was at the time, he knew he would be sure to lose his seed, and spill it down the back of her throat like an undisciplined horny teenager within the next minute if she kept that up. Then, not only would she have 'won' the first round, he would have spoiled and tarnished that first experience with such an immature slight of premature ejaculation.

"I got this. Who in the fuck do this chick think she is? That Heats *versus* Knicks *game. Lebron banging out with Mello. Lebron fakes left, right, drives straight down the middle...down the middle...of those fat luscious titties..."*

Tanisha's milk chocolate cleavage spilled out the top of her sundress; her D-cup displayed in a black paisley push-up bra appeared twice their normal size on her already petite frame. The thought of sliding his shaft between them, right into her mouth, flooded his thoughts.

"No! Focus. What the fuck!? Focus. Not on that! Think of something else. Anything else! Go back to the game. Anything but how I want to slide my shit right between those fat ass titties pressed together. Press them together, and slide right in between them, directly into her mouth, one of Veronica's specialties. NO! Focus. Focus. Focus on...ok, there we go."

Two slow moving shadows became the remedy to help quell the fire in his loins; Malik caught them out the corner of his eye. It also took that brief distraction to direct Malik's attention to the rest of the room.

Sparsely furnished. Plush, bubblegum colored carpet, candy cane wallpaper, two dressers painted with various candies which displayed many of the like – bubblegum, lollipops, hard candies, chocolates. End tables lined with large glass vials; strawberry, chocolate, caramel, honey. Several posters of retro showgirls back-dropped in candy themes, with...two, sliding glass patio doors displaying a spectacular view of a secluded trail cut into the grounds, connecting each cabin hidden in that forest of forbidden pleasure.

Malik remained focused on those two, slow moving shadows, shadows that soon revealed themselves to be a couple traversing across the trail, enjoying a casual walk on that beautiful summer day. With Tanisha's back to them, she hadn't spotted them. She had no clue that the first sight of them stumbling upon that petite, brown-skinned girl on her knees, with her head in that guy's lap, performing her fallacious skills so beautifully on him, that her special show slowed their pace.

After a real good look, four eyes focused in utter intrigue; the salacious spectacle stopped them dead in their tracks.

Malik wasn't the least bit surprised by their fascination.

This was Veronica we were talking about, performing on him with the skills of a veteran porn star. A few more sucks, a calculated, circular flick of her wrist up and down his shaft, tilting her head back to suck on his balls, coincidentally dropped both of their mouths in shock. Not surprising. They changed course and carefully inched their way towards the door.

Malik and Tanisha's blatant act of voyeurism sure went down much smoother considering that couple just so happened to be walking the trail, completely nude.

$$ $$ $$

Booking reservations for the weekend to one of the three top nudist colonies in the tri-state was almost two months in the making. Malik always had a thing for nature, and the whole natural aspect of sexuality. His Adam to Tanisha's Eve. So exploring the more carnal side of sex in nature with Tanisha (even if she hadn't known it yet) just seemed to be the only logical progression of things to come in their relationship.

"I swear, Sandr...my bad. Veronica. You got that shit down pact," Malik stressed, reclining even further, as if to fully luxuriate in the phenomenal head that pornographic pseudo-personality was giving him. Only he knew the gesture was more to give the couple standing right outside those double glass doors a better view.

"You...haven't...seen...nothing...yet," Tanisha vowed between breaths, polishing his magic stick between her lips in complete admiration. "I'll show you just what a *PhD* can do. Mensa ain't got shit on this brain, or better yet, this...*throat*.

What I call...*deep knowledge.* Just wait till I show you how I graduated with the grand fina..." Tanisha noticed how she didn't have Malik's undivided anymore, how his attempts at controlling his wandering eyes exposed the truth of their surroundings.

Tanisha slowed the bobbing of her head, finally lifted her lips from the head of his dick, lips lewdly dripping saliva, both hands coated, and rolled her head over her shoulder to see...

"*Oh my God!*"

There was a damn couple invading their privacy at their door, just standing there, observing.

And *what the fuck* — they were both *naked!*

The woman, white, a fiery redhead with perky breasts, b-cup, maybe, a neatly shaved triangle down below, (proof that the drapes matched the carpet), stood about five foot six with a slim, athletic build. The guy, also white, light brown hair wrapped in a tight ponytail, about five foot ten, who stood protectively by her side, came equipped with a figure very similar.

The manner in which they stood there, there was no question in Tanisha's mind that they caught most of her handiwork, and what her lips and tongue could do to a dick. They both stood firmly in place. Both wore perverse smirks stuck on their faces like masks. Both stared down on her shamelessly. Both were entranced at that petite, brown-skinned exhibitionist showcasing her talent.

Tanisha didn't find herself so shocked that her performance pushed them to be so bold as to want a front row seat to the action. In fact, one of the biggest turn ons for Tanisha was the idea of being watched by complete strangers performing the most obscene acts — sucking dick ranking on the top of that list. Her husband knew that. She just normally didn't have their sexcapades sprung up on her without notice.

Tanisha returned to her husband before her, squinted at him perversely.

The look he gave her in return...busted!

That motherfucker set her up. Executed a sting operation that caught her out, red-handed.

Better yet: on her knees, lips wet, dick in her mouth, taking it halfway down her throat.

That naked couple, them catching her in such a compromising position, it had to be his doing. A mysterious couple that caught her out in that mysterious room, on her hands and knees, her head in her husband's lap, her lips shiny, still literally holding his rock hard shaft in her hand, doing something so lewd and raunchy it was supposed to remain a secret in their bedroom – his doing. She stared up at him, gauged him, wanted confirmation. Malik lightly shrugged, smirked, gave her a sly wink.

Yeah, he got her.

"Oh, so you wanna play like this, negro? Put me out there to perform? Ok. Gloves off. Let's fucking play."

Tanisha smiled, and winked back at him. She completely ignored the couple in their presence; her pretended unawareness of those exploring eyes made the act more salacious. Tanisha helped Malik to remove his jeans and boxers, dropped them down to his ankles, took them off completely. She exaggerated the way she wrapped her lips back around the head of his dick again, that time without a shred of shame.

Time to take the center stage...act one...Showtime!

"Yeah," Malik slurred, "You like that we got company, don't you?"

The question was unnecessary; he already knew the answer.

Tanisha kept her eyes locked dead center into his. There was no denying the slight shift in her body at Malik's inquiry; it was done not to accommodate him, but to give that voyeuristic couple an unobstructed visual of her every move.

"Tanisha doesn't. Tanisha would have fucking *killed* you if you pulled some shit like that on her. But...I'm not Tanisha. This is Veronica, and Veronica *loves* shit like this." Tanisha lewdly slurped all over his fat dick in her mouth, worked her hand up and down his slick shaft, and exaggerated the way she bobbed her head in his lap. "When she knows there's others enjoying her skills, she loves to get a little extra…*nasty* with it. Be that raunchy, filthy, freaky ass bitch she knows you love so much."

With a few calculated bobs of her head, Tanisha prepared herself, warmed herself up, and opened her throat; Malik melted into an ecstatic sigh when she took him all the way down to his neatly trimmed pubic hairs. Malik tried to keep his eyes on his saliva-glistened shaft disappearing between Tanisha's ovaled, suckling lips, but his head weakly fell back, his eyes rolled in his head behind lust-heavy slits.

Rolled until he heard…

Tap! Tap! Tap!

$$ $$ $$

The light rap on their patio door window could have been seen as inevitable.

It didn't sway Tanisha for a second.

She was already caught. On her hands and knees, head in her husband's lap, his fat, saliva-coated dick deep down her throat, sucking on it like a top paid porn star who *loved* her work. She was sure that's why Malik brought her there in the first place, to live up to the role. The role of a little nymphomaniac for 'Mr. and Mrs. White birthday suit' that she was sure they would never see again.

Tanisha acted as if she didn't hear the raps, raps that came a second time around, that time even louder. She continued to perform, and display her deep throating ability to perfection, now even more so. Her petite hand reached underneath to caress Malik's balls. She massaged his heavy, bloated sac, primed him for an explosive orgasm; still hadn't decided if she would greedily swallow it all, or take it right in her face as the encore for their audience.

The distraction of that mysterious white couple helped Malik – he knew at any moment he was going to blow – but not nearly as much as he hoped. All he could manage was a slight nod behind strained features, a nod that indicated for them to come in. He bit his bottom lip, squinted, clutched two fistfuls of sheets underneath him, and fought to hold on to his virility as the woman timidly, and cautiously, slid the patio door partially open.

"Hey, good afternoon. How...how are you guys?" the redhead poked her head inside, "We were just taking a little afternoon stroll, when we...when we just happened to...wow," she tried to continue, but found herself too enthralled by Tanisha's performance to form complete sentences. Tanisha continued on like they weren't even there. *Or*, like they were there, and she was auditioning for them, determined to get the part.

"I've never seen you guys here before...and...we...we would really, *really* like to spend some time with you guys while you're here. I'm Charlotte, and this is my husband, Ted. We've kinda new here, only been members for the past year and a half, and...I'm...I'm sorry, but I gotta say this. You are really, really, *really* good at that," she chimed, drawn with the force of earth's gravitational pull over to that couple to get a closer look.

Her partner, Ted, he shadowed her every move. He leaned over her shoulder to get a closer look himself. Take a front row seat to watch that pintsized black woman suck all over that black phallus with a passion he'd never seen. With his wife slightly arched over, just as entranced by her skills, he used that opportunity to run his hands all over his wife's out-thrust ass. He palmed it lovingly, rubbed his body against hers, but kept his eyes glued on Tanisha.

"*Focus. Fuck...focus! Basketball. Football. MMA fighting. Shit!*"

Malik struggled, fought the tingling sensation brewing deep in his balls.

It was about to go down.

Go down in a big way, just as he suspected it would.

Only he didn't expect to run into another couple so soon, or for things to progress that fast; they hadn't even been on the grounds for an hour. Ted's hand trailed a deliberate line down her spine and in between his wife's ass cheeks, quickly found her secret, he sneakily wormed two fingers deep up in Charlotte's tight little opening.

Her mouth dropped in lust, she whimpered out a little, "Oh, honey. That feels sooo good," at the way those fingers tickled her so nicely.

She arched her back even further, anxious, sought deeper penetration, squirmed her thin hips, and reached back to wrap her small hand around her husband's stiff erection. She blindly stroked him up and down from behind, stuck on that little bombshell sucking all over that black dick as if her life depended on it.

"Focus. Fucking...FOCUS!"

Oh, who was he kidding?

It was a lost cause.

How could he resist when Charlotte's moans filled their small room like music from her husband's fingers penetrating her from behind. At how she leaned so close to Tanisha's head that Malik could actually feel her light pant warming his inner thigh. At the way Charlotte not only jerked all over her husband's dick, but gave him a sneaky look in her eyes that screamed all Tanisha had to do was give her the ok, and she would have gladly taken over to finish up the blowjob his wife performed on him like a porn star.

He couldn't.

Malik broke under the pressure, an orgasmic geyser unleashed. He let her have it.

"Oohh...yes. Nice! That is *soooo* beautiful," the redhead

sighed as if she experienced the most beautiful work of art, almost in sync with Malik's cry of ecstasy.

The orgasm that shot out of his body, straight into Tanisha's hungry mouth, was unlike anything he ever experienced, clearly nothing like the few milky ribbons erupting from Ted's erection all over the back of Charlotte's ass and thighs seconds later. The impact of such an explosive release filling her lips didn't cause Tanisha to flinch a hair.

She concluded she wanted it in her mouth, so she continued on, just as intently. She jerked Malik into her wide open mouth, spray painted his semen all over her tongue, and closed her mouth around her husband's dick still spitting up cum to swallow him down with moans and hums as if he was the most delicious drink she ever tasted.

"That was...really, *really* hot," Charlotte commented thickly. "I'm impressed. *Really* impressed."

Tanisha gently squeezed Malik's balls a few times for good measure, really milked him dry – textbook Veronica – then finished up by kissing the tip of his dick to peck away the last bit of essence that bubbled up.

"I'm glad you two enjoyed yourselves." Tanisha finally peeled her attention away from Malik. She got her first real visual of Ted's essence dripping from the tip of his dick, his sperm splayed all over the back of his wife's thighs, added, "It seems almost as much as us," and giggled lightly, proud of how her performance pleased everyone there. "By the way, my name is Veronica, and this is my husband, Link."

Tanisha cleaned the corners of her mouth with her thumbs, and smoothly brushed that dainty sundress from over her shoulders; it fell around her ankles along with her tight matching panty and bra set. She stood before them, nude herself, mirroring that mysterious couple in their midst.

"And if you thought that was hot, my mouth..." she crawled atop of Malik, face forward, reached between his thighs, and positioned his still hard dick for entry, passing occasional glances at the couple behind her, "...just wait till I show you what this ass can do, how I ride it."

The next ***Case File #28 – Malik & Tanisha***, to be continued in:
The Anonymous Black Files 1.2: *The Interviews*

Sixth Interview

"I gotta admit I'm a little surprised. I thought maybe that little...*mishap* you witnessed on our last meeting might have scared you off. That would have been really unfortunate too, considering I'm definitely feeling the flow of how our *Interviews* are traveling, especially that last session. That session was good energy right there.

"With that being said, hopefully that little mishap doesn't have to be included in your final edit. Remember, perception. Say again? Who were those steely-dispositioned individuals that disturbed our last meeting? Were they the reason why I had to pack up and bounce with all of my shi...make such a quick departure from my last office in our first session? Well, to sum it up for you, just as in any relationship, we all have a past, things we may not be so proud of. That's just a part of reality.

"The beauty of enduring such an experience is it not only came as a vivid reminder that we reap what we sow – there are no such things as free passes in life, karma will inevitably unfold – but such a test allowed me to *over*-stand how the enlightened self will respond to such an event. Not just me, but also all of those around me. Kiara being one of them.

"When I was first confronted with such a dilemma, Kiara

could have easily used that as an excuse to part ways with me, and never look back. She didn't. She thugged it out with me, held strong to weather the storm. And just like with any relationship, her blatant display of strength allowed me to appreciate her all the more.

"Speaking of relationships..." Dr. Black laughed, "...a nudist colony. Yeah, Malik and Tanisha even threw me through a loop on that one when I first critiqued that session. How about it, would you do it? What do you think, go to a nudist colony? No comment? Do you realize your *refusal* to comment on it says something in itself? Silent acquiesce. Forget it. I'm not gonna pry cause I don't wanna lose sight of the topic of that last Case File.

"The nudist colony, Malik and Tanisha's high degree of mutual self-disclosure. Their courage and willingness to allow each other to enter into the innermost recesses of their minds, their freedom to express their innermost thoughts, desires, fantasies, giving each other full disclosure to each other's private worlds, and taking a genuine interest in it. For them, to engage in something like that, as a couple, there had to be a prerequisite: they both not only created an atmosphere of trust and acceptance, but they were willing to know, and accept, each other fully; mutual self-disclosure.

"My clients seek my counsel for methods on how to not only maintain, but improve, on their long-term relationships. Several had some idea of where the problems arose in their relationships, and sought clarification. Some were searching for insight on how to keep the spice. Some on the verge of calling it quits, and sought as a last resort the advice of professional counseling.

"Within all of these scenarios, what I found to be the most important key to our sessions, instead of simply toting out textbook theories, is to help them feel comfortable enough, and connected enough, to bring out the innermost feelings within themselves.

"Unfortunately, I've counseled some who internalized their

deepest feelings because they were not sure how to act on them. They suppressed them for a litany of reasons: fear, ridicule, judgment. So these deep feelings remained. Disownment and repression does not equate to a fruitful solution. They are still there. And without a meaningful outlet to channel these thoughts/desires, the disownment of these feelings and desires that are inherently there by nature, will no doubt lead to a chronic state of disharmony within self, which is completely counterintuitive in a committed relationship if complete visibility is the objective.

"Don't get it twisted. Although visibility is the sought out objective, this doesn't mean that every thought lingering in the mind need to be voiced. Judgment is key, not to mention a little wisdom and insight. It takes both to do the math to whether it is necessary to communicate certain feelings, to share certain thoughts and perceptions. How rational would it be for an individual to demand of their lover an expression of everything they think, feel, fantasize, and desire?

"I would never profess to a client such an objective. The object is to create an atmosphere where such disclosure, if necessary, can be freely expressed without fear, judgment, or moral condemnation. This is something I ask my client's to create – an atmosphere where their significant other can freely express their feelings, emotions, thoughts, without the stigma of ridicule, condemnation, or attack.

"When such an environment exists, when there is an atmosphere where there is the freedom to express fantasies, wants, feelings, thoughts, with full confidence that their interests are being fully acknowledged, and genuinely considered, that is a couple who have become the soul, yeah, not sole, the *soul controllers* of their destiny, masters of their unique union.

"Another key component for them to remain the soul controllers of their destiny is to allow for the continual flow of effective communication. This is the essence of mutual self-disclosure: to communicate their feelings, emotions, the hurt or the pain, with their partners displaying a sincere interest in listening.

"For those immersed in the streets, I've learned that this was one of the hardest concepts for them to grasp. For one to simply listen to their significant other, to just be there, available, without succumbing to the impulse of offering ideas, or a solution to the thoughts being communicated to them. Not just gangstas though.

"I noticed this pattern with many of my professional male clientele. It's really simple math if you add it up: men and women think differently. If I solicited any of my brothers, and began to converse with them about my problems – bills, friends, women, children, work – the first thing my dude is gonna do is give me insight on how to *fix* the problem.

"Brainstorm it together, work through different scenarios, come to a solution. Simple. At least on the surface that's how it would seem. Why would I bend his ear, and hold it hostage, if I wasn't searching for help on a fruitful solution to solve my dilemma? That's how most *men* think. Not the case all the time with some *women*. They are such a complex and beautiful creature, aren't they?

"Present the same scenario, and some will seek to simply vent their source of contention, not with the hopes of being offered a solution, but simply with the sole intention of seeking an outlet to get it off their chest. No feedback. No solution. No opinion. Just a simple release. In some instances, that verbal release may even allow them to process a solution themselves.

"The problem is the overwhelming majority of men, who are not in tune with this particular characteristic, will find it virtually impossible to simply sit through this kind of dialog, especially if he feels he has a reasonable solution, and *not* offer his advice. So this is where the million-dollar question presents itself: how will one be able to differentiate when she just wants to express her thoughts, feelings, concerns, and when it is appropriate to give constructive feedback?"

The Anonymous Black Files

$$ $$ $$

"Like I said, that's the million dollar question right there – literally. Cause if I had the answer to that, I'd bottle that method up, and distribute it on the block faster than crack! Seriously, as I mentioned in one of my earlier sessions, the reason why such a universal answer can never be applied to all women is because…bingo! You took the words right out of my mouth – all women are individually unique in their own right. Each one is different, equipped with different issues, and will respond differently based on the circumstances.

"For my brothers in search of deeper insight into their significant other, I encourage them to calibrate their values, thoughts, feelings, and try to synchronize them with their woman's psyche. By doing so, they become less dependent on others for a determination, and are more likely to make that determination themselves. And they should want to make that determination, especially if their failure to gauge the situation leads to feelings of anger.

"These feelings – escalated annoyance, getting heated, becoming angry with your partner – is not only common, it's normal. That's reality, everyday life. The key is to figure out how to express that anger honestly and openly, clearing the air without escalating the situation to the next level. Tanisha had a big problem with that.

"She conditioned herself with a defensive mentality: at the first sign of attack, she flipped the switch, got into battle mode, and assassinated the person's character like she was in a verbal cage match. Coincidentally, she was very good at it. Jon Jones with the mouthpiece. Obviously, this didn't lead to any effective resolution in communication. It only satisfied her lower desires, temporarily, and created the perfect platform to inspire a counterattack. None of which was productive.

"It's an art to cycle through a highly irate state, and still be able to effectively communicate that anger *without* provoking matters to escalate. It's not an easy art to master. But for a couple to advance in their relationship, especially ones who are highly opinionated, and seek to maintain peace and tranquility, learning this art is essential.

"If not, they could expect the opposite: mastering the art of denying, or disowning feelings. The art of deception by smiling, or holding a stone exterior outward, while internalizing this murderous rage on the inside. This is the sworn enemy of effective communication.

"In all of the couples I've counseled, I haven't encountered a couple yet who *hindered* their relationship by honestly expressing their anger. I've counseled several who have by erecting additional barriers by repressing this anger. By turning this individual 'off' in their mind while they were in the middle of voicing their thoughts, thinking, "*I wish this motherfucka would just shut the fuck up.*" By 'solving' these issues of anger by making themselves numb. In the end, remedies like that aren't effective at all.

"What is – communication. The communicating of the negative, the positive, and everything in between, giving their significant other full range of their mental and emotional world. And if you think this concept of communication is self-explanatory, obvious to anyone with any modicum of insight and common sense, you'd be surprised at the number of individuals who fail to grasp this principle.

"What you have to understand is there are instances when someone who is afraid, or questions themselves, to express what they want, they will often resort to *blaming* their significant other for their failure to offer them an objective forum to express it. There is a fear, and an underlying anger, for the individual who knows what they want, but doesn't feel they have the courage to voice it. There is a fear of surrendering your thoughts and feelings to your partner, allowing them to see you mentally naked without confirmation of how they will respond.

"Imagine if Naomi didn't feel comfortable enough in her relationship with Salim to express her yearnings of bisexuality? Imagine if Tanisha wasn't confident that Malik would react positively to her acts of spontaneity when she wanted to role-play to spice up their sex life? What if Zakia couldn't assert herself with random acts of dominance and overt masculinity, which has become such an intricate part of her psyche, that her behavior and sexual assertion have become one in the same? Would this not lead to hurt, resentment, a feeling of isolation and loneliness, even amongst their own partners?

"The beauty of the three *Case Files* that I shared with you is they each have a full understanding of what they want out of life, love, their relationships, and have no fear in expressing it. Not expressing every passing feeling, impulse, urge, thought or fantasy, but being able to create an environment where such an expression is welcome. Not to say that each and every one of their needs will be met every single time. No relationship could ever promise that, because there are some days when they will be experiencing two different mentalities.

"No one can give someone everything they want, when they want it, every time they want it. No one exists primarily for the satisfaction of our every desire, twenty-four-seven. But the knowledge of knowing they can express themselves freely is a relief in itself, instead of feeling like their partner isn't even interested in building on the subject.

"In my initial consultation with some client's, there's been instances where they didn't feel their significant other gave them the forum to freely express themselves *directly*, so they resorted to satisfying their desires *indirectly*, through subtle forms of manipulative behavior. Others that weren't so creative simply said *'Screw this shit'*, and outright cheated. Either way, both of these mentalities constitute a complete breakdown of progress in the relationship, with manipulation being a degree more grimy in my opinion.

"Manipulation comes with the component of insecurity. And if someone feels so insecure that they believe they can't honestly communicate their thoughts, and have to resort to manipulation to get what they want, not only will they sabotage their relationship with their partner, but such a mentality will no doubt spill over into other intimate relationships to sabotage them as well.

"If they felt the desire to manipulate their partner into getting what they want, either by guilt, or by sympathy, they may ultimately succeed in getting what they want, but the consequence of this behavior, once it came to light, would most surely result in resentment and anger. Which is why a policy of honest communication, the courage to be who they truly are, sharing feelings, thoughts and desires, will always reign over any tactic of manipulation.

"This willingness to recognize, and accept, their innermost feelings, and be willing to express them in an honest forum, is not for adults with the mentality of children. Or cowards. Or liars. To the contrary. It is only for those mature enough to accept the conditions that come with it.

"The apex of each relationship that I try to establish with my client's is for each of them to see each other, and to be seen. To appreciate each other, and to be appreciated. To know each other, and to be known by each other. To be given free rein to explore, with permission of the other to be explored. To allow visibility, and to receive it in return.

"Self-discovery. To be led deeper and deeper into their partner's psyche, to be truly fascinated with their partner, of wanting to get to know that person, every day, with the full understanding that this is a never-ending process, being each day they are continually evolving."

The Anonymous Black Files

$$ $$ $$

"This why I find it comical when someone mentions the old cliché: 'love is blind'. Lust may be blind. Intrigue. Even fascination. Not love. Love has the power of seeing the other with the greatest clarity and depth, because love requires knowledge at greater depth and insight.

"I like to test this theory by presenting a scenario to each of my client's. An examination to determine how in tune they are as a couple. One that comes to mind is something I call: *'168 Lessons'*. It's really quite simple. I request that this couple spend an *entire week* alone, absolutely alone, with no distractions. Preferably, in a nice hotel room, with room service, and whatever other necessities they need, so there is no need for them to even leave the room.

"One of my most memorable client's that come to mind when she embarked on this enlightening excursion is Tanisha. When I broke down some of the basic rules that they were to follow – Malik and herself have to remain in the room for the duration of the lesson; no matter what one says to the other, regardless of what is said, they have to remain in the room; no matter what one says to the other, neither can shut down and refuse to participate; all of their discussions have to be personal, meaning no talk of kids, family, friends or business – she initially thought it would be a walk in the park. A vacation.

"She communicated to me that on the first night they joked, clowned, but soon the lines of communication began to flow. That authentic flow of thoughts evolved to tension, then minor beef, but then a strange thing happened: it began to reverse, a new deeper level of intimacy developed. She expressed vividly on that first night that they didn't fuck. They made love, with passion, and an intimacy deeper than any episode she could recall previously. The second day as well, with an even deeper physical connection. After forty-eight hours, and exhausting a healthy portion of their bodily fluids, she concluded, *'Alright, we're good. We can bounce'*.

"Not yet. Remember, those weren't the rules. She recalled the edict I gave them to remain with the original commitment, and in doing so, they continued down the path of communication, and traveled further down the road of deeper intimacy and contact. They began to explore, share, and expose new feelings they've never discussed before, therefore discovering new things within themselves, and their partner.

"The commitment in this lesson forced them into an environment where they were absent any other source of stimulation, but themselves, which taught them deeper levels of intimacy. With this deeper insight into each other, they experienced a gradual deepening of feelings and emotional attachment – they never felt so alive with each other. When that assignment was over, Malik and Tanisha emerged from that room, a week later, happier than when they first went in, with deeper insight of who their partner really was. This is one of the happier endings.

"Sometimes the end result is a realization that the relationship may not serve the needs of the other, and they wish to part ways. Someone without deeper insight may look at something like this as a failure, that my assignment 'broke them up', but in actuality, it's not. It's a revelation. A revelation, and a success, if they conclusively decided to end a relationship that was bound to be empty and end in tragedy anyways.

"When I propose such an assignment to my clients, they react in one of two ways – with excitement or anxiety. Either response provides insight, and becomes a revelation in itself. Do the math: if the idea of spending an entire week with your significant other, with no distractions outside of themselves, makes one or both of them uncomfortable, that says something. The same as if they were both tripping over each other anxious to sign up. Not as an escape from the children, life at home, or the monotony of their environment, but a sincere desire to spend that time alone together.

"You'd be surprised at the number of couples who had difficulties making their relationship work, or who had trouble communicating, but learned how to radically change their relationship by continuing this exercise at least once or twice a year. The reason being is you have many couples who share a life with each other, but due to work, kids, friends, family, and other distractions, never really spend time with each other to really get to know each other. They are an item, together, but are in several ways, apart, still strangers.

"There is no aphrodisiac so powerful, or authentic, as the uncensored flow of communication from one soul to another. This is why, if you do the science to it, you will *over*-stand why sex is so stimulating after a couple vents heartfelt feelings in a screaming match; their pattern of communication has been broken down to its most raw form. Don't get me wrong, venting has its purposes, but to encourage such a vent just to experience some raw sex…naw.

"The best way to ensure explosive sex, every time, I'm talking some *'leave her legs shaking, his toes curling, both getting lightheaded'* type of shit, without the fallout from relational friction is…well, what do you know. That's our time. And just when things started to get good. Here's your next case study. No, no. Don't be impatient. Patience is a virtue. I'll share with you the secret in our next session. Until the next time. Peace."

Case File #35 - Victor & Zakia

Zakia's six-inch, black leather, thigh-high boots clicked in a rhythmic rap. Each step became a slow tap dance across their polished hardwood kitchen floor. She secured a bottle of *Patron*, her drink of choice, retrieved a very expensive crystal tumbler, splashed some in. She knocked down four shots, back to back.

"Delicious."

Strong liquor had the distinct ability to prime and program her mind up to do the most deliciously wicked things, and for a night just as that night, those four shots were just a prelude of what was about to go down.

"Oh where, oh where has my little toy gone? Oh where, oh where can he be?" Zakia sang in a hypnotically fluffy voice that floated across a whisper silent kitchen. She retraced her steps, backtracked out of the kitchen, her stride long and deliberate, and took steps up the spiral staircase to the second floor.

"Come out, come out wherever you are."

Her steps took her past the open bathroom door...*wait a minute*. She took a step back, did a double take: a full-length mirror lined the entire sidewall.

Immaculate.

Zakia smiled devilishly. She found herself entranced by her

reflection. Oh, if only her coworkers could see her now. The image she garnered over the years, and her authoritative stance, shook most of those she encountered to their core. Ice Queen. Ball Crusher. Death in stilettos. Those humorous epithets paled in comparison to how they would label her at the moment.

Hair loose, her auburn-tinted dreads flowed freely down to the center of her back. A mask of heavy make-up adorned powerful features – thick, black eyeliner, a heavy coat of black lipstick enhanced her already thick kissers, blush, mascara. Around her neck, a black leather choker with one-inch silver spikes.

So decadent. So immoral.

Not nearly as immoral as her outfit.

A black leather corset stitched up the front to prop up her exposed breasts. Thin black straps tied her ensemble down in the back as tight as those ties would permit to pronounce her hourglass shape, and expose her flat, unblemished brown stomach; a thin string of diamonds dangled from her pierced belly button. Elbow-length, tight, black leather gloves. One hand clutched the bottle of *Patron*, in the other, a crystal tumbler. A black leather, bikini-style bottom, the face very skimpy, no more than two inches wide in diameter, the sides, thin leather straps; the crotch was conveniently sliced from the yoni to the rear.

Very easy access to gain access inside her.

Thin, white ropes graced her ensemble, an addition courtesy of Zakia. Two of them were circled around her breasts, swelling them to firm cantaloupes; her nipples stood out like fleshy chocolate beads, a little smaller than M&M's, but much sweeter. One was tied tightly around her waist, circled all the way down both thighs to her calves. The restraint trapped blood in select areas to stimulate specific erogenous zones; it heightened her arousal, left her sensitive to the touch.

The ensemble, the additions, made her feel so kinky, so constrained, yet ironically, so in control.

Zakia made it to their bedroom, and stood in the doorway

with her hand on her hip.

"There he is," she said lively at the first sight of Victor sprawled out across their massive king-sized; he lay naked aside from his boxers. He popped up from his reclined position at her swift arrival, scrambled for the TV remote, and fumbled with the buttons to click the power on a huge seventy-six-inch on the far wall; he failed miserably.

"Tsk, tsk, tsk," Zakia kissed her teeth, and shook her head disapprovingly. "Now what did I tell you about this?" She walked over, the height of calm, and picked up the remote by his side; she shook it at him. "I thought I told you to do nothing, absolutely nothing, but sit here and think about what happens to bad little boys when they misbehave, who?" Zakia arched a single eyebrow.

"Their mistress."

"Excuse me? Speak up!" For the first time she raised her voice.

"Their mistress," Victor repeated, that time with more conviction.

"That's better. Now let's see here," Zakia's tone softened again, "Just what was my naughty little boy doing the moment I left him alone for just a few minutes?" All Zakia had to do was click the power for a screen that wasn't so cold to flash back to...a football game.

"This doesn't look like you were doing what you were supposed to be doing – prepping yourself to cater to *my* every demand. This looks like you were indulging in entertainment for *yourself.* Is that the case?"

Zakia pointed the same universal remote at an entertainment system, it lit up.

Rhianna's *'RockStar'* broke the silence in surround sound.

Victor didn't answer her, he was busted. He simply stared at her, his expression blank.

"Get the *fuck* over here," Zakia hissed, then she pointed a sharp finger, which held the bottle, down to the floor by her feet.

By the time she knocked back the remainder of her fifth shot, Victor crawled off the bed to approach. He stood face to face with her. With six inches holding up her thick physique, she stood practically eye level with him. She peered deep into his eyes, and quickly found herself growing irritated at his haughty stance.

"Down on your knees – now!"

$$ $$ $$

The command came out flat, direct. There was hesitation.

Victor began to comply with her demand, but not nearly as fast as she liked; she threw her hand out like a punch for the back of his head, and yanked him down with a firm thrust to her waist. Being the defiant little subject he was clearly making himself out to be, when his lips descended past her breast, he sneakily licked all over her right nipple, even wrapped his lips around her hard protruding nub for a quick suck before she got him to his knees.

"Oh, so you think you're cute?" Zakia sunk her nails into his naked shoulders; she peered down on him menacingly. Victor's response – a mewling whimper, along with a faint hiss, a product of pain fused with pleasure. "When I command you to do something, you do just that, and nothing more. Am I making myself clear to you?"

Her nails sunk in deeper, on the verge of piercing skin.

"Ye...yes, my queen," Victor exhaled in a moan, displaying a more sincere level of respect for her authority.

"Good. Now remove my boots."

Victor did as he was instructed. He reached for the tab on her right boot between her thighs, each tooth clicked in a deliberate...whizzzzzzz. Victor made sure to caress her soft, dark brown flesh as he peeled it away like a banana to reveal her calf, shin, down to her ankle. He went for the other, that time leaning in close enough to ingest a deep inhale. The sweet essence emanating from in between her thighs drew him in like love.

"Just the boots. Don't get cute, or make me have to tell you twice," Zakia threatened, staring down on him from above. "Stop trying to be slick." Victor gave her an ambiguous nod. He unzipped her other boot for Zakia to step out of it. "Good boy."

Zakia turned off from him, poured herself another shot, and made her way over to a leather recliner in the corner of the room. A quick glance over her shoulder, she caught Victor luxuriating in the way her fleshy bubble swayed with each step, how her ass cheeks spilled out the bottom of black leather to form a perfect rounded 'W'. That produced a prevailing smile.

"Now, let's start over again. How are you supposed to serve your queen?" She sunk comfortably in the plush recliner, and kicked her feet up on a matching leather ottoman.

"However my queen desires. Your every wish is my command," Victor related sincerely. He began to rise from his knees to approach her.

"What are you doing? No one said you could get up." Zakia took a light sip; she remained fixated on him with cold, blank eyes. "You come to me, but since you seem to be in need of some humility, you come to me as you are. Crawl."

Victor smirked. He thought about it for a moment as he remained on his knees, then hunched over on all fours. His movements were sleek, the muscles in his arms and shoulders contracting, flexing, the bearings of a panther stalking its prey, his waist slimming, the outline of his dangling manhood swinging like a pendulum from side to side behind a thin veil of black silk.

Zakia remained stoic, a queen perched on her throne; her only movements, an occasional blink, along with a calculated circling of her index finger around the rim of the tumbler that sat on the arm of the recliner.

There was an engraved sterling silver basin by her feet, half-filled with water. A fluffy white washrag floated stilly on the surface. No instructions were necessary. A slice of her eyes from the basin to her feet would suffice. Well, one more time back to the basin. Victor proceeded to wash her. That wasn't the first time he performed such a ritual, only the first time under the guise of punishment.

Once he cleaned them to satisfaction, he leaned over and took her pinky toe into his mouth. He paid attention to each toe in turn, worked his way up to the big one, being mindful of her other foot; his powerful hand caressed and massaged it with the delicate touch of an expert masseuse. Their eyes remained locked the whole time, both engaged in the task of scrutinizing their significant other; Zakia trying to detect traces of arrogance; Victor, fragments of pleasure in his stolid mistress.

A game in which they both took pride in winning. A game which left them both forced to accept a stalemate. That is, until…wait…wait…yeah. Just an inkling of weakness on Zakia's end, a crack in the cement, pushed Victor to lean in experimentally, and plant soft pecks on her right ankle, shin, lower calf, inner knee, all the while closing the distance with his sights set in a direct line in between her thick, brown thighs.

$$ $$ $$

"What are you doing?" Zakia posed ambiguously; she got nothing from Victor. "And what are you looking at?"

Victor didn't even attempt to divert his actions, or his eyes, from directly in between her thighs.

"Heaven," he sighed passionately.

He ran his tongue slowly across her flesh, made a deliberate line up in between her inner thigh.

"Did I give you permission to do that?" Another frigid look, another light sip. No attempt on her end to thwart his advances.

"Correct me if I'm wrong, but your command was to serve you, my queen. Allow me to serve you," Victor reminded.

His hands massaged her inner thighs, he parted them at his leisure, hiked them up to his broad shoulders. The velvety folds of her dark chocolate, moist lips flowered open, slightly, as if a delicate breeze in mid-June ruffled her secret curtains. His parting of her thighs left her totally exposed, the wide-open crotch of her leather bikini bottom allowed for no interference.

He closed the distance, neared her center. Impassioned licks of his tongue, lips kissed, mouth sucked on the soft flesh between her inner thighs, he traveled up slow and deliberate till he finally reached his destination. Victor spread her second fleshy lips open in the most lewd manner, two fingers rolled back that protective layer of flesh that kept her secret hidden, opened her, left her totally exposed, a soft tongue drew delicate, deliberate circles around her protruding clit.

"You serve your queen well," Zakia purred, with fragments of passion filling her voice. She dipped her index finger inside the tumbler, circled her finger in alcohol, and ran the wet tip around her nipple. "But it appears that your actions are more self-serving, than selfless."

She sucked her finger clean, embraced the back of his head. She pressed him deeper in her center, rubbed her pussy all over his face, and forced his lips and tongue to get further acquainted with the inner recesses of her fleshy walls. She tucked him in so deep the entire lower half of his face was practically gone.

"Ooooh...*serve me*. That's it. Serve your queen, you peasant," Zakia breathed. She rolled her slick, alcohol-coated nipple between two fingers, squeezed it, harder, harder, until she winced pleasurably under the pressure. "Don't you ever fucking defy me again. Do you hear me? You do as you're told, and nothing more. Understand?"

"Um hmm," Victor mumbled.

His mouth never left her nectar, his tongue never stopped licking, his lips never stopped sucking. He could sense his wife, her mode in mistress, teetering on the edge. He set out to nefariously tip the scales, shift the balance of power in his favor. Authoritative to subservient. His fingers tore open the already gutted slit in her crotch even further, tore that expensive designer piece of lingerie in half; he dug his face in deeper. He started to munch and suck on her flesh with fervor.

"You...you piece of shit! You destroyed my...that cost over...ohhh, you motherfucking...piece...of...you're gonna...fucking pay for that!" Zakia chanted.

She held Victor's head so tightly against her open snatch she came dangerously close to suffocating him. He continued on, tickled her g-spot with two curling fingers, conquered her with the *'come-here'* trick. He licked, munched, hummed, his tongue hammered her clit in soft taps, sucks, until he dug deep enough in her well to tap the geyser. Zakia broke, opened a spring in her waterfall she really didn't want to open, a reservoir of orgasm from that little slice of heaven that her defiant little servant sucked out, and savored.

"You...bastard. You fffffucking...*bastard!*" Zakia ranted behind panted breaths. She squirmed frantically in her seat, tried to wiggle away from the savagery of his sucking, escape the persistence of his tormenting tongue. "Ok, that's...it. Enough. I said...you had enough!" She tried to nudge his head out from in between her thighs.

She struggled to no avail.

Victor reverted to such a greedy little nymph. The sweet essence he siphoned from her sex marked a silent victory for him.

"Dominate me? Picture that. I own *this shit!"*

A wet finger coated in her climax found her back door, her kryptonite. He rubbed it delicately, gently, applied pressure, slipped it in to the first digit, continued licking.

"What did I...tell...you? I told you to...ohhh...I said...that's it.

Stop trying...stop trying to turn me out, you motherfucker," Zakia whined, conflicted from the sensation. She was torn, needed to recalibrate. Unsure if she should squirm away from his touch, and regroup, or allow him to continue, and conquer.

"You don't ever...like to listen. I told you to... oh, you greedy fucking bastard!" Zakia cried in a throaty moan.

Another valve opened, another wave of an explosive orgasm shot through her body like electricity, that second cascade shook her to her core. She could feel it pouring out from in between her thighs. Victor was actually sucking the life out of her, literally, draining the very essence from her being, and the motherfucker wouldn't stop.

"That's what you get for trying to run shit. You can't fuck with me. I run this!"

"You *stupid* motherfucka!" Zakia hissed, collecting her breath, along with her composure. She finally managed to separate his lips from her center, nudge his head out from in between her thighs. "Did I tell you to do all of that? Did I? When I command you to stop, you fucking stop!" Zakia shoved him away with a foot to his chest; he landed firmly on his ass a few feet away.

Zakia situated herself in the recliner, her chest rose and fell in a light pant, a film of perspiration glistened across her forehead. She scraped together the remaining traces of dignity she clearly lost in their brief battle, and pierced Victor with evil squinted eyes. A perverse, victorious smirk rippled across his lips. The whole lower half of his face was drenched, practically dripping in her essence. In the process of attacking that pussy, his erection popped out through the slit of his boxers. It pointed like a flagpole to the ceiling. Neither of them could deny what he was doing.

Exploiting her weak spots.

To slip a finger in her back door, with his tongue on her clit, *after* he already made her orgasm, that was one of her weaknesses, her button to push to open the floodgates. And he pushed it perfectly. Knocked her down off her high horse, obliterated her cocky little stance, the sought after position of authority she tried to wield like a weapon, and reduced her to a whimpering, moaning, shriveling feminine wreck. She found herself steamed at the role-reversal he managed to pull off.

"Mercy's for the weak," he always reminded. He was right.

For that, he had to pay.

$$ $$ $$

"Get the fuck up. Get your ass in the bed!" Zakia commanded. She branded a cat-o-nine-tails menacingly in her right hand. "Take those off before you even take another step!"

The leather tails of her twelve-inch whip kissed a light sting across Victor's muscled back. He shed his boxers in two steps, kicked them off to lie on his back, nude, across the center of their bed. All traces of delicacy vanished from Zakia's being. She stalked him, walked a half circle around the foot of the bed, dragged her tool of torture along his legs, waist, chest, arms. Victor remained attentive, obediently complying to her every demand with a silent vigilance.

His eyes kept finding Zakia's secret spot; from her crotch, and all the way down to the center of her thighs, a shiny film of moisture glowed like an over application of baby oil. But that there was no baby oil. He did that. That was his work. Yeah, he pushed the envelope on their little battle of dominance, but that was just the right recipe to bring out the beast in Zakia.

"Mercy's for the weak."

"You don't like to listen. You're a hard-headed motherfucka." The whip whisked through the air, slashed across the top of Victor's naked thigh. On Victor's end, no reaction. Zakia walked methodically to circle the bed. "So I got just the right punishment to teach your not knowing how to listen ass." The bottom of his feet felt the sharp sting of those thin strips of leather. "I'm gonna teach your ass how to listen if it's the last thing I do."

Zakia brought that whip down for a final time across his abs, that time harder than all of the previous times combined; it echoed in their spacious room. Victor flinched for the first time, tightened his jaw, teeth clenched, hissed.

Zakia smiled.

She could break him. Break him like every other time in the past. She quickly straddled him, sat on his thighs. The unintended invitation of all that ass, so close, just within hands reach, was too tempting – Victor reached down to fill both hands full of her fleshy cheeks. He palmed it in a grip so tight that he sliced her lewdly open from behind.

"You're really gonna keep testing me, aren't you?" It took some effort, but Zakia peeled his hands from her backside; she lifted them over his head. "Your behavior is only making things worse."

There were padded handcuffs attached to the outer rinds of their headboard. Victor resisted, slightly. Not fully fighting her aggression, more for show, like she was really overpowering to take him. He could have easily bucked her one hundred and sixty pounds frame from over him like a wild bull, tossed her clear across the room, but what fun would that have been? So with a little fight in him, he allowed her to cuff his left wrist, then his right above his head.

"Now, you're gonna apologize. Beg me for my forgiveness for your total lack of respect."

Zakia pointed a sharp finger in his face. The hint of a smirk that began to really piss Zakia off twitched on the corner of Victor's top lip. He said nothing. They held each other's gaze, a battle of wits, a mental standoff, until Victor flinched forward to lick the tip of her finger. Zakia slapped him lightly across the cheek.

"You think this shit is a joke? You know, you're really trying the last little bit of my patience," Zakia growled through clenched teeth. She sunk her nails into his chest, came dangerously close to breaking skin. Victor let out a pleasurable sigh, still no words, no concession. She leaned over, dove at his neck, her teeth found the exposed side of his jugular.

Zakia bit down, sunk her fangs into his flesh, even tugged at him like a wild animal to tear at his skin. The handcuffs rattled above his head, left Victor helpless underneath her. All he could do was squirm, moan, and accept that slice of delectable torture. With each powerful rake of her nails down his chest, or clutch of his flesh between her jaws – she seemed to almost instinctively know just when to release the pressure before she drew blood – Victor's erection ballooned up in spurts. Zakia felt his pressure against her thigh; she cut her eyes down to it.

"Hmmm, and just what do we have here?" Zakia wrapped her hand around him at the base. "You got the nerve to think you actually deserve *pleasure* after all the shit you pulled?"

She tugged at his hardness, pimp-slapped it silly from side to side like that hardened slab of masculinity disrespected her personally; an abuse that coincidentally stiffened him even harder. He felt like a flesh rock between her nimble fingers.

She squinted at him, smirked.

Yet again, as the evening unfolded, still early into the night, and she could see the pendulum of power swinging back in her favor. Maintain her position. *No mercy.* Zakia sunk her teeth into the side of his neck again, hard, bit and almost drew blood, softened, licked and sucked his injury. His shoulder, bit hard, licked, sucked. Proceeded in that hard-soft process down over his chest, nipples, abs until she made it to his stiff erection.

She lifted her eyes to peer up at him, and melted into a wicked snarl.

"O...ok, ok, I'm sorry," Victor said, finally expressing genuine signs of fear from the intense look in her eyes. Zakia flashed her teeth up at him in an exaggerated smile, chattered her teeth a few times like a human wind-up chatterbox. "Za...Zakia, for real. Al...alright, don't...not there. Don't...don't bite me there," Victor chanted, twisting his arms in the handcuffs, trying to squirm from the demented presence hovering over his erection.

"Oh, so now you're not so tough anymore, are you?" Zakia mocked. Her lips closed the distance to the head of his erection, so close Victor could feel the heat of her breath warming him. "Let's see here. Now just what should I do to a defiant, disrespectful motherfucka like you?"

$$ $$ $$

Zakia no longer paid attention to Victor.

His rock hard erection less than an inch from her face held her sole attention.

A clear drop of pre-cum bubbled up on the tip. Zakia squeezed his dick up for it to overflow and roll down the underside of his shaft. She quickly leaned in to lick it up, from the base, all the way to the head, then wrapped her teeth around the tip. She lifted her gaze up to him again, met eyes, with only the head of him in her mouth, and sunk her teeth into him lightly.

"Ok, Ok! Zakia, I should have...yo, chill. Aghhh, shit! Alright! Alright, I should have listened...to you," Victor chanted, conflicted from the feeling. Hard and soft, her warm, wet mouth, the soft suck, back to the light bite. A soft, wet tongue, then teeth. She repeated the process – pleasure mixed with pain, agony with desire. "Zakia, I may have crossed the line when..."

"Why do you keep calling me that? Zakia? How are you to address me adorned in this attire?" Zakia squeezed a tight grip on his shaft, and gave it a firm yank as if she was trying to pull it off.

"Mistress," Victor blurted. Zakia's eyes lower slits. She didn't let up off the pressure, she gritted her teeth, and squeezed him even tighter. "Your highness," Victor hurled, popping any title of nobility that came to mind. With the other hand, Zakia reached for his balls; she wrapped them tightly in her clutch, squeezed. "My queen! MY QUEEN!" Victor chanted, staring down on her with terrified eyes.

With both of her hands filled with his crown jewels, and her mouth, more specifically, her teeth, hovering menacingly over him, Victor knew he was completely at her mercy.

"Better," Zakia sighed.

She softened her hard stance, gently massaged his bloated sac, stroked the length of his shaft delicately; punished him with the hard, then rewarded him with the soft.

"But you were still such a disrespectful motherfucka. So disrespectful. Grabbing at my ass so crazy like that when nobody told you to. Ripping my expensive lingerie in two, destroying it. Licking at my chest, my delicious nipples. Eating from my garden, indulging in its forbidden fruit, even drinking from the fountain of youth as if you are worthy of such divine nourishment. You defied me. Tried to make a mockery of my authority. This cannot, and will not, be tolerated."

Zakia held his erection less than an inch from her mouth, brushed her lips up against the head of his dick, swiped it over the surface, spoke to him as if she was speaking to it. What appeared to be an accidental sweep between her lips, or swipe of her tongue over the head, was clearly no accident. She could feel how each word of chastisement hurled down on him excited Victor all the more. Each sharp scold enticing him, each harsh rebuke throbbing him more intently between her fingers.

"You're nothing but a mortal. You're not worthy enough to partake in the pleasures of the gods. For your act of disobedience, Icarus, flying too close to the sun, you need to be punished. *Severely* punished. I'm sorry. But this is the *only* way you will learn."

Zakia wrapped her warm, wet lips around him. She sucked on him so passionately, and slid her hand so smoothly up and down his saliva-coated shaft it tickled him. She fed on him like a ravenous harlot, until she engulfed nearly two/thirds of him down her throat.

"That's...that's it, my queen. Pun...punish me. I fucked up. I'm such a...disrespectful, ungrateful, stupid motherfucka. Nothing but a mortal. A pea...peasant. Don't...let me...get away with...no stupid shit... like that. I...I deserve to be...ohhh, yeah, I deserve to be...punished for...for my disobedience," Victor popped in ecstatic breaths.

He stared down on her in complete admiration.

Zakia worked him over so beautifully with her eyes closed, so focused, so intense, sucking softly, a delicious rhythm, licking on the head in her mouth, feeding more of his stick between her lips, deep throating him while stroking him tenderly with a circular twist of her wrist, that Victor wasn't quite sure who was more into it – him or her.

He was getting close. His moans traveled throughout the room, handcuffs rattled, his arms flailed in their binds above him until he clutched tight fistfuls on the headboard. He thrust his hips up in her face in short jabs, his body tensed up. The moment Zakia sensed his imminent release, she exploded her lips and hand from his erection to shut down all sensation in an instant.

"NO! No!" Victor blurted, as if she yanked the plug on his life support machine, "Don't stop. Keep...keep *punishing* me. I fucked up. Teach me a lesson. Keep teaching me...a lesson," Victor pleaded in a whiny voice.

"Oh, don't worry. I will. I'm gonna punish your ass till you learn. I promise you that," Zakia insisted with a mischievous smirk.

She waited several moments, long enough for Victor to calm down, gave his erection that throbbed so uncontrollably some time to recover, then went right back to work on him. The process was repeated slowly, at least four more times over the course of a half hour, left him with blue balls, until she reduced

Victor into a shriveling wreck, practically crying, begging for relief.

"Shut up! Shut your fucking mouth, and stop your whining, you little bitch!" Zakia hurled like a capture with no conscience on inflicting torture on her victim. She slapped him across the face for good measure. "That shit ain't cute no more, is it? In fact, that was only the beginning. Let me stop playing games with you. *Mercy's for the weak,* remember? Your words. Not mine. You only condemned yourself."

Zakia peeled that tattered bikini bottom down over her thick, chocolate thighs, tossed them across the room like trash, crawled over his waist, and squatted over him with her feet planted on the bed by his sides. She used two fingers to flower herself open right above his stiff erection.

"I'm gonna teach you..." Zakia lowered herself for her soaking wet lips that practically dripped to nibble on his head, "...not to ever..." she lowered herself a little more, swallowed him in to about a quarter, "...ever..." half, "...ever..." three-quarters, "...*ever* forget who the fuck you're fucking with!"

Zakia inadvertently lost her breath when she eased herself down to nestle her waist snugly in his lap; she swallowed all nine inches of him in one stroke, deep in her belly.

"*Damn it! Shit!*"

She had to take a moment in her mind to regain her composure.

Taunting and teasing him like that for so long, one of the longest ever, left him harder than she ever recalled him being. She could feel him in the bottom of her stomach. His erection felt like a foot of flesh steel lodged deep in her womb.

"*Take a breath. Slow things down. Remember who's running the show here, who's in charge. Me. Not him. Me!*"

$$ \$\$\ \$\$\ \$\$ $$

Zakia collected herself. She had to.

Teasing him for so long, close to forty-five minutes straight, with the intention of tormenting him, actually became a double-edged sword to wound her. Zakia enjoyed sucking Victor off. Over the years, she developed a profound love for it; the idea of his throbbing erection between her lips exciting her like no other. In their games of dominance, the scales of pleasure could be balanced in the act of intense oral.

On the one side, the pleasure *he* received.

On the other, the power *she* wielded controlling that distribution of pleasure.

A pendulum of power that swayed to and fro in the moment, but that night was different.

Fully engulfing herself in the moment, that evening, she discovered another facet of pleasure tickling him with her tonsils. Channeling the essence of *Linda Lovelace*, the original deep throat, Zakia found a second clitoris deep in the back of her throat. And with this newfound discovery, this revelation, Zakia unknowingly got herself so horny, so soaking wet, so hot and bothered, that when she slid all of his thickness up in herself, she slipped, and almost exposed herself. She forced herself to choke back the sounds of ecstasy dangerously close from escaping her throat from the intense pleasure she received.

Had to.

Had to hold those carnal cards close to her chest.

Bluff him after fluffing him.

She could know that in her own mind, but not Victor. He was to be punished. And punished he will be. A punishment Zakia planned out. A punishment she knew just how to administer on him, despite those newfound, unforeseen pleasurable events.

No mercy.

Zakia went back to work on his neck with her teeth, biting,

nibbling, sucking as hard as suction would permit, remaining perfectly still on his stiffness. Victor tried in vain to roll his hips underneath her, get some motion going, some friction, stroke in tight wetness, all to no avail. Zakia refused, read his intentions, squirmed herself firmly on his lap, and took him in even deeper. She touched erogenous zones within herself, poker faced her pleasure, and successfully limited his movements to nothing.

"Stop...fucking moving," Zakia commanded through clenched teeth, controlling, refusing to be controlled. She sunk her teeth into the side of his neck again, bit, and punished him because of his unknowing pleasure. "Stop...stop trying to get your shit off."

"Zakia...I mean, your highness...I mean, my queen. Alright. Alright! You taught me. I promise you, I will never, *ever* disrespect you like that again," Victor professed, with his voice cracking in agony.

Zakia heard the sincerity in his voice, witnessed complete submission in his eyes. She peered down on him, contemplating, a goddess over mankind, then very slowly, and very deliberately, and very methodically, opened the gates of heaven. She lifted herself up to the head, right to the tip, and gave him two, good, up and down, soaking wet, tight strokes; in and out...in and out, *Kegals* on point, pussy on virginity. She massaged him within her velvety folds with more proficiency than a geisha who mastered the art of *Kama Sutra*.

Victor's eyes fluttered, rolled in his head, his lips twisted into a half smile, mouth agape in lust, he exhaled a throaty, "Ahhh, shit...yeeeaaahhhh," that carried throughout the entire bedroom.

Just as quick, heaven's gates were slammed closed; Zakia sat back snugly in his lap, stiff, cold, grew frigid again, cut off all forms of pleasure.

"That's it. No more. You're not worthy of such magnificence. You didn't even deserve that," Zakia taunted, massaging his chest, staring down on him with a prevailing look, back in full control.

"Stop...stop doing that shit! You're *torturing* me, my queen. I said I learned my lesson. What else do I have to *say?* What else do I have to *do?"*

Zakia smiled down on him, squirmed in his lap, purred, "Would you like me to continue? You'd like to feel *everything* I have to offer, wouldn't you?"

"Ye...Yes! Yes...please. *Please!"*

"Are you sorry?"

"I'm sorry. I'm *soooo* sorry."

"Who am I?"

"My queen! My most honorable queen. An Asiatic goddess on earth."

Zakia thought about it, concluded that was worthy of a few more strokes.

"Look at you. So pathetic. You're such a little bitch. Fucking pathetic, little, sniveling bitch."

Zakia began to ride him, slow. Excruciatingly slow, right up to the tip, then gradually back down, easing herself deep in his lap, squirming lewdly and corkscrewing her waist on the down stroke to swallow every inch that he had to offer, staring at him with sinister eyes the whole time.

"I knew I could break you. Conquer your pathetic ass. Knew it would only be a matter of time before I made you submit."

"I'm broken, my queen. *I submit.* I'm a little bitch. Just please...whatever you do, don't stop. *Please* don't stop. I *beg* you. I give up. This pleasure...this pussy...it feels *soooo* fucking good, my queen. Just please... whatever you do...don't...don't stop."

Signaling his utter defeat, along with tingling pricks of ecstatic shocks all over her body that she fought to conceal for the last hour, Zakia conceded, did the honors.

She gradually increased the speed, the intensity, concentrated, rode up and down on his thickness so smoothly, so rhythmically, created a harmony so perfect – snapping her waist, squeezing her vaginal muscles on him, sawing her clit, pummeling her g-spot, taking him in from the tip to the hilt – that it took her mere minutes to get herself off to another earth shattering orgasm.

"You...ffffuck. Fuck! Do it. Do...it. I give you...permission...to fucking...cum. Fucking cum...*now!* Do it now! Fucking...cum in me!" Zakia demanded.

She pushed herself to the brink of sanity, continued to fuck Victor, hard, bounced in his lap viciously, squirmed in circles with him deep in her, determined to violently fuck the cum out of his dick. The entire bed shook, rocked, the headboard banged against the wall. A fuck so ferocious the white rope binds tying her breasts tight fell free, along with the binds threaded up her thighs.

Sweat bubbled up across her forehead, her dreads bounced chaotically, body jerked, ass twerked, she didn't let up. Not until she accomplished her mission. Not until she heard Victor cry out in agony, and felt one of the most explosive orgasms she ever felt from her husband flooding her in torrents to fill her insides.

Zakia made sure to keep going, made sure she milked him for everything he had, tap his reservoir dry, make sure he never forgot who provided him with such a feeling. After collapsing across his chest, and panting like athletes recovering from a triathlon, Zakia finally uncuffed him to release him from his binds.

"Za...Zakia, my queen. My beautiful...Asiatic queen," Victor panted, flat out on his back, completely spent; he barely had enough energy to massage the indented rings around his wrists from the cuffs tearing into his skin, "That was...I don't know what got into you tonight, but that...that was the best nut I ever experienced," he added, slowly rolling over to prop himself against the headboard.

Zakia rolled out of bed with an indelible smile, glowing; she trudged in slow steps like a warrior who just stepped off the battlefield towards the bathroom to do some much needed clean up.

"But..." Victor's single word response, and the way he said it, stopped her dead in her tracks, "...as good as that nut was, and all of the wonderful, delightful, deliciously wicked things you managed to pull out of your bag of tricks, there's just one tincy, wincey, tiny, little problem that I think I need to remind you of."

The smile immediately fell from Zakia's face, her eyes fell closed, her head lowered to her chest.

"I didn't say those three magic words."

Zakia shot back around to face him. "No, fuck that! You copped out. I won! I had you *begging* like a little bitch. *'I'm broken, my queen...I submit...I'm a little bitch...Just please...whatever you do, don't stop...Please don't stop...I beg you...I give up...Just please...whatever you do...don't...don't stop',*" Zakia whined, mocking his desperate pleas.

Victor laughed heartily, his deep baritone carrying.

"You're absolutely right. I was copping a plea like a motherfucka. A straight biiach! I can't lie, what you did to me tonight, how you managed to squeeze paradise around me so tight, how you were so wet, the way you blessed me with your blessings so good, I would have said *anything* to make sure you didn't stop. Well, *almost* anything. Need I remind you, my sweet Asiatic, Nubian queen, my African goddess, that *wasn't* the deal. Our 'safe word', our word of submission, was *Pyramids of Giza*. And to my recollection, that's the *only* word, or should I say, three words, that never came out of my mouth. Which means – you didn't win, *I* did!"

The painful truth smacked Zakia across the face like a street pimp handing out discipline. He was right. Whenever they indulged in the act of *S&M*, in that specific game they played, they always made sure to give each other 'safe words' to ensure things didn't get out of hand, or when the other person conceded. That was the bet they made several nights prior over a game of *Scrabble*.

The Anonymous Black Files

Zakia won.

Victor was to be her 'servant' for the night, her mortal to praise her in worship.

One who was the most unbecoming in defeat, Victor posed another challenge of his own: run it back, double or nothing. Why not? He would win that second game, so he thought. And even if he didn't, it wouldn't matter anyways. There was no way, regardless of what she doled out, that she would ever be able to make him cop out, and say those three words of concession.

Zakia laughed at the thought of it. Easy money as far as she was concerned. Second game, she blew him out. Chalk that up as *two* nights she would have him at her complete disposal.

Yet, as she took inventory of him reclined across the headboard – the various teeth marks, the fingernail scratches painted all over his upper half, even what appeared to be three or four hickies tarnishing his neck and chest – she had to admit that no matter what she put him through, even the new addition of delaying his orgasm in oral for the longest record to date, she didn't succeed in making him cop out.

Zakia sucked her teeth, rolled her eyes at him, and turned to storm out of the room.

"And oh, hey baby, by the way..." Victor called out, "...make sure to wear something nice and humbling for next weekend. Preferably the French maid outfit – with no panties. I don't want any interference. I plan on going straight to work on you, because I know I'm gonna have to practically *kill you* to make you gracefully bow out. I will. Make you bow out, that it. And if I don't," Victor shrugged, "I can assure you, I'm gonna have a fucking field day tearing your ass up trying to make you wave the white flag."

The next ***Case File #37 – Victor & Zakia***, to be continued in:
The Anonymous Black Files 1.2: *The Interviews*

Seventh Interview

"Peace, peace. How are you doing? You look a little frustrated. Yeah, I know. Construction has been hell for the past three days around here. What is it, about six blocks? You had to park about a half mile away? Seriously? That bad, huh? Sorry to hear that. Minor inconvenience. Don't let it damper your whole day. Drink? Take the edge off a little something."

Dr. Black approaches the bar in the corner, fix himself and the journalist a drink.

"Look on the brighter side of things. Glass half-full, we're seven interviews in right now. We covered a lot of ground. Self-acceptance. Individualism. Psychological visibility. Complimentary sexual personalities. Rhythm and energy. Self-esteem. Mutual self-disclosure. Communication. Self-discovery. As I'm sure you could imagine, I couldn't possibly elaborate fully on each of those issues due to time constraints, only partially shine light on how I enlighten my client's, give you slices of sunlight on the topics we built on, how my theory is structured. A little unorthodox, I know, but I assure you, no doubt effective."

The journalist hands over the last thumb drive, sips his drink.

"Victor and Zakia. They evolved so beautifully from our

original sessions, mainly Zakia. Thinking back to the end of our first session, only one principle comes to mind: self-alienation. Sexual self-alienation for that matter. A form of alienation that stems from a particular state of mind.

"Do the one: self-alienation. A sense of personal unreality. A sense of losing touch with self. A sense of failing to *over*-stand how to express those feelings felt. Zakia learned to accept that her sexual responses were in actuality an expression of herself, always an expression of who she was, whether or not she chose to experience them that way. When she ironed out the kinks on her self-esteem and it became relatively healthy, when she found herself in harmony with self, that is when she found the act of sex a natural and spontaneous expression of self, a joyous experience of self, her mate, and of life.

"Prior to my travels with Zakia, I noticed how she visualized, and utilized sex – as a weapon. Her sexuality, her femininity, her magnetic attraction, all weapons in her arsenal that she wielded to her advantage to *level the playing field* against her masculine counterparts.

"She would never admit her underlying motives, not even to herself in the beginning – those feelings of inferiority to men. Instead, she masked this blemish with overt aggression, and not in a constructive manner, which only submerged her deeper in denial, and convinced herself that that was an effective way to approach her relationships. Today, she acknowledges this view, and has re-examined the methods she used.

"Don't get me wrong. She still views sex as an opportunity to establish her position, or his, but expanded this approach in a more constructive, productive manner. At the end of the day, Zakia is always going to be Zakia. What I offered her is alternatives, ways to view her relationship from not only her position, but the position of Victor.

"Zakia learned that the bedroom is like a metaphysical arena where she played out the basic drama of her existence. Victor and Zakia are unique as a couple, both who will admittedly concede to their strong preoccupation with power. Not necessarily a bad thing. Power in itself isn't bad. To be assertive, dominant, aggressive, traits not necessarily negative in it of itself. It's the *manner* in which someone goes about expressing these traits, their motivation, and their intent behind the exertion.

"Victor and Zakia, as was clearly demonstrated in their case studies, both seem to find their greatest peaks of sexual intensity engaged in *S&M*, or sadomasochistic experiences. Sometimes it could be pain, the ability to inflict and/or endure it. Sometimes it could be to explore the depths of humiliation and degradation, a sport in which they reverse the roles of power to peak each other in pleasurable punishment.

"The thing about sex is when it is experienced with an individual who has a love affair with life, it explodes and overflows in a torrent of joy and excitement. When two souls who are alike experience it, entities of like-mind like Victor and Zakia, it can abound into an act of worship, overflowing the boundaries of flesh and spirit to manifest the deepest values of their existence.

"This can only be experienced when an individual's sexuality is integrated with self, not at war with other cardinal values of self. Only if they are not divided against self – which some may refer to as a split between mind and body, spirit and flesh, admiration and passion – can they truly be free to fully enjoy self, that of their partner, and take pride and admiration, in the direction of their sexual desires no matter how foreign it may be considered to another.

"Zakia can now project a guiltless, joyous attitude towards sex. Towards her sexual feelings, her responses. Towards her body, the body of Victor, and view their sex as a vehicle of self-worship where they can experience the height of being alive through their physical. Through Salim and Naomi's willingness to reciprocate in the addition of another female in their sexual repertoire can they continually reaffirm that their sex is a source of joy to each other. Through Malik and Tanisha's spontaneous acts of role-playing can they experience sex as the ultimate celebration of love.

"Reality check: it isn't all about sex. Personally, I couldn't imagine a very fulfilling relationship between a healthy, vibrant couple *without* it, but it surely isn't the end all in a relationship. Simply because threesomes, or role-playing, or *S&M* alone cannot sustain a relationship across the test of years, decades, cannot tip the scales for all the weight a relationship must carry.

"Outside of the other trials and tribulations in a relationship, a Salim, or a Tanisha, or a Victor must factor in the traits of admiration in their partner. To admire someone is big in the context of relationships. I say this considering a scenario that touched home with me on a personal level."

$$ $$ $$

"I was traveling through life with this woman after I acquired knowledge of self and became enlightened to the very teachings I impart on my clients, and I had an odd revelation when I sat down and did the math to our relationship. She treated me like gold, was intelligent, nice career, really beautiful, a phenomenal body, I mean one of the toughest in my eyes – ass on fat, waist on slim, thighs on thick, chest all firm, skin the color of hazelnut coffee, just as smooth too – with a sexual repertoire that was out of this world.

"The problem, simply put – she was a *super* bitch! Able to curse someone out faster than a speeding bullet, leap buildings in a single bound just to flip out on them if she didn't get her way. As a person, she had a very dark, ugly aura about her. She was the general manager of a large marketing firm, and she treated everyone under her supervision like straight shit. Her family, surprisingly few friends, weren't immune. They were all verbal punching bags whenever she felt the urge to take swings at them.

"Anyone who approached her, she spit straight venom on them, like it was an insult to find her approachable. Bottom line, despite the A-plus treatment she'd given to me, and the very select few in her close circle, the cold venom she unleashed on everyone else crippled the ability for me to admire her as a person. When one admires another, there is a sense of pride in one's choice of partner, confirmation in judgment, a sense of feeling visible, appreciated, loved.

"Naomi spoke, in different terms, of how she admired Salim for the way he took care of his responsibilities as a man, the homage he paid to his elders, the respect he garnered from family and friends. Victor admired Zakia for her drive and determination to excel in her career, her temperament to remain level headed in trying situations. Malik admired Tanisha for her ability to remain optimistic despite the odds, her bright aura, and style of livening up dark situations.

"Their admiration melded into a deeper experience of love, an experience where each other's happiness, and self-development, became extremely important to each other. Where they allowed each other to enter into their own private world where very few, if any, had ever entered. As a result, this allowed for a deeper level of commitment.

"There is no question in Salim's mind the importance Naomi has in his life. Not only is she essential to his happiness, he has come to be at complete peace with it. His self-interest has swelled outside of self to include Naomi. Her happiness, her wellbeing, has become a matter of personal, selfish concern. They remain individuals in their own right, but their union has allowed them to form a unique bond, an allegiance within themselves. *Them against the world.*

"They became extensions of each other. If someone harms one, they are in essence, harming the other. Strictly speaking, the protection, preservation, and respect of their relationship became the highest priority within the range and scope of their abilities.

"I say within the scope of their abilities because, Victor and Zakia for example, entered into each other's lives at a time when some would say the 'stars were aligned', their passions and aspirations were congruent with the path life was unfolding for them, which allowed their relationship to be experienced as a joy and nourishment for both. But let's not forget – change and growth are the very essence of life. Motion is life. Stagnation is death. If the species of man is not continually moving forward, he is moving backwards.

"What if there came a time in Malik and Tanisha's evolution where their paths diverged, where they found their needs and values propelling them in different directions? As painful as the revelation would be for them, they may have to face reality that they had to part ways. It would do neither of them any good to cling, to resist, to hang on to a relationship that is nonproductive out of fear of venturing off to explore new and unchartered territory. As they say: 'to put oneself back on the market'.

"Should it be considered that their time together was a waste? If they were to both grasp the bigger picture, I don't think either of them would come to that conclusion. They both gave each other beautiful children, life experiences, the good and the bad times to grow on, and memories to be cherished because of it.

"Flip side of the same coin: what if their love matured to a level of mutual self-advancement? Would it be so foreign in their selfish passion for each other to demand sexual exclusivity? The majority of the couples I counsel wouldn't think so. The love and feelings they have for each other has led them to view sex as more than just a physical act.

"It has become an exclusive vehicle to express the depths of their love. Not just a marriage of their bodies, but their souls. So to share, or allow someone else access to something so personal, is almost unthinkable. Almost. And only for some. There are exceptions. Salim and Naomi for example."

$$ $$ $$

"Their relationship is so unique because although they pledged an eternal union to one another, they do not deny their sexuality, or the explicit fact of being sexual beings. They both fully accept the love they have for each other, but cannot deny the sexual attraction they have for other women, specifically women with a particular physical disposition: urban model, video vixenesque.

"This is the state of their relationship at the present moment. Who knows? Maybe in the future, one or both will evolve past the threesome phase, and demand that same sexual exclusivity I spoke of. Only time will tell. While others, after the fascination phase has faded, and the attractiveness of others begin to catch their eyes again, which is inevitable, maintain the policy of *'look, but don't touch'*, Salim and Naomi overcame this temptation by mutually engaging in ménage a trios to satisfy this urge.

"Is this system for everyone? Of course not. In my assessment of couples who commit to long-term exclusive relationships, those who won't necessarily be so easily guided by such temptation, are those who venture into them in the second half of their lives. Forties, fifties, by this age, most have more than likely quenched most of the sexual curiosity they harbored, making it more likely to preserve a path of sexual exclusivity.

"In their early twenties, even thirties, that's an entirely different story altogether. The likelihood of a couple in their twenties committing to a long-term relationship, and remaining sexually exclusive, *across their lifetimes*, is highly, *highly* unlikely.

"Its simple math: couples in their early twenties aren't normally sufficiently developed, or seasoned enough, to maintain a commitment of sexual exclusivity across a lifetime. Evolution, a shift in values, growth, change, let's not forget to mention outright immaturity. All variables that are bound to take place in those earlier years that will be fertile ground for the seeds of temptation to grow which would lure them to 'cheat'. Impossible? Absolutely not. Odds I'd be willing to bet on? Yeah right.

"What's interesting is contrary to what many believe to be the primary factor of cheating — sexual frustration — isn't the leading cause at all. Normally, in their youth, the urge to push the envelope on their sexual boundaries are the norm. Sexual exploration and curiosity is common in their daily diet.

"Some would even assume the desire was led by someone who was more sexually attractive than their partner. Now while this is the case, sometimes, I couldn't tell you how many times women expressed their confusion as to why their man cheated with not only someone they considered uglier than them, but didn't, in their opinion, tote any desirable characteristics. What they failed to grasp is when someone cheats, sneaks out, engages in an outside encounter with another, it could never be simply chalked up as sexual attraction.

"It could be the desire for novelty and variety. It could be to satisfy the curiosity of the sexual legend someone carries with them. Shiieet! The reputation I carried with me when I was in the game for how I laid that pipe game down was…oh, sorry. Never mind. Back to what I was saying.

"It could be a sense that they were missing out on something. A desire to confirm they are still attractive and desirable to the sought after sex. A boost to their ego. A retaliatory tactic to return the hurt or infidelity of their partner. A chance encounter with a blast from the past who seemed unattainable previously, and when the opportunity presented itself, became too tempting to resist. A fight, an argument, the birth of a new child, new children. Attention. Or it could be as simple as the person seeking a change to break them out of the boredom of what they consider a mundane relationship.

"The reasons are endless. Whatever the case, once someone passes the threshold of fantasy to reality, there will be consequences behind it. For every *action* there is a *reaction*. But every reaction doesn't have to be a negative one. If a mature couple, analyzing their relationship from a broad spectrum, realizes they began with one policy, which ran its course, or failed to fulfill the needs of each other, they can simply evolve to something more suitable for each of them.

"Whatever they choose to incorporate – role-playing, *S&M*, or even another individual – into their union, the key is for the both of them to be honest. Honest with what they feel, their preferences, their newly acquired tastes, the person they are becoming, because it would do neither of them any good to lie to themselves, or their partner. This kind of dishonesty only erects walls, creates psychological masks that they'll wear to hide behind, because it won't truly be them, only the façade they're portraying.

"*Denzel Washington*, and *Angela Basseting* their way through life with their significant other. When Tanisha first came to me, she spoke adamantly about her knowledge of Malik not only viewing porn on the low, but his unspoken obsession with other women. She called him out on it. Pointed out how she continued to catch him out, repeatedly, red-handed, staring at other women's breasts, asses, their provocative outfits, their beauty.

"Then when confronted, Malik would always minimize her concerns, downplay her intuition, which only sparked the flame of jealousy. That ugly, green-headed monster of envy was awakened in her when his actions led to feelings of being threatened, rejected, abandoned, or the perception of interest in another.

"Now while others may have experienced these feelings due to an inferior sense of self-esteem, I didn't see that as the case with Tanisha. She wasn't threatened by those other women, even when she agreed they were, in her opinion, physically more appealing than her. What got her was Malik's denial about it.

"He insulted her intelligence. She couldn't understand why Malik would lie about finding attraction in the Beyoncé's, the Lupita Nyong'o's, the Kim & Chloe Kardashians, the Priyanka Chopra's, the Lucy Liu's, and the Jennifer Lopez's of the world, when it was so evidently clear that those women were revered by hundreds of millions for their beauty, along with their other redeeming qualities.

"What concerned her was if he would lie about something so trivial, something she considered natural, what other things would he lie about? What Malik never knew in his attempts to spare her feelings was the wedge he was shoving between them. By denying those feelings, by refusing to acknowledge Tanisha's instincts, going so far as to twist reality in her head, he unknowingly sabotaged their relationship almost to the point of them not recovering.

"Only when he came clean to those true lies of his feminine fantasies did he clear the air to allow Tanisha to not only learn to trust him again, but cater to his desires by taking on the persona of different women in their role-playing routines, something she wanted to explore anyways.

"Fortunately for Malik and Tanisha, along with several other couples, is their love, maturity, and desire to overcome the obstacles and hardships of committed life together allowed them to tolerate temporary moments of frustration, alienation, solitude, and distressing conflicts, instead of tossing in the towel and calling it quits."

$$ $$ $$

"It appears in this enlightened age of technology and endless access to others, more and more couples have little to no staying power, little or no tolerance to see past the immediate moment or perceive a broader perspective outside of the moment, reducing the sum of their associations to the mercy of the next argument. There is no way something meaningful and worthwhile can survive in an environment so fragile.

"One of the principles I advocate is to learn the ability to absorb the essence of our partner in all instances. It takes time, maturity, and wisdom to step outside of the immediate moment, mainly in the heat of a dispute, to analyze the essence of this person, and the relationship. But this is crucial, especially if we expect to make a long-term relationship last. Especially if we are wise enough to *over*-stand that when we profess to love someone, and commit our lives to them, we knowingly, or unknowingly, sign on for the long haul, good or bad.

"We are to expect certain *rights* from them in the process: the right to be respected, the right to have our thoughts and feelings acknowledged, the right to be treated with honor and dignity, the right to be given emotional support. *Not* the right to never get heated with them, or disagree with their opinions, behaviors, but the right to know that this person always has their back, and will be on their side. The late, great Tupac said it best: *Ride or die*.

"Studying the lessons in the *Five*, the *Knowledge* degree in the 1-40 describes how the planet earth is approximately 25,000 miles in circumference, and being that the original man makes his history equal to his surroundings, the planet earth, which is symbolic to the original woman, he *renews his history* every 25,000 years as well.

"Now while it is irrelevant to delve into the deeper science behind this teaching, being there is a lot of symbolism in the parable, I can say this concept of renewing, or redefining can, and should, be applied to relationships. The years of this renewing period can vary – five, seven, nine – but a definite reconstructing period should take place. Just like how we evolve and go through different stages of development, so does the relationship.

"In the beginning, what I describe as the *Fascination/Infatuation* phase, for the most part, everything is all good. The excitement of experiencing new thoughts, reactions, a body that connects to our body in a different way, sexually, mentally, spiritually, becomes a stimulating charge. The first stage.

"The second stage, the *Committal* stage, is when the excitement of exploring each other sexually, mentally, the thrill of figuring out this 'new' individual loses its spark due to the exposure of being in the presence of this individual daily.

"This is where the flaws which were initially minimal rise to the surface, where unique qualities once revered becomes common, where what was once viewed as new becomes routine. There could also be a sense of harmony in the union created, an unspoken peace at the prospect of *over*-standing this new addition in your life, a sense of stability and comfort at the knowledge of having another half that has your back. The second stage.

"Then there is the third stage, the *Metamorphosis* stage, where one begins to see clearly that the individual they first encountered years, decades ago, is no longer the same. Time, life, their experiences have changed them, and those subtle changes over the years have now become fully manifest. Where the harsh reality of truth has to be faced – this is not the same person I initially committed to.

"In this stage, the relationship is tested the most. For those who fear change, there may be an attempt to struggle to recapture the past, fight against time to recover remnants of the person they fell in love with, reignite the spark of those first moments.

"Sadly they can't. It's impossible. So instead of welcoming the process of growth, evolving with the flow of the relationship, there is hostility, a resistance, a negative energy, and in the extreme, accusations that become self-sabotaging. His newfound interest in exercising and concern for his appearance *has* to be because he is cheating. Her desire to further her education *has* to be motivated by a desire to move on to bigger and better things, *someone* better. *Where* is all this coming from? *What* motivated it? *Who?*

"In this stage many couples part, not because they grew apart, but because one of them fought the reality of growth, evolution. One of them tried to stop time, and remain on a moment that passed. When one failed to flow with the changing currents, lacked the inner security of the other, and closed their third eye to the emergence of what could have been a new beginning for the both of them.

"Remember that *rhythm and energy* I spoke of in a relationship? Well, there is also a system. And in any system, if one part changes, the other must change with it in order to maintain equilibrium."

Dr. Black pounds on the edge of his desk, two fists produce harmony.

"Two hands, one beat. Same rhythm, same flow. But what if…(one hand beats faster, the other slower)…they don't flow together? Disequilibrium. You gotta flow with it. That's just life. Continual motion. If you are not moving *forward* in life, then you are moving *backwards*. Like I said, stagnation is a slow death. You either evolve with life, or decay with it. Grow with your partner, or watch the relationship die before your very eyes. Always be in the moment – feel it, love it, cherish it, experience it – then let it go, and move on to the next moment, the next adventure.

"When you embrace that change, when you flow with life, fluid as water, when you become the advocate of your partner's dreams and aspirations, that's when a couple will truly stand the chance of, in the immortal words of Keith Sweat, *'Making it last forever'*.

"What do you know, that's our time. No, not just for today, our whole interview in general. Hopefully you gained some insight from the *Case Files* that I shared with you, along with our sessions. Maybe in the future, based on the public's response to this interview, we could do a follow-up with some additional *Case Files*. What is it you ask, more sessions exploring different forms of sexuality? Something like that. I was never one to spoil a surprise.

"What I can assure you is they'll give you much deeper insight on the mentality, and the motivation, behind the science of their relationships. Maybe it'll even teach you something about yourself. If, and until then, my friend. Peace."

Epilogue

"If I'm not mistaken, don't you have…" Kiara stopped short, she swept her fingers over the face of a twelve-inch *IPad* to check Dr. Black's itinerary, "…I don't see any meetings scheduled for today." She placed the *IPad* down, and double-checked his schedule by scanning over a huge day calendar on the center of her desk. "What about that journalist from the magazine? I don't see him here either. Are you done with that?"

Dr. Black approached the brass and glass wet bar in the corner of the office, turned over two crystal tumblers. "That I am." Cubed ice clinked to a swirly stop at the bottom of each glass, several fingers of Courvoisier bathed them to about a quarter. "We had our final interview last week. I even got the first copy of the magazine to read the final edit prior to release."

Dr. Black took a light sip of his drink before he placed the second tumbler on the center of Kiara's desk, directly over the calendar she couldn't seem to cease scrutinizing.

"Black, it's not even twelve in the afternoon," Kiara said, blindly brushing the tumbler aside. "And when did you get it? Better yet, why haven't I seen it yet?" Kiara added, locked into the screen, her fingers typing out over seventy words per minute.

Dr. Black smiled, placed his index finger under her chin to

lift her head up to him, said, "Kiara, relax. Sit with me for a minute. Check it out," and took Kiara by the hand.

Kiara looked into his eyes, shook her head, sighed.

"One minute. Just one. I got a ton of stuff to do."

Dr. Black led her across the office to a plush, brown leather loveseat. It was as if the weight of her clerical duties, which consumed her all morning, became lost after she sunk comfortably into the cool material and took her first hearty sip.

"I think it came out pretty good. I read it about three times."

Dr. Black placed the magazine on Kiara's lap, and took a load off to nestle himself warmly by her side. The specific article had a yellow Post-it labeling the exact page. Kiara flipped it open, and read. After thoroughly reviewing the entire three pages, she gave her final approving nod.

"Nice. I noticed how he didn't mention the minor incident he witnessed. I wonder what you said to convince him to omit that," Kiara posed, followed by a casual sip.

"The same thing I said to convince another special someone in my corner. A brother know how to be persuasive when he needs to be," Dr. Black uttered smoothly, resting his hand on her thigh just above the hem of her tight skirt.

"Oh, so it sounds like you *manipulated* and *lied* to convince him to see things your way. Is that what you're saying? That you manipulated and lied, to get *me*?" Kiara arched a single eyebrow. She didn't resist his large hand sinking halfway between the warmth of her naked thighs; he gave it a firm squeeze.

"Of course not. It's not considered a lie or manipulation if you simply remain...*conservative* with the facts," Dr. Black said slyly. Kiara nudged the side of his leg with hers, gave him a playful elbow in the ribs. "Naw, seriously. I simply told him what he needed to know. Like I told him in an earlier interview: you can lie to those around you, all with their own set of consequences that come along with it. But with you being my wife for close to a decade, you know I would never lie to you about anything.

"For a journalist who's recording my every word to document it in some nationwide magazine publication, that's a whole different story – literally. I had to navigate and direct the course of the facts he documented, made sure he didn't paint me in a negative light, which you see he didn't. Not to mention, take into consideration the publication he wrote for.

"You know how the hood looks at anything relatively close to snitching as being sacrilegious, even if it isn't. If I told him we were ducking and dodging them boys who worked for that cartel because they think I had something to do with one of their bosses getting knocked with a life sentence, he would have rightfully assumed that I snitched on him. That would have tainted everything else that came after that.

"Little did he know, the individuals who ran down on us in our meeting were actually the FEDS. Government agents who failed countless attempts to get me to roll over on my former connect. A sting operation I'll never participate in. Not that I believe those individuals aren't guilty of the crimes the FEDS accuse them of, that's not the point. The point is, *I'm* not going to be a part of any indictments being filed against them. If the FEDS indict them, which I'm sure they will if those individuals continue down the course of that same lifestyle, it will be because they succumbed to their own fate, without my assistance.

"I told him, perception. Believe *none* of what you hear, and only *half* of what you see. Fortunately, I believe the rapport we built up over the weeks allowed him to sense the genuine type of individual I was, and made him feel comfortable enough to print exactly what I wanted him to print."

"And the *Case Files* of the couples you gave him? How many were there, two, three?"

"Three couples, two sessions each. Salim and Naomi. Malik and Tanisha. Victor and Zakia. The three I felt the most comfortable with, who've been together the longest. Some of my favorite couples being their tastes are so...diverse." Dr. Black's hand made contact with the silky material in the center of Kiara's thighs. He proceeded to brush her delicately in a circular massage above her sensitivity.

Kiara arched a single eyebrow.

$$ $$ $$

"I wonder what his response would have been if he knew *we* experimented with several of the exercises those couples engaged in? How it was your, shall I say, *subliminal persuasion* which encouraged those other couples to engage in such activities," Kiara mewled as the sensation of eighty proof liquor and her husband's frisky, exploring hand gave her that warm tingly feeling all over.

"What could he do but tip his hat, pay homage, and salute? Think about it: aside from those *Case Files*, what other couple do you think he encountered with such diverse tastes?"

"Yet, with all of your pride in your handiwork, I noticed how you failed to tell him about us. For all he knows, I was simply the general manager of this firm."

"All done for a reason. It crossed my mind to enlighten him to the true nature of our relationship, to show him just how effective a husband and wife team can be when they work together, but I decided against that. I figured that might have distracted him from the true purpose of our interview – to display my methods that I verified through the actual *Case Files* I let him review.

"I wanted him to analyze Salim and Naomi, Malik and Tanisha, Victor and Zakia, objectively. How they maintained the spark in their relationship, instead of being sidetracked and distracted with ours. Study *their* chemistry instead of watching *us* to determine if he could detect any flaws in the day-to-day workings of a couple who engaged in the same kinds of extracurricular activities."

Dr. Black nursed a few more sips, and savored the delicious spirit, before he rested the tumbler on a glass coffee table before them. He guided Kiara onto his lap, straddled all five-foot-six, one hundred and sixty-seven pounds of her over him, face forward. Dr. Black welcomed the weight of her healthy physique. She melted onto his frame, took that dominant position over him, but ironically, remained with the same passive persona. He caressed her waist, thighs, and hips lovingly before he massaged her firm bubble in sheer admiration.

"Yeah, I'm sure that's the *only* reason why you didn't inform him of the true nature of our relationship," Kiara said, with her lip curled into a sly smirk. She unclipped two pins from her tight bun, her long wavy hair fanned out over her shoulders, veiled most of her caramel face. "Are you sure it had nothing to do with the fact that you didn't want him to view your wife through the lens of a Naomi, or a Tanisha, or even better, a Zakia?"

Kiara leaned forward, planted her lips softly over his, gave him a light peck.

"Maybe..." Dr. Black returned ambiguously; he kissed her back, and removed her black specs to get a clear visual of her light grey eyes, "...but again, like I said, everything is done for a reason."

He slowly unbuttoned Kiara's grey blazer, peeled it from her back, tossed it blindly over his shoulder. Her tight, white dress shirt, he removed each button to expose her white, paisley embroidered bra. He planted soft kisses on her flesh, danced his tongue between her milky caramel cleavage.

"I gave him those files because I wanted him to do the math to the benefits of what can occur when a couple can triumph over any adversity they face in their relationship. When they have complimentary personalities, an equal sexual appetite, and can successfully navigate through the complexities of their relationships."

The Anonymous Black Files

Dr. Black removed his own blazer; Kiara helped him unbutton his dress shirt.

"What a Salim, or a Tanisha, or a Zakia has done. But remember, we do have other files. Those who weren't close to the couples on the drives I gave him."

"The failures," Kiara mentioned.

"Harsh. I wouldn't necessarily label them failures, because how could any of them *fail* if they *learned* from their experiences? A failure is one who recognizes a course of action isn't working for them, yet continue to proceed down the same path fully aware of what the outcome would be. You know the saying: *the definition of insanity is to continue doing the same thing, and expecting different results.* I believe most of our client's would consider themselves successful in the way they conduct themselves in their relationships, except of course, for those who aren't."

"The ones I consider your little...social experiments?"

"Don't make it sound so dirty. I wouldn't label them *social experiments*. Such a term can lean towards a negative. I build on the positive. Besides, can we even classify couples like those as our actual clients, considering the...*undocumented retainer* for one of those clients alone could cover the lease on this office for the next five years, with their *Interviews* and *Case Files* playing out more like confessionals than retaining any insight on counseling?

"Couples like *Khalid and Ashanti:* a high-stakes stick-up artist with his Instagram model partner in crime. *Desmond and Elisha:* an up-and-coming NBA great, and his behind-the-scenes significant other. *Rasheed and Veronique:* an incredibly wealthy power couple flaunting an open relation with America's elite. Couples who choose scandalous means to maintain that companionship with their partner, and are really only interviewed to gain deeper insight into their psychology. Couples that I counsel, yet omit to inform them of the consequences of their actions to allow them to hopefully see the error of their own ways.

"For those brothers still knee deep in the 'trap', those sistas who grind to get that money by any means, yet try to sustain a relationship, who chose to manipulate, coerce, scheme, and deceive their partners, I simply allowed for the natural course of events to play through with the hopes that they would eventually come to terms and learn the error of their ways.

"Some have. Unfortunately, some haven't. But even then, I wouldn't consider them failures on a whole because *I* learned something from their scandalous episodes, and imparted that wisdom on our clients. So just like everything in life, it can be viewed as a learning experience. And you have to admit, some of their files are absolutely insane! Come to think of it, I think that's what I'll do next."

"And what will that be?"

"Demonstrate the *opposite* side of my teachings. That magazine wasn't the first publication to request an exclusive interview, and I'm sure they won't be the last. I only agreed to do that interview because, well, you know. But I think I might do that. Compile a few of those other individual's files together to show..."

Dr. Black and Kiara both shot their attention to the office door when it was thrust open with such force that it smashed against the wall behind it. Three huge, burly men in all black – leather jackets, gold chains over hairy chests, hair slicked back in hair gel, at least eight hundred pounds of flesh divided between them – protectively sandwiched a relatively smaller man in comparison donned in an expensive suit.

They swarmed the office with the impact of a human tsunami, spilled inside, then just as quick, closed the door behind them.

$$ $$ $$

"Well, well, well. I hope I'm not interrupting anything," the man in the middle mentioned behind a twisted smirk. One look at the half-dressed couple – that feminine half with her skirt hiked up around her waist, straddling her masculine lover – told him that he had.

Kiara reacted.

She shoved her hand into the crevice of the love seat to withdraw her nickel-plated equalizer – a snub-nosed .357. Those two burly behemoths weren't more than a few seconds behind her – they both whipped out handguns from hidden shoulder holsters to take aim on that couple still partially entwined in an amorous embrace.

"Easy, Kiara. After everything we've been through, I assumed you'd welcome me in a more hospitable manner," the finely dressed gentleman said quite calm considering he spoke behind the barrel of Kiara's weapon.

The muscle enveloping him remained stiff as statues, their guns fixed on that beautiful, half-dressed almond-skinned African with her dress shirt open, white lace bra exposed, taking aim on their boss with the focus of a trained assassin. After a moment, and an obvious stalemate between the three, Dr. Black reached out to lower Kiara's weapon to remove the man out of the line of fire; he smoothly eased his wife up off his lap, careful not to misinterpret any sudden movements on their part.

It was only then that his trained goons reluctantly lowered their weapons as well; they weren't concealed back in their holsters, they simply dangled those heavy caliber weapons in their hands like diligent soldiers, on point to attack if that feisty little vixen even thought of playing the role of a light-skinned *Wonder Woman* again.

"That's better."

The gentleman, completely unfazed by the gesture of a loaded weapon coming so close to taking him off this plane of existence, sunk heavily into one of the plush leather recliners Dr. Black's client's normally sought counsel in. He sat back, crossed one leg over the other, interlaced his numerous gold ringed, chubby fingers, and held up his chin as if he was pondering deep thoughts. His goons stood protectively behind him at his left and right.

"This is a really nice office you have here, much better than the last. I like it. Makes me feel all nice and cozy. What do you think, fellas? Care to take a load off, relax, and spill your souls to the good doctor here? Get his advice on how to psychologically cope with all of the sins you committed?" The comment incited a low murmur of chuckles from his illicit security.

"Oh, I forgot. That's not what you do. You're one of those *other* kinds of doctors. You like to talk about sex, sucking and fucking, shit like that. That's why Gino came to see you in the first place, to work on the issues between him and his wife, Sara. You do some kind of sex therapy thing, right?"

Dr. Black studied the man in their midst for a moment, turned to his wife, said, "Kiara, would you please excuse us. Give us a few minutes," noticing how his wife didn't move a muscle from his side.

"I ain't leaving you. I ain't going a motherfu…"

"Kiara," Dr. Black cut her short, he had an intense look in his eyes.

Kiara hesitated, her dress shirt still open, her partial nudity lost in the moment of their unexpected guests. Her handgun hung her arm, she refused to budge, words on the tip of her tongue, but with another assuring nod from her husband, she finally lowered sad eyes, and turned away from him. With an evil roll of her eyes at the individuals who so rudely intruded, she carefully secured the hammer on her weapon, transferred it from her hand into her husband's with a stern nod, closed her shirt, and proceeded towards the entrance.

With his wife making her departure, out of harm's way, Dr. Black let out an internal sigh, said, "Tony, what's going on? How can I help you?" and placed that nickel-plated, mini hand cannon in the top center drawer of his desk.

"Did I ever tell you how much I love that girl?" Tony mentioned, following Kiara's every move, mainly her ass, until she disappeared around the corner. "Now *that's* a woman right there. Militant, stern, knows how to follow orders, absolutely beautiful, with a body men would kill for. All with that killer instinct in her eyes. That woman's a killer, literally, you do know that, right? What do you got going on with her? I know you've been together for awhile, working together, but is it something serious? Or, did you just brainwash her like what all of you other quacks do, and you're just screwing her beautiful brains out whenever you feel like sticking your cock in something?"

Dr. Black didn't dignify that with a comment.

He didn't even blink, he simply stared at Tony with deadpan eyes.

"No matter." Tony waved his hand to one of the men behind him, nodded to the bar; he went off to fix Tony a drink. "I was just in the neighborhood, and thought I'd do you the courtesy and stop by, pay you a little visit. I haven't heard from you in a while. You wouldn't be trying to dodge me, would you?" Tony's weighty cohort returned with a single tumbler, he handed it over to his boss.

"I'm not dodging you, Tony. I'm just trying to run my firm, everything legit, on the up and up."

"Up and up?" Tony got a good laugh out of that. "Yeah, I guess that's why Gino started working with you in the first place. You *were* in fact a legitimate doctor at one point. That's how we were able to move our product with you undetected for so long. Hell, I'm sure from all the money you made with the help of my family, that we practically funded this entire little venture you got going on here. And things would have continued to run smoothly, you make your money, we make ours, that is until that unfortunate little incident popped an unsettling question mark over your head."

Tony's lively demeanor instantly faded, all in sync with the smirks of his cohorts twisting their grills into evil scowls.

"I told you before, Tony. You know I had nothing to do with that. Why would I knowingly put myself, my family, my friends in harm's way? I knew the rules, and I didn't break them. When the time came, and I got caught up in that little...I took responsibility, and my punishment, like a man. I handled mine. I'm not a rat, Tony. You should be able to look me in my eyes, man to man, and know it."

Dr. Black spoke with such conviction that even if he wasn't telling the truth, his confidence had the effect of causing Tony to show pause. Tony took his advice – he leaned forward in his seat, the leather behind him creaking from the release of pressure, he placed his drink on the coffee table before them, and stared Dr. Black directly in his eyes.

There was an intense stare down between them, each one trying to detect traces of deceit, insecurity, fear. After a moment of complete silence washing over the entire office, an uncomfortable silence, Tony let out a light chuckle again.

"Maybe I would, maybe I wouldn't. After all, you are a psychologist, one who studies the human mind, master of illusions," Tony said dramatically, waving a single hand in the air suggesting his propensity to twist reality to suit his purpose. "Which is the main reason why I came here in the first place. Contrary to what you may think, I didn't come here to do you any harm. I would get no pleasure in doing that. That's not good for business. No, I came here to present an offer to you. After discussing it over with my family, we decided to give you an opportunity to make amends. Get back into our good graces."

Dr. Black sat up at full attention.

"Tony, no disrespect. But I told you, I'm no longer in that life. Everything I do now is legit."

Tony appeared to be growing frustrated, as much as he attempted to mask it.

"Are you sure? Because the last time I checked I don't think anybody in my family, myself included, gave you the approval to simply walk away from your obligations. You do remember your obligations, don't you? You made some very important commitments to some very important people. We trusted you, welcomed you into our family, and took care of you when you were in need of assistance, on several occasions. I don't think they're gonna take too kindly to you turning down this generous offer.

"But..." Tony grunted when he pulled his weighty frame to his feet, "...it is your choice. America. Land of the free, home of the brave, natural rights, yada, yada, yada, all that good stuff. I'll just go back to my family and relate how..." Tony cleared his throat, "...you turned down our generous offer. Hopefully they'll be as forgiving to you and your family, as I'm sure you counsel your client's to be when someone turns their back on them."

With that, Tony threw one last disturbing smirk at Dr. Black, eyed him up and down, then kept his eyes down on the carpet beneath his feet, a signal that spoke louder than words, and turned for the door.

Dr. Black observed Tony in silence; one of his goons opened the door for him. Tony was moments away from stepping out before Dr. Black shook his head in defeat, and said, "Tony, wait." Dr. Black met him at the door. "I'm appreciative of everything that you've done for me, and if there's a way I can repay that gratitude, I would never want to insult you, or your family, by turning it down. How can I help you?"

Tony stood in the entrance, took a moment, gradually cracked a dim smile, said, "Here," and dug into his inner jacket pocket to retrieve a white envelope.

"Smart man. I knew you'd come to your senses. The instructions are inside. It's a little different from your previous assignments, but I'm sure you can handle it. Like you said, everything you've been doing recently has been on the up and up, so you're the last person anyone would look at for this type of job. Unfortunately, if you fail to complete it, it'll be like you never took it in the first place. Which means, how can I say this...it would be in your best interest to make sure you get it done. Again, for you and your family's sake. I'll be in touch."

Tony left Dr. Black standing by the door with that single white envelope in his hand. Kiara entered the office to see him staring down on it in a trance, reluctant to even open it. She took his side, placed a soft hand on his shoulder; Dr. Black didn't even recognize she was standing there.

"Baby, what is it?" Kiara asked softly, almost scared to hear the answer.

It took a moment, but Dr. Black finally broke from his rift to peer at her on his side.

With a heavy sigh, and an even heavier aura of dejection, he said weakly, "Something to let me know that right when I thought I was out, they did something to pull me right back in."

To be continued in:
The Anonymous Black Files 2.0: *Deception*

Book Club Question

The Anonymous Black Files is not only a thought provoking read, but it is geared to initiate further discussion. Here are some questions regarding the *Case Files* to initiate dialogue:

Salim & Naomi

1. Salim and Naomi chose threesomes to spice up their marriage. Is this something you would experiment with? Why/why not?
2. Should couples (married/unmarried) experiment with this fetish?
3. Do you agree/disagree with Salim and Naomi's perspective on why threesomes work for them?
4. Will threesomes strengthen or weaken a relationship?

Malik & Tanisha

1. Malik and Tanisha engaged in role-playing/voyeurism. Is this something you would experiment with?

2. Is role-playing a productive way to spice up a relationship? How so?
3. Would you view your mate in a different light based on the role they portrayed?
4. How far would you go in a role-playing scenario?

Victor & Zakia

1. Victor and Zakia found the height of their sexual pleasure engaged in *S&M*. Is this something you would experiment with?
2. Are there degrees of *S&M*? If so, what are they?
3. Does *S&M* work better with long-time couples, or consenting flings?
4. Is *S&M* a constructive way to enhance a love relationship?

Relational Survey

Additional questions to continue exploring the mind of your significant other:

1. Is it important for full disclosure of your past, or are there some things that should be left unsaid?
2. Was man/woman designed for monogamy?
3. Do you wish you slept with more or fewer mates? Why?
4. What makes your partner unique in contrast to relationships from your past?
5. Can you recall your best sexual experience? Why was it so special?
6. When did you know you were in love with your mate?
7. Does love hurt?
8. Are you passive or aggressive in your relationship? Is there a benefit in either style?
9. Do you believe great sex can evolve into love?
10. Can a relationship survive without sex?

Turn the page for a sneak peek into the sequel...

The Anonymous Black Files 1.2: The Interviews

The *Case Files* were only the beginning.

Return to a world where the renowned sex therapist, *Dr. Anonymous Black*, inspires his audience to reflect on every intimate relationship they ever been in. A world where psychological principles push his readers to challenge the motivating factors that lured them to their significant other in the first place.

Discover what drives Naomi to seek out and secure voluptuous vixens to engage in *threesomes* with her husband, Salim. Study Tanisha's true source of creativity, and what prompts her to set the tone to embark on *voyeuristic* sexual escapades with her husband, Malik. Learn who will finally conquer (or concede) in their feisty, *S&M* games of domination and discipline between the professional power couple, Victor and Zakia.

The Anonymous Black Files 1.2: The Interviews concludes the *Classified Case Files* of all three couples, answers all riddles, and delivers a deeper understanding of their worlds, in their own words, of what inspires these adventurous couples to seek out and explore their innermost decadent desires.

It's only human nature to seek out an outlet to have our desires fulfilled.

Who knows?

Maybe the methods of one, two, or even all three of these unorthodox couples will inspire you to seek out and explore some of those decadent desires yourself.

Date: January 29th, 20—
Time: 10:39 am
Case File #10S – Personal Interview
Client: Salim

Salim (S): Now ain't this a motherfucking bitch!

Dr. Anonymous Black (AB): *Salim, my brother.*

(Dr. Black embraced Salim's hand in a loud, echoing palm in the center of his office, pulled him close to his chest, both men all smiles; they gave each other a tight, brotherly hug).

(S): If it ain't the one and only...

(AB): *Ah, you know when I'm wearing the therapy hat that I go by Dr. Anonymous Black, right?*

(S): (Chuckles) No doubt. No doubt. (An inspective eye swept around the office, Salim gave a slight nod). Doing big thangs, family. Respect soldier. I salute. Every time we cross paths, I can't help but to think about how we came up, the struggle. Two levels of intelligence who rose up from that savagery in them streets, cutting up concrete, to falling victim, bidding in the belly. You take me back, my brother. Come to think of it, yo, you remember that lil badass correction officer that you were trading thoughts with? What was her name again, Rodriguez, Rivera? Something like that, right? Eva Mendez looking-like chick with the baddest body in the building. Whatever happened to her? You linked with her on the free cipher?

(AB): *Come on, fam. Seriously? You're sharper than that. Don't buy into urban legends, street myths. None of what you hear, half of what you see, remember? Besides, that nonsense was a minute ago, a past life. Life evolved. I moved on to bigger and better things.*

(S): You sure did. (Light laughter). Shit that I'm sure funded all of this. I respect game. I respect even more that lil gig you had going on with that clique out of New York. The Fucinno family, right? Or was it Pallentino? I heard you were doing some pretty good numbers with them. That is until...

(AB): *Salim, again. All in a past life, my peoples. I'm not living like that anymore. I shed that coat of a hustler to slip on the jacket of a counselor, a negative for a positive. Which is the reason why I wanted you to come into my office and build with me. I wanted to ask you some questions.*

(S): (Salim inspects Dr. Black strangely, stiffens, posture defensive). Why'd you tell me to come without Naomi? What are you talking about, what kind of questions? You ain't got no open cases, do you?

(AB): (Dr. Black laughs). *Cut the shit. You know I ain't about that life. I'm not working undercover for the FEDS. No questions about the street game, or the mud we played in, washing dirty money trying to make it clean. I wanted to talk to you about your relationship. How you eventually settled down, and married Naomi.*

. . .

(S): (Salim relaxes tense features) Just Naomi, no street life?

(AB): *Of course. Remember how we used to pick each other's brains about all the shortys…excuse me, women in our lives behind that G-wall? Well, I noticed how you, a straight gangsta, a brother who not only had nuff women in the past, but had a crazy variety to choose from, when it came to settling down, out of all of them you chose Naomi. Why?*

(S): I mean, it's a long story.

(AB): *I'm your therapist, and we got all the time in the world. So let the long story begin.*

(S): (Salim rests comfortably in a plush leather loveseat across Dr. Black). Naomi, what can I say? With her I just knew.

(AB): *How?*

(Dr. Black constructs a blunt, *Kush*, strawberry leaf, lights it, *inhale…exhale*, extends it to Salim).

(S): Mother Earth's natural therapy. Some things never change. (Salim smirks, took a heavy toke, grew more lax; two professionals echoing sentiments of times past). How did I know? To be straight up, I didn't know at first. She was like finding a needle in a haystack. Remember that brown-skinned cutie, TT, Taryn, I used to rock with? I thought she was official. Pretty, body tough as shit, ass fat as fuck, a career, only one child. But the longer I traveled with her on a mental level, the more I started to see she had issues. For one, she was suspect with her baby's father. I think she was still letting kid tap that ass on the low, late night. So I really didn't trust her for that. For two, she kept a couple of male 'friends' around her. Now you know I ain't insecure with mines, but come on now. All of them brothers taking her out, buying her gifts, clothes, jewelry, but y'all just 'friends'? Even if she was keeping it one hundred about how she felt about them, it's only common sense how they felt about her. That shit was tacky. The other females – too clingy, too money hungry, too angry, too annoying, basically psychologically fucked up from dealing with too many clowns in the past. Then the flip side: some either had a tough body and not a tough enough face, or vice versa; good face, not a tough enough body. Or, they had the looks, and the body, but wasn't about shit. Had her shit going on financially, but the mental, her whole relational psychology, was foul. Some with no ambition, and had they hand out expecting a hitter to take care of them just cause they throat was deep, they offered three inputs, and could put a porn star to shame. Basically, prostitution disguised in the form of a girlfriend. All types of shit. They just never seem to have the full package. That is until I hooked up with Naomi. She had it all. Face, body, sex appeal, ambition, was about her business, and was a straight feminine gangsta designed in dark chocolate flesh.

(AB): And the sex?
(The blunt changed hands).

(S): Shit! My dude, she put it down better than any other woman I ever had in my life. You know I done had my fair share of sampling all different forms of flesh: white girls, my fair share of the sistas, nuff Spanish girls, you gotta love the medas. A few Asians, all of them chicks was tight as fuck. A couple Middle-

Easterns. Even one lil badass exchange student from India. All tough in their own individual right. But when it came to Naomi, she blew every last one of them out of the water. You see, in my experience, for a female to be that good sexually, eight out of ten times, she done let half the hood run through her, and got that ass passed around like a Philly blunt in a cipher of goons to get that nice. And you already know what's coming with that – a crazy reputation, psychological issues, a fucked up view of men, topped off with the possibility that she probably gonna be that hoe, even if it's on the low, for the rest of her life. For Naomi, it only took three or four brothers, and years of experimenting and practice with me for her to get that nice.

(AB): *How do you know? No offense, but that could be a bold faced lie. She could be lying to you about the numbers. You know what they say – whatever number a woman gives you, multiply that number by three.*

(S): If that was any other woman, *anyone*, I would have thought the same thing. With her, I don't know. I just believe her. That was one of the other things that was different with her than any other female I've dealt with – we kept it one hundred with each other, no matter what. I lost track of how many times we sat down together, sparked a couple of them green things, went shot for shot on some of that brown juice, and just picked each other's brain. We talked about everything. Fam, *everything*. Past relationships. All the shit I been through, the shit she been through. What we like, don't like. What worked, what didn't. What we gonna do to get that money, our boundaries. Everything. And the more I traveled with her, the more I realized how much I was feeling her, and how I ain't wanna let that go. I ain't never feel that way for nobody else. You know what time it is. A brother used to run through them chicks like clothes, not giving a fuck if they stayed or left after I got that nut off, knowing it was another ten more just like her that I had on speed dial. Not her. I never felt that way about Naomi. Never. She was one of the ones I didn't want to lose. *Couldn't* lose. *Refused* to lose. Not only was she official in the sex department, but like I said, she was always about her business. When I was in them streets hustling cracks, my queen was always by my side helping me to bag my shit up till I copped that first kilo. All of the times she could have dipped into my money stash, and clipped me for some of my paper on the low, what ninety percent of them other chicks would have done, she never touched my paper, not even once. Which just made me want to spoil the shit out of her, which is exactly what I did. When I flipped that first kilo to cop two, she was the one telling me to think bigger than the game. Not on some preaching shit, but to be smart about it. Use that as a stepping stone cause I couldn't hustle forever. To stack up enough dough to get out, get a business, and go legit. She planted them seeds in my mind. She made me see the full potential and limitations of that dope game so clear it was like she was holding up a glass of water to the streets. Then when I took that fall and got knocked with that bid, she was the one to hold it down for me like a soldier, and trooped that shit out with me when damn near everyone else left me for dead. Then when I came home, and told her I wanted to try my hand at running a music promotion company, get out the drug game for good, instead of her even saying one word negative about that shit, like I couldn't do it, or where was I gonna get the money from, or anything else, she just had my back, one hundred percent. Shit, she even surprised me and told me she stacked close to fifty stacks from the work I was pumping before, gave it all to me, and told me she got faith in me. For that, my dude, I just fell in love with that woman and knew no matter what, I wasn't never gonna let that go.

. . .

(AB): *You started talking about your sex life. How Naomi was nice under them sheets.*

(The blunts exchanged hands.)

(S): The nicest!

(AB): *That wasn't it. It was something else you were telling me that was special about her.*

(S): Yeah, when we were building one day, she threw it out there that she not only fantasizes about getting it on with females, but she had a little thing going on in the past with one of her old college roommates.

(AB): *What did you initially think about that?*

(S): What do you think? I'm an *official* gangsta, my dude. One hundred percent street soldier. So you already know – I was *loving* that shit! (They both share a hearty laugh). When she first put me on, I thought she was stuntin'. Just by chance, we went out to this nightclub one night, and I was sporting her heavy cause I knew I had one of the baddest queens up in that shit. In my eyes, she had every female in there fucked up. The next thing I know, I notice how a few of them fallen angels were sweatin' the god. Well, I *thought* they were just sweatin' me. Come to find out they were sweatin' the *both* of us. That's when Naomi started asking me what I thought about them. I told you, we keep it one hundred with each other, all the way, so I kept it one hundred with her, and told her what I *really* thought. One vixen had a body so bananas – hourglass shape, fat chest, slim waist, thighs like tree trunks, *Megan thee Stallion* ass, twerk game on ten – that I told her a brother ain't got no choice but to smash that shit from the back. Another, with her lips so full and thick, we both knew what her specialty had to be. Then *she* started commenting on them. One that was so sexy even she couldn't take her eyes off her. How looking into the eyes of another she could tell that she was a stone cold freak in bed. How one had this strut that was out of this world, like that queen who was glowing in neon lights was packing gold between her thighs. How one had moves that were so hypnotic on that dance floor that anyone with eyes could get lost in her trance. We just kept going back and forth pointing them out. My dude, it was like she was one of my goons, my homies, and I was just chopping it up with one on my team. That's when she asked me if I thought she could pull this chick that everyone in the club was drooling over. I told her *I* could bag her, but she couldn't. I guess she didn't take too kindly to me doubting her like that. She ran down on that woman, without hesitation, kicked her game at her, and we ended up inviting that fallen angel home with us that night. The rest is history.

(AB): *Did it bother you? That she let you know how she got down?*

(S): With her little college fling, at first it did, cause I wasn't sure if there were real feelings there. Having fun, exploring her sexuality, experimenting with a female is one thing. An emotional investment, dividing her heart between me and someone else, is something completely different. In the end, when I knew my wifey was only in love with me, and was only experimenting, naw. Shit, my dude, she like what I like.

(AB): *Did y'all ever have any issues with it?*

(S): Issues like what?

(AB): *The most obvious: she treat you to that lil redbone, or Spanish mommi, or lil chocolate cutie, then one night when Naomi ain't there, you and that other chick start getting it in on the low.*

(S): My dude, again, if that was *any* other female, I would have used that as a *license* to be jumping that shit off left and right with them other chicks. But, and I know this shit may sound crazy coming from the cloth we were cut from, I wouldn't even disrespect my wifey like that. Not only would I be playing her after she went out of her way to bless me like that with another female, but I would be going back on the one thing she asked me not to do – never cheat on her.

(AB): *Have you ever cheated on her?*

(S): To be honest, yeah. I did, once. Not with someone we ever did a threesome with. I was smart enough to never play with fire so close to a bomb. My incident, my slip happened when I took this trip to Miami on a business trip. I met this lil badass Cuban chick. About nineteen, twenty, could barely speak a lick of English, straight off the boat, literally. Mommi was about five-foot-three, one-thirty, had skin the color of pure honey, jet-black, curly hair down to her ass, and a body like one of them specimens out of a '*Straight Stuntin*' magazine – all tits, ass, and thighs, flat stomach, no fat, looking to make her come up in the modeling industry. Long story short, she was on the set of one of my promotions, I spit that thug's ether at her, got her back up to the hotel where I was staying, and kept my dick up in that lil young thang for the entire weekend. Strange thing happened though. When I was laid up in bed next to her, panting and sweating, thinking of all the wild shit we did, it finally hit me – I was in love with Naomi. Truly, genuinely in love. I know that may sound like the craziest time in the world to find out you in love with somebody – after a long weekend of doing the freakiest shit I could think of to a lil immigrant from Cuba – but that's just how it happened. All the shit I was doing with this stranger, was the same shit me and Naomi was doing. But instead of it just being an empty physical act, with me and Naomi, she took it to the mental, emotional, even spiritual. Not only that. Me and my wifey shared much more than just mind-blowing sex sessions. That's when I realized no matter how good the sex session, no matter how pretty, or stacked the other woman's body is, or how talented she could be in bed, it just wasn't worth losing my wifey over it. Sex, fucking, is only one thing, and can't balance on *one side of the scale* all of the other shit my wife had to offer *on the other side*. Besides, why lose my wifey by risking it with a fling when I could just put my wifey down, and we *both* get at her together? In the end, my experience with that Cuban girl left me wishing Naomi was there so we could have shared her together. After that day, I made a decision – I decided then and there that I was gonna give my wifey *one hundred percent*, being every other female that I dealt with before her only got a *fraction* of me; a few nuts here, a little time there. Basically, the leftovers from the other chicks I was cheating on them with. So from that day forward, I never cheated again.

(AB): *You mentioned your desire to share that Cuban female with Naomi, being you knew she was into threesomes and other women. What if, after all of the looking out for you that she did, treating you to other females, that she wanted the same in return: another brother in bed with you both?*

. . .

(S): (In mid-inhale, Salim choked on a mouthful of smoke). Is you...(cough...cough)...is you fucking crazy? *Share*...my *wife*...with another *man!* You sound crazy as all hell.

(AB): *No disrespect intended. I thought that was a legitimate question. After all, I figure if she made the effort to invite women into the bedroom to please you, that if she wanted to indulge in that same form of pleasure with another man, that you would be willing to make the same efforts to please her.*

(S): (Salim appears incredibly angry, the idea alone inciting mental images of death). First of all, me sharing my wife, not some lil ratchet, but *my wife*, someone I took *vows* with, someone I would bleed for, die for, with another man, is out of the fucking question. Never gonna happen. Ever! And it ain't got nothing to do with making that same effort to please her. I do please her, myself, well, and by getting it in with other females. But, if the cost of me indulging in a lil threesome every now and then with another female, was the price of letting some other hitter touch my shit, I would have never agreed to do that shit in the first place. You see, there's a big difference between the two.

(AB): *Which is?*

(S): Which is, she's bi-sexual and likes women. I'm *not* bi-sexual, I don't sleep with men. When we invite a female into bed with us, we can *both* enjoy her, together. It's a team thing. If we brought another... (shakes head, rolls eyes, dark thoughts circulating)...*brother* into bed with us, what would I get out of that? Nothing! It would be basically the both of us tag teaming and running through her. Just gangbanging her. When it comes to my wife, I'm stingy as fuck, and ain't down to divide her up with no other...*man*. Trust, my dude, you already know I was heavy in them streets, and indulged in all of the games the goons play. So back in my days, me and my team done associated with cliques of females that served the team just on the strength of who we were. I ain't just coming off the top of my head with this shit, I lived it. And every time we got on a sex session, and put one, or more, of them chicks through it, mostly a team of females getting down with our team on some *mini-orgy, free for all* type shit, wasn't nobody doing no shit like that with their wifey. Nobody!

(AB): *You can't say nobody. You can only speak for yourself. Personally, I've talked to brothers myself who invited women, along with other brothers in their bed, who even swapped partners, to spice up their sex lives.*

(S): Well, whoever them brothers is that you talking bout, them idiots is crazy!

(AB): *Your opinion.*

(S): Which is all that matters when it comes down to *my wife – my* opinion of her. Why, would you share *your* queen with another man?

(AB): (Dr. Black smiles ambiguously). *Nice reversal, but this isn't about me right now. My opinion, and how I view my relationship with my woman is unique. I'm sure there's some things my significant other and I would do that other couples wouldn't think of doing, for their own reasons. Just like I'm sure, positive, there's some things they do we wouldn't dream of.* That's why it's so important to choose someone who you're compatible with. Don't get me wrong, I'm not passing judgment on another brother who would share his woman with another man. I told you, I've met, and counseled quite a few couples who's into that – swapping mates, threesomes with females and males, participating in orgies. So I guess the better question I should have posed to you, which you already answered, is: what if she did ask you for something like that? A threesome with another man?

(S): Then I would know she wasn't the one for me. To quote a phrase you taught me: one of the most important things in making a relationship work is making sure we're both compatible. If my wife felt she needed to get trains ran on her by two, three, or more guys, then we surely wouldn't be compatible. Your credibility and word alone makes me believe you when you say some brothers might actually enjoy something like that. They may even feel a twisted sense of pride watching their woman take on two or three grown men, and handle them all to exhaustion. I promise you, I'm just not one of them. What I find pleasure in, what gets me off, is watching Naomi turn another female out. Watching her eat pussy, knowing for the rest of her life that chick will remember my wife's lips from the pleasurable head she gave them. Or, watching my wife thug a chick out, making them bless her, guiding their head between her thighs, how a gangsta would when a chick be sucking them off. Hearing her coach them chicks on how to bless her right, so within the span of one session, my wifey done taught them chicks how to be pro's at that shit. That's what *I* get off on. Women on women. No men. That's what me and my wife got in common, among many other things. Which is why I love her so much, and couldn't see living my life without her. (The blunt exchanged hands).

. . .

The Anonymous Black Files

(AB): *And with that, that's our time. As always, you know it was a pleasure building with you, giving me some time to pick your brain. Before I go, about that Italian family I was running with. You remember them Bloods that was selling them dirty burners on the north end? How could I get into contact with...well, let me shut this audio off being this interview is officially over, and discuss some matters of a more personal nature.*

Audio Disconnected...

Made in the USA
Middletown, DE
15 March 2022